"IF I RELEASE THE PRESSURE
YOU CAN KISS LOS ANGELES GOOD-BYE."

The bag. The bag in his hand. My God. Sheridan was right. He's got the last bomb in that bag!

"There's a manual override in the detonator," Jeffries said. "The first five interlocks are released. I'm holding down the last switch."

Goddammit to hell! We can't touch him. If he just relaxes the pressure, just a bit, the bomb detonates . . .

Martin Caidin's
ALMOST MIDNIGHT

A stunning suspense novel that
will stop your pulse!

D1319671

Almost Midnight

MARTIN CAIDIN

BANTAM BOOKS · TORONTO · NEW YORK · LONDON

To those flying twins,
JOHN and JEFF HAWKE

*This low-priced Bantam Book
has been completely reset in a type face
designed for easy reading, and was printed
from new plates. It contains the complete
text of the original hard-cover edition.*
NOT ONE WORD HAS BEEN OMITTED.

ALMOST MIDNIGHT

*A Bantam Book / published by arrangement with
William Morrow and Company, Inc.*

PRINTING HISTORY
Morrow edition published 1971
Bantam edition published April 1974

1

Far below them the city glowed softly. Thin moonlight brushed a winding river in subdued reflection. The man studying the city from three thousand feet ignored the roar of engine and wind. He paid scant attention to the aesthetics of the scene displayed before him while he studied a bridge forming an unmistakable illumined pathway across the river. From the bridge his gaze traveled north along a lighted highway to a traffic circle with the crawling glow of cars. The traffic circle oriented him properly. He moved his head slightly to pick out, a half-mile distant, a large rectangular structure, almost invisible but for floodlights splaying high fountains. He glanced at his watch, his face unmoving. *Just about now*, he thought, *the automatic timers should trip*. A moment later yellow lights flashed into view atop the rectangular building. The man smiled. *A perfect invitation to the First National Bank of Banning, Georgia.* From this high the flashing lights seemed a single source-point. But they formed a perfect triangle ten feet to the sides, providing excellent perspective for height and distance. Only the day before, the man in the airplane had placed those lights on the roof of the bank. The large building stood on a gentle bluff within the city. Encased in shallow cylinders the lights remained invisible to anyone on the ground. Not so from the air. The man glanced again at his watch and tapped the shoulder of the pilot seated before him. He pointed toward the flashing yellow.

The pilot nodded. "Got it," he shouted above the engine roar. "How's the wind?"

His passenger shifted beneath the parachute straps binding his stocky frame. He waited to reply, studying their drift across the ground. He glanced again at the yellow lights atop the bank. Even as he formed his

1

answer he thought of the bulky package he and another man, disguised as air-conditioning servicemen, had placed on the bank roof the day before. They hid the canvas containers behind the rooftop air-conditioning units. Quickly they laid out the three lights and connected the timer to set them flashing many hours later. Before they left the roof they worked expertly on the alarm locking mechanism of the door. They returned to their truck and drove off.

Now the man in the small airplane was about to return. He nodded to himself and again touched the pilot's shoulder. He leaned forward to be heard more clearly. "Wind's just right," he called. "Come up just south of that traffic circle. Got it?" The pilot nodded vigorously. His passenger clapped him smartly on the arm and started from the small cabin. Moments later he clung to the wing strut, one foot on the metal step leading to the cabin. Poised on the edge of space he was completely at ease. No fear of height or his impending fall reached him. After more than a thousand jumps this was his element. He judged his position and again checked their drift. Before the pilot could feel the sudden motion the man behind him vanished, spinning away and below. The pilot continued flying straight ahead. In moments there would be nothing to mark where the plane had been.

He twisted expertly as the wind snatched him from the plane. Face down, the city arrayed clearly before him, he arched his body and extended his limbs in controlled fall. Only for a moment. His body stabilized, he brought in both hands, grasped the D-ring in his right and then whipped out his arms. The chute blossomed with a thin *crack*. Then silence until traffic whispered up to him. He concentrated on his descent. He had to be perfect the first time; there wouldn't be a second. Hands on the control toggles, he turned expertly, working the wind, the black nylon canopy invisible from the ground. A high overcast eliminated moon and stars to render him a wraith sliding from the sky. The three flashing yellow lights separated with greater speed to give him a perfect coordinate. He judged the position

2

of the rooftop air-conditioning structure to assure his clearing the sharp concrete edges. The building loomed up, and he angled the chute upwind just before he touched. Then he was down with a muffled thump, rolling once, coming swiftly to his feet, collapsing the canopy before the wind could drag it to the edge of the roof.

He took a deep breath, glanced at his watch and enjoyed the luxury of a broad grin. Then he bent to his tasks. He laid out the parachute neatly, opened the canvas-shrouded package he and his associate had secreted there the day before. He removed a large deflated, rubberized balloon and deployed it within the parachute canopy, securing the latter to the roof. He used a dim flashlight to check a tube connection and spun the valves of two compact cylinders. He listened to helium sighing through the line and for several seconds studied the flow gauge. He grunted in satisfaction; it would be ready by the time he was through downstairs.

He turned to his left and grasped the handle of a large rubberized bag. He walked briskly to the door he had modified some eighteen hours earlier. The door swung open silently. After several seconds he again nodded with satisfaction. The alarm was still disconnected. He moved quickly, using the flashlight sparingly. His jump boots, with cushioned heels and soles, made no more sound than would a cat. Finally he stood before the thick bank vault. He smiled to himself; the massive steel circle was virtually impregnable.

But not the wall. Studying the construction blueprints had told him—them—what they needed to know. The man knelt to the bag, extracted a ring-shaped explosive charge nearly three feet in diameter. He fastened the charge to a side wall of the main vault, snapped in the detonator wires and uncoiled the wire around a corner of the vault. Another glance at his watch; he cursed softly. He returned to the bag and then moved through the bank, setting small containers on the floor, twisting a timing device in each container.

He paused deliberately, forcing himself to review every step in his mind. It was all done exactly as he'd

3

rehearsed a hundred times. He walked to the detonator control, braced himself and closed the switch. The explosion crashed through the bank, pummeling him with concussion. He ignored his ringing ears and moved swiftly to the gaping hole ripped in the wall. Inside, he worked with the knowledge of a man who knew where to look for what he wanted. His hands moved swiftly, stuffing bundled currency into zippered bags attached to his parachute harness. He pulled the zippers closed, more than one hundred thousand dollars on his body. There was more, but time was running out fast.

Almost at the same moment he heard the first sirens. He laughed harshly, ducking through the hole in the wall, moving at a steady run for the stairs. A backward glance showed him the flashing lights of police cars. The scene vanished as sharp explosions boomed through the building and smoke poured from canisters he'd placed on the floor. Within seconds the police could see only that smoke. The man was pushing his way through the rooftop door when more explosions cracked behind him. He heard the sound of breaking glass. More of his little packages left behind. The timers reached their limits and detonated explosive charges, sending bullets smashing through the plate glass fronting the bank. For all the police knew a fire raged within the bank, and desperate men were firing at them. They'd be in no hurry to force their entry. Whoever was in the bank was trapped.

The man in black reached the roof, closed and jammed the single entrance door behind him, muffling the intermittent explosions. He ran to the parachute, heaving and twisting like a thing alive from the helium balloon struggling to break free. From the rooftop the din of puzzled and angry men reached him. Engines and screaming sirens. The more noise and confusion the better. The man checked the cylinder gauges. Everything was ready. He ran a strap around the helium cylinders and hooked the strap to a buckle of his parachute harness. He'd leave nothing behind.

He snapped the clasp rings of his parachute harness to the balloon-parachute connectors. He glanced about him. Good. The wind still blew toward the back of the

4

bank building. Away from the police. He braced himself and jerked the snap release to the balloon. Silently, shrouded in darkness, the black balloon ascended from the roof, drifting before the wind.

The police milled outside the bank, heeding shouts to take cover as the desperate men within continued to fire at them.

The balloon drifted at four thousand feet, a bulbous shadow against the soft clouded dawn. The man suspended in the parachute harness checked once more the coded radio transmitter. He showed his impatience, glancing alternately at his watch and the lightening sky. Then he heard the engine sound. Behind him. He twisted in the harness, searching out the familiar profile of the low-wing Pawnee. He kept his eyes glued to the airplane as it swung in a wide circle about him, the pilot waving.

The man in the parachute harness studied the ground, checked his wind drift. He reached up to pull the vent release of the balloon. But the descent was too slow, and he pulled another release to puncture the balloon. Like a great dying beast the rubberized container deflated. Moving slowly, with perfect control, the falling man released his snap locks to the balloon and dropped away. For several seconds he fell like an arrow, hands at his sides, head down. Then his arms and legs spread-eagled and he turned in the manner of a highspeed glider, diving swiftly. He looked behind him to assure his clearance. His hand jerked the D-ring of his emergency chest-pack, and nylon cracked open above him.

The streaming balloon rustled past him to thud with a small cloud of dust into an open field. Moments later the parachutist was on the ground. He moved quickly, rolling up his chute, and ran to where the balloon and his other parachute lay in a crumpled heap. By the time he reached the balloon the Pawnee was settling to earth to his right, taxiing awkwardly to him. The man on the ground ran to the plane with his gear. Standing on the wing he opened the hopper door where chemicals usually were stored. He tossed in his equipment, climbed

5

into the hopper and pulled the door closed. He felt the roar of power as the pilot opened the throttle. For several seconds the wheels bouncing over the rough ground jarred him. Then it was smooth as the plane lifted steadily.

The man patted the zippered bags with more than a hundred thousand dollars within them. He smiled as he thought of the Pawnee flying low over the fields and trees before it climbed to altitude.

Nothing was more common in this part of the country than a crop duster flying low early in the morning.

"You plan on getting some while we're up there?"

Captain Ben Michaels glanced to his left. He shook his head slowly at the wide grin on the face of Dick Chambers. "Major, don't you ever think of anything except ass?"

Chambers laughed. "I remember once or twice I thought of something else." The major pursed his lips and appeared deep in thought. "Of course," he went on, mock-serious, "it's hard to recall *exactly* when."

"Hah! I'll bet."

"Never mind the questions, boy," the major persisted. "Just pay attention to what you're asked. You plan on getting any while—"

"Up there? In Alaska? For Christ's sake, we're going to be way out in the boonies," Michaels protested. "Won't be a white woman around for five hundred miles. Nothing but Eskimos and moose."

"So what's wrong with a good-looking moose? Course, you gotta walk a mite far to get kissed, but—"

"Good Lord!" The expletive sounded from behind them. The two pilots turned to their flight engineer. Captain Myron Smith studied them with open disdain. "I wish you two animals, you especially, Major, could hear what you sound like. It's rutting season all year round."

Chambers raised his brows. "Oh, ho! Words of wisdom from our religious fanatic." Chambers poked his copilot and jerked a thumb back at Smith. "You hear the message, Ben? Our good flight engineer is about to begin reading to us from the Bible."

Myron Smith scowled darkly. He took poorly to his crew's ill-concealed amusement of his background. The flight engineer had studied several years for the priesthood and he hadn't been able to rub off the urge to set his friends on the straight and narrow. He knew he overdid it, but he couldn't help himself. Especially with their pilot. Dick Chambers operated like a seminal factory that might be closed down any day. He flushed at Chambers' remark about the Bible. It was true enough. He always carried one with him. And with the load they were carrying in the C-130 he especially felt its comfort. Those atomic bombs back there in the deep belly of their transport. He shuddered. He forced himself back to the pilot's mockery.

"The Bible, huh?" Smith said. "It would be an improvement over that trash *you* read!" His retort was made with more heat than intended.

Chambers laughed. "Trash! The finest erotica ever to come from the pen and he calls it trash!" Chambers half twisted in his seat and stabbed his finger at the flight engineer. "Listen to me, my fine-feathered theological freak. The only difference between what I read and that well-worn volume you're toting around is that *my* erotica is at least honest, while the Bible just covers it all up in a nice blanket of do-good hypocrisy. Not only that, but—"

"Hold it, *hold it!*" Captain Ben Michaels waved his arms frantically to head off the stormy exchange he knew was coming. "Not now, you guys. For Christ's sake, can't we make just one lousy flight without you two going at it? You're beating my ears to a pulp!"

Dick Chambers shrugged. What the hell, he *had* been on Myron's back pretty strong lately. "Okay, okay," he sighed. "It's time for coffee anyway." He turned and gestured to the radioman, farther back in the flight deck of the big transport. "Hey Gus. How's the coffeepot doing?"

Lieutenant Gus Johnson waved airily. "Coming right up."

Captain Myron Smith settled back with a mug of steaming coffee. He felt his anger washing away slowly and reprimanded himself for a fool. He knew he left himself wide open for the ribbing the crew gave him with such enthusiasm. He knew at times he sounded stuffy and overbearing. Like a hillbilly preacher shouting of damnation and salvation. He sighed weari-

8

ly. He lacked cause for umbrage with these men. They were a great crew. Wonderful men. Every one of them a proven combat veteran. Every one of them with awards for valor and courage from that stinking mess in Vietnam.

You had to be proven to fly the mission they were on right now. Transporting five atomic bombs from Tennessee to Elmendorf in Alaska. Myron Smith had been proven, like the others, in Vietnam. Ninety Ranch-Hand missions in creaking old C-123s, spraying powerful chemicals across verdant countryside, defoliating the areas used by the Cong for staging bases. Myron Smith sighed. At least that was infinitely better than hurling napalm against villages in which women and children cowered against the flaming hell from the skies.

He couldn't keep his thoughts from the rounded steel containers with their terrible cargo. *The* weapons. Nuclear. Each encased in its own thick steel shell. He thought of the thick steel and laughed without mirth. Thick was a matter of relative speaking. *Nothing* was thick to those weapons, destined for operational readiness with swift attack bombers in the Alaskan cold. Readiness for strikes against northern bases of the Soviets.

Myron Smith knew that as flight engineer in the cargo transport carrying the bombs to Alaska he would never be called upon to unleash that atomic hell against living beings. He doubted he could ever go that far. Not for love of country or for family or for any other reason. Nothing could justify such horror. He drained the coffee mug and cursed to himself. He *must* stop this line of thought. He had no business wearing this uniform if this was the cross he had to bear.

He wondered what the others thought about the bombs. *If* they even thought of what they were carrying with them. Oh, not that they didn't know about the weapons. But to *think* about them. To force your thoughts to consider in slow, exquisite detail what they were doing. The two pilots didn't seem to care. Major Dick Chambers and Captain Ben Michaels. He wondered what were their thoughts, if they wrestled with themselves about their savage cargo. Myron Smith didn't know what they thought. The two pilots were skilled, brave men who refused to discuss the morality of atomic bombs and their roles in setting up their use. "That's *your* bag, baby," the major had snapped at him one day when Smith pressed the subject. "Go tell it to your Bible but stay the hell off my back. And that's an *order*." He meant it, Smith knew. He felt, deep within him, that Chambers had crossed his own private Styx to appear so callous about it all.

Myron Smith thought about the others. Lieutenant Gus Johnson. He looked at the radioman studying his navigation instruments. He's too young, thought Smith. He grew up in a world where atomic and hydrogen bombs were as common as jets and satellites. He hasn't the slightest comprehension of . . . Myron Smith shook his head sadly in unspoken sympathy for the lack of conflict within Johnson.

The remaining two men were different. Master Sergeant Paul Slavick was their Loadmaster. He didn't care *what* they carried in the big C-130. Slavish Slavick, they called him. All the sergeant cared about was doing his job. Whatever they brought aboard the airplane had to be stowed, tied down, chained securely to the machine. Slavick tended his cargo as if it were a matter of life or death. Myron Smith had to admit he was right. If cargo shifted suddenly in rough air it could tear the heart out of their transport and kill them all. Slavick tended his cargo and ignored the rest of the world.

Kelly was another matter. Master Sergeant Joe Kelly. The Weapons Guard. Keeper of the atom. A hulking brute of a man, startlingly intelligent, but with a fanatical dedication to guarding the bombs they were transporting to Alaska. He's been brainwashed, thought Myron Smith. Eight years in SAC. Eight years of wearing a .38 on his hip, of carrying a sub-machine gun cradled in his arms like a precious infant. Eight years of protecting the nuclear seeds against interlopers. That was his job. He went along with the C-130 crew to assure that only authorized personnel went anywhere near the bombs. Kelly would shoot the guts out of his own crew if they tried to touch the bombs. He had a

10

list of names and complete identification of the officers assigned to receive the nukes. Anyone else—everyone—was to be regarded with malignant suspicion.

Does he have even the slightest concept of what he's guarding? The question bothered Myron Smith who had thought overlong on that subject. Rocking gently in the big turboprop transport at twenty-five thousand feet with five atomic bombs only a few feet away was unreal to him. The bombs intruded upon his peace of mind. They gnawed at him, their presence forcing his mind to dwell on their terrible caress, should they ever be unleashed.

The weapons they carried were fully ready for combat use. That alone was frightening. It helped—not as much as it should, Smith thought with a sour grimace—to know they were rigged with elaborate safety systems to prevent the fission process from starting until safety arming locks were released. Smith knew, as did the others who had been briefed in detail about their cargo, that fire or explosion would not set off the weapons. They needed to know this. Their airplane might suffer mechanical difficulty during their delivery mission. The Air Force far preferred its crews to deliver the weapons safely to ground in an emergency landing than for them to bail out and leave the bombs to be destroyed in the ensuing crash. Those bombs cost more than two million dollars each. The Air Force didn't want its investment thrown away by a frightened crew. So they were briefed in exhaustive detail. Experts proved to them again and again just how safe were those bombs. Myron Smith had the uncomfortable feeling that someone was protesting too much about such safety.

Yet their existed a casual air about carrying five atomic bombs from Tennessee to Alaska. Sergeant Kelly carried both a sidearm and his ever-present automatic weapon. The remainder of the crew were armed only with .38 revolvers. Myron Smith wondered just what he would, or could, do with the popgun strapped to his waist. Who would he shoot? Who wanted such terrible devices anyway? Except, he thought darkly, governments who planned day and night for the most effective means of killing and destroying.

11

He couldn't ward off the depressive mood that settled darkly about him. Parkers Air Force Base, near Nashville, was his home field and he was weary to the bone of living with atom bombs in all directions. The Air Force maintained a secret nuclear weapons modification center at Parkers where the nukes were brought in for servicing, refitting and modification with new arming fuses and devices. Then they were loaded aboard transports like their C-130 and flown to different fields around the world for loading aboard tactical fighters and bombers. Myron Smith estimated he'd played nursemaid, as flight engineer, to possibly four hundred nukes. Their crew had flown them across four continents.

The weapons were nothing like the monster hydrogen bombs carried by SAC. Unless you *knew* what lay concealed within the dull-metal canisters in the cargo deck of the C-130 there wasn't any way of identifying the weapons. He thought in detail of the bombs and he felt the stirrings of nausea in his stomach. Each bomb, before it was fitted to its missile carrier, was only eleven inches in diameter and nineteen inches in length.

Yet it would explode with the force of three hundred thousand tons of high explosives. Three hundred kilotons! Myron Smith thought of Hiroshima and the first bomb, and he thought that each weapon they carried would explode with a force fifteen times greater than the bomb at Hiroshima. They carried five bombs. An appalling sight of cities smashed flat, of writhing mushroom clouds, roared through his mind. He struggled to guide his thoughts elsewhere, forced his mind to their airplane, to its flight.

He glanced through the windshield, then directed his gaze to the left of Dick Chambers, to the side windows. Even from twenty-five thousand feet he saw the ground clearly. The desert air was unusually clear and they could see tremendous distances. He waited to study Monument Valley from the air. Its great buttresses and deep-red color, splashed across the Utah-Arizona border, always filled him with a sense of wonder. They might almost be God's work, he thought. He glanced at his watch. They should be there soon. He studied the

12

instrument panel. In a few minutes Michaels would switch their VHF homer to the next VOR site. They'd alter course by several degrees and Monument Valley would appear below and to their left. Myron Smith released his seat lock and slid closer to the front of the flight deck to get a better view.

Their route took them from Parkers Air Force Base near Nashville across the southwestern United States. They were flying a wide detour around a severe weather front to the north. They'd fly to the west coast, turn to the north and then cut across the Pacific to Alaska. Because of their cargo their precise route was controlled rigidly. At all costs they must avoid flying over major cities or large concentrations of population.

Monument Valley would soon be coming into sight. Myron Smith leaned forward. To his front and right Ben Michaels dialed in the frequency for the Monument Valley VOR. The new numbers appeared in their window guide. Moments later the homing needle began to move fitfully. Michaels adjusted the autopilot a hair to compensate for an unexpected crosswind. Behind Myron Smith the radioman, Gus Johnson, started to call in their position report to the VOR station.

The homing indicator went dead.

"What the hell?" That from Ben Michaels. He twisted the frequency control several times. To no avail.

"Hey, Gus, you raise Monument Valley yet?"

Gus Johnson shook his head. "Can't get 'em. Looks like they're off the air."

"Something's always wrong with that goddamned station," Dick Chambers muttered. "I think they play with themselves or something down there." The pilot glanced at his chart and called to their radioman. "Gus, how long before we pick up the next VOR?"

Johnson replied immediately. "We should come into range in about thirty minutes, Major."

"No sweat," Chambers mumbled. VOR stations were always going off the air for one reason or another. Mechanical breakdowns and electronic gremlins plagued the VHF equipment. It didn't matter. They were out of touch with any ground station now and would remain that way for another thirty minutes or so. They'd report into the next station. There'd be a mild flap on the ground, Chambers thought. When you carried nukes you were supposed to be under radar track at all times. Well, they sure weren't now. There was nothing below them in all directions but rock and desert. That's their bag, Chambers thought. Let them worry about it. He glanced at his watch and noted the time. Exactly 3:14 P.M. local. He made a notation on his knee pad. Just for the record. He—

"Hey, Major!"

Chambers started at the urgent sound in the voice. "Slavick here, sir! Look out to your left. About eight o'clock. I'll be damned if those aren't P-fifty-ones out there!"

Chambers pressed himself to the side window. He couldn't believe it but they were there, all right. Two long-nosed, sleek P-51 fighters. "Christ, I didn't know we still had fifty-ones active," Chambers said to his copilot.

"I don't know," Michaels said doubtfully. "I think the Air Commandos—they're a Hurlburt in Florida—they've put them back into service."

Chambers studied the two fighters sliding in toward them. "They've got ANG on the tail," he said.

Myron Smith leaned forward. "That would be Air National Guard, wouldn't it?"

"Yeah. Could be," Chambers replied slowly. He was still doubtful. "But what would they be doing up here with—hey, Gus, he's signaling for radio talk. Go to guard channel and see if you can pick him up."

Chambers proved to be right. Michaels already had his headset on, and Chambers and Smith grabbed theirs.

"*. . . emergency. Repeat, emergency. Our orders are for you to land immediately. You can see the runway dead ahead about twenty miles. Start your descent now. Over.*"

Chambers stared at Michaels. "Emergency? Land immediately? What the hell is this all about?"

"I don't know," his copilot said quickly. "But whatever it is I don't like it. There's something funny here,

14

Dick. No one would send up anybody from ANG. And they sure as hell wouldn't be using fifty-ones."

"Damn right they wouldn't," Chambers growled. He grabbed for his microphone. "Nine-eight-two to the Mustang to our left. I don't know what this is all about but I don't appreciate games like this. We're not landing anywhere. I haven't the foggiest about any emergency. You read me? Over."

"Start your descent now. That's an order. Repeat, that is an order."

"You can shove your order," Chambers snarled. "We're not going any—*Jesus Christ!*"

Brilliant lights sparkled across the front of the transport.

"Tracers! The son of a bitch is firing tracers at us!" Slavick yelled from the cargo hold.

"Gus! Get out a mayday!" Chambers barked to the radioman. "Tell somebody what's going on!" He paused only a moment. "Slavick!"

"Yes, sir!"

"Where's that second fighter?"

"He's sitting off to our right and behind us, sir. Slightly above. He's the one that fired—"

"Okay," Chambers snapped. "Just keep an eye on him. Gus, did you get anyone?"

"No, sir," the radioman replied quickly. "With that VOR station dead we're out of reach."

It hit them at the same time. They were out of radio touch. But if they turned around, fast, and started back along their original course, they'd be in radio contact in just a few minutes. Cursing, Chambers switched off the automatic pilot and grabbed the controls.

He wasn't thirty degrees in the turn when the tracers blazed only scant feet from the cockpit. Chambers hauled the big transport back to level flight.

The voice from the fighter to his left stayed calm and positive. *"The field's only fifteen miles ahead of you now, Nine-eight-two. Land straight in. And tell your boy to stay off the radio."*

They stared in disbelief at each other.

"You've got just ten seconds. You get the next burst in the cockpit."

15

Lieutenant Colonel Paul Beyersdorf stared through the window at a row of trees almost wilting from the blazing California sun. There were some good things about Norton Air Force Base, but this damned heat, and the smog rolling in from the coast ... Beyersdorf turned his head to look at General Sheridan.

He looks like a robot sitting there. If I know the Old Man he's building up a head of steam. This thing could wreck his career if he doesn't start coming up with the right answers. Damnit, what's holding up Reider, anyway? Sheridan will tear off his head like he's wringing a chicken's neck. If this meeting doesn't get under way pretty soon we won't be able to live with the Old Man for a month. Christ. A quarter to ten already and—

Lieutenant Colonel Paul Beyersdorf broke off his rumination as a sergeant entered the conference room. The sergeant's uniform looked as if the man had stepped straight from a recruiting poster (thank God for small favors, thought Beyersdorf) and he was crisply spit-and-polish. He did everything but click his heels as he addressed the general.

"Sir, report from Base Operations." General Sheridan waited for the sergeant to continue.

"It's Colonel Reider, sir." Every man in the room stiffened. "He'll be on the ground in a few minutes. His aircraft had a flameout, left engine, sir, and an electrical failure. They weren't able to report until a few moments ago, and he requested we inform you immediately."

The general nodded slowly. Beyersdorf knew he had already whipped through his mind virtually every element of what might have happened in the air with Colonel Reider. Just the few words reported by the sergeant told Sheridan a detailed, interwoven story.

Hank Reider—Colonel Hank Reider from Tactical Air Command Headquarters, Division of Aerospace Safety —was flying his own B-57 from Virginia to Norton Air Force Base, California for the emergency meeting. Not too far out, no more than a few hundred miles, anyway, the left engine of the B-57 flamed out. Unless they were carrying weapons stores, and they weren't, Beyersdorf knew, there wasn't much sweat to losing the one engine. The B-57 could hack it on just one. But there was that matter of the electrical failure and *that* meant emergency. If Reider hadn't put down somewhere en route then, on the face of it, he was violating his own safety requirements. On the face of it, anyway. But maybe there had been some rotten weather in the area, and letting down through the soup with heavy rain and turbulence, and only one engine going for you, *and* with your electrical systems acting up, was begging for trouble. If Reider could keep the twin-jet bomber over the weather with one engine he was playing it smart. Radar had him on ground track and when he didn't report in on schedule, and they failed to raise him, they'd know he'd lost power somewhere, and they'd anticipate what any good pilot would do. Continue with his original flight plan. You could always tell what was happening by what a pilot *did*. Because of power from only one engine, Reider's ground speed would have dropped. Air Traffic Control knew there hadn't been any sudden flow increase in the jetstream. Reduced speed and radio silence, and the en route weather, and the continued flight of the B-57, meant only one thing. The colonel was pushing on to Norton Air Force Base because that was the safest, the wisest move to make. Not even the wrath of General Sheridan could have forced Hank Reider to push his luck to the point of being foolish. And the general knew it.

General Sheridan looked up. "Thank you, Sergeant." Nothing else. The non-com didn't bother to ask if there were a message. He knew better than that. Had Sheridan wanted to send back word he would have said so without prompting. The sergeant snapped out, "Thank you, sir," and did an about-face that would have brought a smile to a Prussian martinet.

17

Arthur Sheridan wished for the comforts of a nice, flaming, lethal emergency where his life hung in the balance between disaster and his skill. Then everything was cut and dry. You flew like you never flew before and you rammed the fear crawling up your throat back down where the hell it belonged because you couldn't afford the luxury of being terrified. You defied the law of gravity and you squeezed every last ounce from aerodynamics and you used muscle. If you didn't hack it, the failure couldn't really *hurt* you. Undoubtedly it would kill you. Arthur Sheridan had never really been afraid of death. He'd like something to say about his last flight, sure. There were plenty of ways to die in the air. You didn't ram huge bombers through demanding combat-ready operations without someone paying the piper. Someone, somewhere, was bound to get snared by the law of averages. Anyone and everyone who was good *knew* it would always be "the other guy." You lived with death all around you and after a while you'd even Indian-wrestle the son of a bitch.

Arthur Sheridan felt the only way to treat death was in the same manner with which the ancient Greeks treated migraine headache. With contempt.

He couldn't treat with contempt what he faced now. Which is why he wished he were back in the cockpit of a B-52 or even that slab-winged terror of a B-58. There he knew what he faced. No shadows or phantoms to bring slivers of pain deep into your brain.

He wondered if Beyersdorf were aware of his fierce headache. He never knew just how much his aide really knew. Beyersdorf was a walking computer. The best. He knew what Sheridan was shooting for and without ever having it discussed openly he was doing his best to support him. Well, Sheridan thought dryly, I need all the help I can get right now. How in the name of hell does a large transport, in clear air in the middle of the United States, just disappear from the face of the earth?

He had the question but not the answer. And people demanded that he come up with the answer. Fast. Because it wasn't any ordinary transport that had vanished. Nothing's ordinary about an airplane carrying five nukes in its fat belly. Where's that C-130? The

18

Pentagon was breathing down the neck of General Brownell. Breathing, hell. They were blowing flames down his shirt collar. Lieutenant General David A. Brownell was the Inspector General of the Air Force. Brigadier General Arthur S. Sheridan was his Director of Aerospace Safety. Brownell ordered Sheridan: "Drop everything you're doing. *Immediately.* Get on the stick. Find that goddamned airplane. Find those triple-damned atomic bombs it was carrying." The C-130 hadn't been missing long enough for an official report to the White House, but that was only a matter of hours, another day at the most. This meeting, held up until the presence of Hank Reider, was proof of the laterally mushrooming effect. Several government agencies were represented here and unless they had the answers to the questions all were asking, the White House would land with both feet in the middle of the picture.

No, the general thought. Not in the middle of the picture. Squarely on the back of my neck. He grinned ruefully to himself with the thought that it was a powerful and muscular neck. It should be, he grunted (drawing a questioning look from Beyersdorf). It's been hit enough times to stand almost anything.

Arthur Sheridan stood six feet two inches tall and weighed in at a husky 210 pounds. His thick neck and powerful shoulders, his slab stomach and the balanced walk of a crack pilot and practicing athlete, gave the impression of solid physical strength and great self-confidence. All of which was true. All of which could fit the description of two thousand other pilots. All were cast from the same mold. They met the same wicked requirements of physical conditioning and mental alertness, they had to cut the same frame of mind. The Hollywood stereotype of a crack pilot in the Air Force had become accepted by the public. As damned well it should, Sheridan argued. Because it's true. You give a man the command of a twelve-million-dollar airplane, place ten men's lives under his fingers, tell him he's in charge of two hydrogen bombs each with an explosive power of thirty million tons of TNT, and what do you expect to find in the left seat of that B-52—a clerk from a department store?

Like many of his peers, Arthur Sheridan wanted command. Not of one airplane or a flight or a squadron or even a group. He wanted the command that brought stars instead of silver eagles to his shoulders. He wanted top rank and if he had anything to say about it he'd make the top. He believed himself to be a man who could do the job better than those crowding around him. He hewed to the principles of Curt LeMay when he created the Strategic Air Command. That the world would go to hell in a handbasket the moment the Russians felt they could squeeze out a clear superiority. Of course, his wrecked marriage might prove an obstacle to his aspirations. Normally that would be true, since the headshrinkers made ominous overtones that wrecked marriages hint darkly of emotional instability and—and so much crap, Sheridan reflected with an interruption of his own thoughts. The skullbinders didn't consider that your wife might just be a plain, ordinary bitch. Or God knew what. Besides, in SAC, divorce was an occupational disease. More than forty percent of all first-line pilots in the Command went through divorce. The strain killed family relationships. In his own case Sheridan remained inflexibly on call to the requirements and the demands of his uniform and the wings he wore. It was no more complicated than that. It wrecked *his* home life. Beth divorced him shortly after his second son was born, and Sheridan was secretly pleased with the arrangement that gave him two fine sons and also relieved him of the prosaic responsibilities such fatherhood entailed. If nothing else, he was honest with his failings as a husband and father. He philosophized that no man can be everything.

But every man, he knew, must take advantage of rare moments life throws up for grabs. Fate chuckled when it threw Sheridan's opportunity to him, as it so often did in the business of flying the great machines with their terrible nuclear cargo. If you survived an impossible situation, SAC was dutifully grateful and noted the fact on your records. You received few accolades. You were in the left seat of a giant machine carrying thermonuclear weapons because you were the best in the business. But every so often the inevitable emergency transcended individual survival or even the survival of the crew and the saving of a crippled twelve-million-dollar airplane. Every now and then the gods tossed the dice and a national disaster teetered on the skill, the courage, the intelligence of a single human being.

The next time the gods tossed the dice they came up with the name of Arthur Sheridan.

It started out easily enough. A long-range mission over the Arctic with a balls-out combat bomb run on a simulated target. Eighteen hours in the air. Except they never made the mission scheduled. Fifteen minutes after takeoff the electrical systems went to hell. The crew reported fire from the bomb bay. No sooner did he receive this chilling report when the controls stiffened beneath Sheridan's hands; the power boost system had screwed up and he and his copilot were forced to fly manually a machine weighing 450,000 pounds. Sheridan ordered the crew on emergency oxygen and depressurized the airplane so the men could get into the huge cubicles where they carried two thirty-megaton hydrogen bombs. His radioman flashed out the emergency, and the command system of SAC stiffened perceptibly. His men extinguished the flames but there seemed every danger they'd leap back into existence. They had a bad short somewhere in the system and things were going to hell in a handbasket. Then the radios went out. The flight engineer started shutting down systems as fast as he could because there was now real danger the fuel systems would be affected by the electrical failures. They might all disappear in a single blinding sheet of flame if that happened.

Sheridan weighed the long and short of it. Finally the radioman managed to activate their single-frequency standby transmitter. They couldn't receive but at least Sheridan could let the ground know what was happening. He didn't have any good news to report. Electrical systems failure. Fire; extinguished but ready to reap-

21

pear at any moment. Radio failure. Difficulties with the flight control system. There was more. Failure of the electrical system meant he couldn't operate his gear or his flaps. *That* meant he couldn't slow the monster to a speed where he could land safely, even if he bellied it in. They'd still be going so fast by the time they reached the end of even the longest runway available they'd go off the overrun into open country. And he didn't know how much longer he could retain control of the giant.

The gods tossed the dice and everything ended up in the lap of Sheridan. No one else could help.

Sheridan fought the airplane over an open area and ordered his crew to bail out. One by one eight men tumbled from the crippled bomber. It was Sheridan's plan to bail out his crew, take the B-52 over a desolate area to the north of his home base, set it into a dive, and explode himself from the plane with his ejection seat.

Then a warning light flashed on the panel. Sheridan's blood ran cold. The copilot to his right, who had started from the plane, went white. He lowered himself slowly back into his seat.

The arming light for one of the hydrogen bombs was on.

Was it a faulty switch? They had no way of knowing. What they did know was they couldn't bail out and leave the airplane to crash. Even in isolated country. Thirty million tons of high explosives might be the result. It was snowing in the Dakotas. The lethal fallout could extend over tens of thousands of square miles. Somehow they had to *land* the airplane. Later, reflected Sheridan and his copilot, they realized they'd never thought of their own lives. Not with thirty megatons ticking away behind them.

What happened next was history. Nearly two hundred miles to the north a SAC field lay buried under heavy snow. Sheridan radioed the nearest field and told them what he planned to do. They confirmed his message by sending up flares. Sheridan headed the bomber and its frightening cargo to the north. There men were already at work. Frantic work. Using every snowplow and bulldozer on the field. Not to clear the runway but to bank snow at one end of the longest runway on the field.

Without flaps, without landing gear, Sheridan and his copilot fought the giant machine to earth. They landed on the belly of the huge bomber, fighting the rudder madly to stay headed down the runway. Snow erupted in tremendous plumes as the B-52 slammed ahead, for thousands of feet decelerating slowly, giving up her great speed with reluctance. No one had left the field. There'd been no evacuation. If Sheridan made even one mistake and that bomb went off the fireball would have been more than six miles in diameter. For fifteen miles beyond that the destruction would have been total. There wasn't anywhere to run, no place to hide.

The B-52 burst into the high snow near the runway's end. Engines tore loose, metal crumpled, and Sheridan and the copilot took a fierce buffeting in their seat harness. The airplane stopped with a final dinosaur cry of protest, half-buried in snow. Sheridan couldn't move, refused to be helped from the plane until the ordnance teams came in through an emergency hatch and reached the bombs. Not until they confirmed the bombs were safe did Sheridan move.

A week later his thick crop of hair was almost completely white.

It was worth it. The Pentagon tapped him for advancement. There was a new star in his life.

Silver, on his shoulder.

He'd made it, all right. Brigadier general. His first assignment, sensibly enough after his performance with the B-52 that night, was the Director of Aerospace Safety. After that—with a top record behind him— higher echelon command. Either the Pentagon or command in the field. And two stars waiting just over the hill.

Then this accursed missing C-130. With five nukes. Vanished. He knew if he didn't get to the bottom of this maddening problem a question mark could well obscure the sight of the two stars waiting for him. This was another "put up or shut up" deal. Only this time he

23

was working with events beyond his control. He didn't have all the information he needed so desperately. You could fight the controls of a crippled machine. But the machine he now sought had vanished into thin air.

"It took us a while to track it down," Fred Elliott said. "But once we had the first few pieces the rest fell into place." Fred Elliott paused to consult his notes. He had been sent on priority order to Norton Air Force Base from the Los Angeles office of the Federal Aviation Administration. Elliott was a tall, spare man with thinning sandy hair. His lankiness gave no hint of the great power in his oversized hands. He gained his startling grip, which he made careful to control, during years of flying the last powerful piston-engine fighters in the Navy. But Sheridan didn't give a damn about his military service. What counted to him was that Fred Elliott was an air traffic specialist for the FAA and, at Sheridan's request, had been assigned at once to the mystery of the missing C-130.

"Whoever pulled this caper," Elliott went on, "is strictly professional."

"Why do you say that?" Sheridan demanded.

Elliott smiled thinly. "General, these people have been in the flying game for a long time. Everything they've done has the mark of the pro. They didn't miss a trick."

General Sheridan tried not to exhibit the dismay he felt. That C-130 wasn't just missing. Someone had gained control of it. Forced it down.

But who—and how—would force down an Air Force transport in flight! And how did they know exactly when and where to strike? There'd be hell to pay on this from the Pentagon. Colonel Hank Reider from Tactical Air Command, still in his flight clothing at the conference table, would take the brunt of it. No matter he didn't have a thing to do with what had happened. Reider was from TAC Headquarters and a TAC plane had disappeared with its cargo of five nukes, and there wasn't anyone *else* to blame. At least for the moment. Sheridan reprimanded himself sharply. That sort of thinking wouldn't do anyone a bit of good.

The devil with who might get blamed or catch the short end of the stick. The job was to find that airplane. But he couldn't shake the sick feeling that persisted in his stomach.

"The details, the report, I mean," continued Elliott, "is available to your office, of course. I came here rather much in a rush without making extra copies, but they're being prepared for you right now."

Sheridan nodded. He glanced around the table. Besides Beyersdorf, Hank Reider and Fred Elliott, there was Bill Thorp from the Civil Aeronautics Board. Thorp was as well known outside the CAB as within that organization for his crusty appearance and attitude. He affected rumpled clothes and a casual air behind which existed the mind of a born sleuth, a reputation he had earned through twenty years of investigating aircraft accidents. Beyersdorf had put through a specific request for Thorp with CAB in Washington. The CAB was the official government agency for aircraft accident investigations, and Beyersdorf had the feeling that despite the considerable talents available right there at Norton Air Force Base, they would need the help of the best skills they could borrow. At this moment no one could make the unargued statement that the C-130 had suffered an accident but there wasn't any question of there being a full-blown disaster on their hands.

Sheridan returned his gaze to Elliott. "Have you added to your report what other information we've been able to give you?"

"Not in final form, but essentially, we've got a picture that's taking place," the FAA man said.

"Would you mind running it through once more? I'd like the rest of you," Sheridan directed his words to the group, "to make notes as we go along. It might close a few of the holes." He nodded to Elliott to pick up the story.

"Well, as I said, this smacks of a professional touch all the way," he began. "It's important to get that straight from the beginning because it lets us make some strong assumptions as to what's happened. Beyond the hard information we already have."

"You can add something to that, Fred," Sheridan broke in. He didn't wait for a response but went on. "Whoever's got that airplane, or is responsible for it being missing, had to know more than how this business operates. He had a detailed flight schedule of an Air Force aircraft. A classified schedule, I might add. Colonel," he turned to Reider, "what's the exact classification on delivery flights of nuclear weapons?"

"Secret, sir." Sheridan knew the answer but wanted it stated by Reider.

"And the dissemination?" Sheridan prompted.

"One copy by the weapons people, of course," Reider replied. "Operations has three copies, the flight crew receive one, and security receives a copy. We file with Headquarters USAF, and we code-transmit to the destination."

"What about FAA?"

"No, sir," Reider said. "They handle the flight plans, of course, but we never identify a flight as nuclear, even in code. We code the flight plan that it's a critical flight but that could fit any one of several categories."

Lieutenant Colonel Paul Beyersdorf motioned for attention. "I don't think we have any choice, General. Somehow, whoever's involved was able to get their hands on our delivery scheduling for nuclear weapons, and—"

"You can't be positive about that," Reider protested. "We don't know that they knew there were nukes aboard that one-thirty."

"No, we don't," Beyersdorf replied smoothly, keeping his voice level, "but it's one of those assumptions we're going to live with."

Beyersdorf could understand Reider's protest. If nuclear bomb scheduling were known to someone outside the severely limited circle to whom delivery orders went, then TAC's security was going to be in for a wicked housecleaning.

Sheridan motioned to Fred Elliott. "Let's take care of the airplane being out of contact," the FAA man said. "Both radio and radar. As you know, the FSS at Monument Valley never did pick up the flight. Several minutes before the flight plan showed the one-thirty as scheduled to enter their area all power was lost." Elliott looked around the table. "It was *not* a power failure," he emphasized, and selected one sheet of paper from those before him.

"For a period of thirty-five minutes the one-thirty was to have been within control of Monument Valley," Elliott continued. "As you're all aware, our standard procedure if an aircraft fails to report, especially on an IFR flight plan, is for an immediate emergency situation to be declared. We spend a few minutes checking down the line, the last station over which the aircraft reported, and so on. If we don't confirm its position or contact the aircraft by radio, we go to immediate alert down the line. Whoever went after that airplane knew all this." Elliott frowned. "They knew it down to the last detail because they made sure that the station, first, would never pick up the airplane, and, second, that any failure of the airplane to report in would be obscured by loss of power on the ground.

"Obviously, timing was everything. These, ah, people, knew the exact route of the C-one-thirty, and they knew its schedule. I feel they must have checked on its progress during its flight. We're running a check right now, in fact, to see if any queries came in about the airplane. But to get back to what I was saying. These people knew that if Monument Valley FSS was knocked out then there would be a period of approximately thirty-five minutes while that one-thirty would be out of contact with *any* station. Again, that's out of contact both in voice and radar." Elliott consulted his notes again. "The airplane was scheduled to enter control of Monument Valley at, umm, the nearest we can make it out, at three-fourteen P.M. That's local time." Elliott looked up and glanced at each man in turn.

"Precisely at nine minutes past three P.M., again that's local time." Elliott was very careful with his notations about time, he didn't want to cause any confusion with Greenwich Mean Time, or Zulu, as it was known, and he used local time because of what he was about to say, "at three-o-nine P.M. local, the power system to the Monument Valley FSS was blown." He paused to let his words sink in. He knew that until this moment

27

Colonel Reider was unaware of this fact, and the colonel answered him with an exclamation.

"Blown?"

"That's right, Colonel. Blown. A beautiful job, I might add, from what we've learned. Experts."

Colonel Reider stared at the FAA man, who picked up his story. "They blew the power lines leading to the FSS station. They backed themselves up, too. A bomb wrecked the generating plant. That took care of the power cables to the remote station. The Monument Valley VOR and radar are about three miles from the FSS itself, so they were able to knock out power without anyone seeing them."

"No hope of identification?" Beyersdorf threw out the question with little hope for a productive answer.

"Uh-uh. We didn't find a thing except where the explosives were used," Elliott mused. "The FBI's making their own investigation right now, of course, and—"

"FBI? Why the FBI?" Hank Reider appeared startled that more agencies were being involved. His question was an unspoken hope they might solve the mystery on their own.

"Why, of course the FBI," Elliott said. "Federal property has been destroyed, and outside an, well, not on Federal land. We're tenants in that area. The FBI's the appropriate agency to—"

Reider gestured unhappily. "I'm sorry to have broken in," he said.

Elliott hesitated, frowning, as if he were concerned that somehow he might have insulted Reider with the news that the FBI had been brought in. General Sheridan shared Reider's feelings. They had enough on their hands without Hoover's legions swooping down upon them. And they'd be only the beginning, Sheridan knew. The security agencies of the government went hog-wild over a situation like this one. Unless they found that one-thirty in not too much more time, the CIA would come sneaking in their back window, convinced that once again the Russians had put over one more grandiose scheme. And if the CIA crawled into bed with them, then the National Security Agency

28

would come snuggling under the bedcovers from the other side. That's all we need, Sheridan glowered. A three-ring circus. He had new information the others lacked. For a moment he felt the urge to withhold that information, to use everything they had to solve the mystery on their own. No one wanted the other agencies crowding in and fighting for the spoils of credit. Sheridan warned himself to avoid that sort of thinking and to concentrate on what had to be done.

". . . nothing from any of our air traffic control centers," Elliott was saying. "We don't record unidentified aircraft that show up on radar, of course. There are thousands of them every day." Again he shuffled his papers. "The only thing that might bear on this," he hedged carefully, "is a report from San Francisco Center. One of the controllers thought it was unusual enough to have made a note of it." They waited. "Later in the day, some hours after the Monument Valley FSS was knocked out, they tracked a large aircraft through their area, westbound."

A sudden shifting of position rewarded Elliott's statement. "By itself, that wasn't unusual," he added. "But we got a strong transponder track, and the airplane continued westbound over the Pacific. It wasn't on any flight plan, by the way, which is why the controller felt justified in noting the fact."

"What about NORAD?" Reider barked. "Why weren't they—"

"They were, Colonel," Beyersdorf said, a moment before Sheridan started to speak. "NORAD got the report from FAA when the unknown penetrated the ADIZ, and . . ." Sheridan knew the details. The moment the unknown radar target crossed the west coast on its westerly heading and penetrated the Air Defense Identification Zone, FAA notified the Air Force. North American Air Defense Command had already picked up the radar target on its own scopes. What happened next was standard procedure. No, Sheridan corrected. It should have been standard procedure, but it wasn't. Two fighters scrambled immediately to investigate the unknown. They never got to it. The target they sought

29

flew at high speed. Not so great the fighters, capable of more than a thousand miles per hour, couldn't get to it quickly. But the target flew off into a severe weather system hanging over the coast and the fighters found themselves in the midst of violent thunderstorms. Severe turbulence and then a savage barrage of hailstones killed all chances of homing in on the unknown. Two more fighters were scrambled along the track of the elusive quarry but failed to detect anything in the air.

The target—the unknown aircraft—had vanished.

They were right back where they started.

Arthur Sheridan, the moment he received the first details of the missing C-130, hadn't wasted a moment. He closeted himself with Paul Beyersdorf and the two men did everything they could to recreate the events as they transpired with the C-130 transport. Could the airplane have suffered some onboard disaster during flight and the pilots attempted an emergency landing? The area of immediate interest involved the many thousands of square miles where no radar coverage existed. That same night, as the emergency bulletins of the missing aircraft came to his deak, Sheridan acted swiftly. Search planes were sent off on carefully spaced grids to study the entire area. Leaving nothing undone Sheridan requested SAC Headquarters to fly an RS-71 mission throughout the entire area. Not photographic. Infrared. The black reconnaissance plane crisscrossed the search area with infrared cameras, recording any areas of unusual heat during the night hours.

The search crews found nothing, but the RS-71 mission paid off in spades. It gave them one of their few tangible leads as to what had happened.

In the area covered by the RS-71, its pilot flying blindly, trusting to his instruments, there were twenty-two abondoned airfields. All of them, at one time, had been active in training new pilots. That was during World War II, now decades past. Sheridan played his hunch that, somehow, their invisible adversaries had forced down the C-130. If this had indeed happened, then there was an outside chance that whatever took place on the ground might have left a thermal signature. Nothing that would have showed up in daytime but that would reveal itself to cameras that took their pictures in the infrared part of the spectrum.

The long shot paid off. On one picture an abandoned runway that allegedly had not been used in many years showed several source-points of heat. They shouldn't have been there. The old concrete runways, heated during the day by the sun, cooled less rapidly than the surrounding desert. But they cooled more or less at an average rate of heat dissipation. On this one runway that commanded their attention they saw several points of heat. As if parts of the runway had been heated to very high temperatures and took more time to cool off than the surrounding concrete.

The pictures were delivered to Sheridan and his experts at four o'clock in the morning. By six o'clock, in the early desert dawn, Sheridan and Beyersdorf were in a T-38 on their way to the Air Force field nearest the abandoned airstrip. There they boarded a helicopter and set out for the airstrip. Sheridan ordered the pilot not to land on the strip or even to fly over it. He didn't want the powerful downwash of the rotors disturbing any impressions that might have been left in the dusty sand of the field.

They walked to the old runway and their suspicions were confirmed. "Any questions?" Sheridan threw at Beyersdorf. The query was redundant. Both men saw the tire tracks made by the heavy C-130. They were unmistakable. They saw where the airplane had landed. They also saw the signature of its gear where it had taken off again.

They found other signs that painted a picture for them. "See here?" Sheridan pointed to the ground and paced off the distance between several other signs of tire treads. "Nothing else made those marks except a P-51."

Beyersdorf looked at him.

Sheridan nodded and answered the questions Beyersdorf would ask. "Sure. The tread is exactly that of the

31

fifty-one. Can't be a Jug," he said, shaking his head. "There isn't a single P-forty-seven flying in the country. It's a tail-dragger, all right. You can see where the tail wheel swiveled, here," he pointed again to the ground. "It might have been a P-thirty-eight but there's no sign of a nose wheel in the gear tracks. Has to be a fifty-one. Besides, nothing else that's flying could keep up with the one-thirty in the air."

They both drew the same conclusion at that point. There weren't any P-51s active in the Air Force. No, that's not true, Sheridan thought as quickly as he drew the false conclusion. The First Air Commando Wing at Eglin, in Florida, had a bunch of rebuilt P-51 fighters. He told Beyersdorf to check the Wing on the whereabouts of every one of its fighters for the past forty-eight hours, but he knew what the answer would be. They'd know precisely where every plane had been. And none of them, he was certain, would have been out here in the desert.

They found a few other things on the abandoned runway. The tire marks of another airplane. From the looks of things it was a tricycle-gear ship, heavy enough to be twin-engine. Sheridan ordered a crack team from his headquarters to get to the scene as fast as they could. And because his men weren't up on that many civilian types he made his next move with deliberation. He requested help from the Civil Aeronautics Board. The CAB sent Bill Thorp with his own team. They took pictures of the tire marks and then took plaster casts of the dusty sand.

"Either a Queen Air or King Air," Thorp told him a few hours later. "Beech, twin-engine, carries six to nine people, either model. No question of it."

They'd found a few other things Sheridan had expected. The burned-out container of a smoke bomb, for one. The smoke canister burned with fierce heat. It had provided their first clue. The scorched area on the runway picked up by the sensitive infrared film of the RS-71 cameras.

They found something Sheridan *didn't* expect. Three empty cartridge cases. They hadn't been on the desert more than a day or two. The brass still shone in the bright desert sun. Their caliber was .30-.30. A powerful hunting rifle. That had been fired recently.

At whom?

There had been only one target, Sheridan knew. The crew of the C-130. But only three empty shells. Why only three?

"So that's how it adds up so far," Sheridan addressed the small group in his conference room. "A few facts, a great deal of supposition. But let's take what we've got and see what we come up with. Take it with a grain of salt because one false assumption can lead us down the wrong road."

"A C-one-thirty, carrying five nukes, is missing. It vanished, first, under conditions of clear weather and without any indication the aircraft was in difficulty. No radio reports or anything else. It seems clear that it didn't crash. It *appears* that somehow it was forced down at an abandoned airfield. All this took place immediately after the FAA radio and radar facilities tracking its IFR flight plan were deliberately knocked out of action. By pros, as Mr. Elliott has emphasized.

"This brings us to that old airstrip. The evidence appears conclusive, and I'm going by that evidence, that the C-one-thirty landed there—that it was forced down. Who did the forcing we don't know. How it was forced down is something else. We have evidence on the ground that a P-fifty-one, at least one P-fifty-one, but likely one or two more, was involved. Okay. We can assume, and rather safely, I believe, that people on the ground were waiting for the C-one-thirty to be forced down at that particular field. The smoke bomb was used for identification and for wind direction.

"There were plenty of footprints on the ground. There was also the track of what appears to be a twin-engine aircraft on the ground. The tire marks get pretty well mixed together on the runway, but we have more than enough to identify the airplane, through Mr. Thorp's office, as a Beech, and most likely a Queen Air or a King Air. We've scoured the entire area surround-

33

ing the airstrip. No vehicle marks of any kind. It seems obvious, to me it is obvious unless I'm proved wrong, that the twin-engine aircraft was used to bring people into that field to prepare for the C-one-thirty landing.

"Now for the shell casings. I've explained these were of .30-.30 caliber. About as common as you can get. No way to trace them. Security is putting them through ballistics tests but they won't be able to tell us any more than we know already," Sheridan said unhappily.

"This brings us to the question of what happened to, with, the Charley one-thirty. It took off from that airstrip. We don't *know* what happened beyond that point. It had approximately two thousand miles range still in the tanks. The only clue we've got as to where it might have flown is the radar reports from San Francisco Center. And all that tells us is that they had an unknown cross through their area, westbound, and that the airplane had an operating transponder. By itself that doesn't mean much. What does have a bearing on all this is that every other large airplane appears to have been accounted for. I say 'appears' because we're covering only military and scheduled commercial. We haven't had time to check on all the others that might be involved. You all know that could include several thousand airplanes. Not only that, but a small airplane with a transponder could show the same radar scope signature as a larger aircraft. We'll see what we can do with that information, but I personally don't believe it's going to be very much.

"This brings us to the attempted intercepts. Two separate scrambles by two aircraft each and both abortive in producing results. It ends there."

Arthur Sheridan's blue eyes stared piercingly at them. "Which brings us to the crux of the matter. The problem no longer is one of a missing crew and its airplane. Or even five missing nuclear weapons.

"The problem is that from all the evidence we've gathered so far . . ." He hesitated to give voice to the thoughts they must already be sharing.

"A group, and we have no idea who it is, with

34

whatever God knows what in mind, have hijacked an Air Force transport."

"They've got five atomic bombs in their hands."

The next question didn't need voice.

What would they do with them?

4

The apartment manager grunted from behind his desk. He didn't bother coming to his feet. Why bother? The fancy clothes on the nigger didn't impress him. Same for the man. No goddamned nigger ever impressed Charlie Jackson. He'd run this apartment house for eight years now and he had no complaints from his tenants. He wanted to keep it that way. Not having niggers with their dope and wild parties was one way he'd done his job. But you couldn't just throw 'em out any more. Not with all that civil rights crap from Washington, you couldn't. You had to talk with 'em, act polite, like. Make a show of it. Charlie Jackson smiled to himself. This wasn't the first colored son of a bitch tried to get in this building. None of 'em made it yet. He played it his own way. He talked to 'em, all right. Let 'em know just where they stood. Leave no questions. Stick the needle in. In a couple of minutes they knew the story, all right. Charlie Jackson didn't want no trouble. He ran a good apartment house and by God no frigging lawyers in Washington were gonna mess *him* up. Kansas City knew how to take care of its niggers. They had their side of town and the white folk had theirs, and they could mix all they wanted to in the restaurants and the movie shows and all that crap, but they didn't have to rub assholes in the same toilet. Charlie Jackson looked at the man standing before his desk and appraised him carefully.

One of them smart ones. Give 'em a little education and they think they own the whole goddamned country. He knew the type. College, no doubt. College, shit! he thought. They push 'em through and give 'em a piece of paper, and they think they're educated. I bet he was in the Army, too, Charlie Jackson thought. So what? So was I and twenty million other guys and *we*

36

don't think the world owes us a goddamned living. This one carries himself well, all right. Stands there proud as a peacock waiting for Charlie Jackson to show his ass.

"Whaddya' say your name was, boy?"

Charlie Jackson almost burst into laughter as he saw the nigger go rigid. That "boy" got 'em every time.

"Moore. Gene Moore, and I'm interested in a one-bedroom apartment, Mr. Jackson."

Charlie Jackson studied his cigar. He removed it slowly from his teeth and turned it in his fingers, studying that cigar as if there wasn't anything or anyone else in the room. After a long pause he looked up again. "Sure y'are," he said, injecting sarcasm into his voice. "Y'got money?"

The Negro stiffened again, and Charlie Jackson felt the urge to slap his knee. He was getting to this one, all right. He watched Gene Moore tighten his lips before he spoke.

"Yes, I've got the money for the apartment, Jackson. Whatever it costs I've got it."

"*Mister* Jackson to you, boy."

"The name isn't 'boy,' *Mister* Jackson. It's Moore. *Mister* Moore."

Jackson chuckled aloud. "Sure, sure. Don't get your feathers riled, boy." Jackson looked up with his eyes large and round. "Well, I should have said mister there, shouldn't I?"

Gene Moore didn't respond to the bait. "May I see an apartment, please?"

"Well, now, that depends," Jackson said.

"The color of my money is green, not black," Moore said coldly.

"Yeah. Suppose it is, all right." He leaned back in the chair, studying the other man. "Of course, I'd like to see it first. It's just that I got no urge to go traipsing all around this building showing you a place and then find out you been spoofing me. Y'understand how I feel, don't you?"

For a long moment the Negro didn't respond. Finally he lowered his valise to the floor. Never taking his eyes from Jackson he reached for his wallet and extracted a sheaf of twenty-dollar bills. Jackson's eyes widened.

37

"That all your own money, boy? You didn't steal it or nothin', did you, now? Because——"

"That's enough." The words came out flat and hard and Jackson bristled at the no-nonsense tone from this nigger. He started to his feet, the anger clear on his face.

"Knock it off, Jackson," Moore said, openly sure of himself. "You've played your little game and you've had your fun. It's enough. Either show me the apartment or refuse me. One way or the other." He stared Jackson down.

The manager stood eye to eye with him. "Or else you show up with some goddam civil rights group and a roomful of lawyers who're all screaming injustice, huh? That what you're gonna' do?"

Gene Moore shrugged. "It's all up to you, *Mister* Jackson."

"Yeah, I know," Jackson said heavily. He opened his desk drawer and withdrew a large ring with many keys. "Okay, let's go." He gestured to the suitcase. "You can leave that here."

"No thanks, I'll carry it with me."

"Think somebody gonna steal it, huh?" Jackson sneered.

"The apartment, please."

Jackson took him to 402. He took him there walking up the stairs instead of taking the elevator. Jackson mumbled that the elevator was all tied up. The thought of the nigger hauling that heavy suitcase up those stairs and then back down again pleased the apartment manager. Teach the son of a bitch a lesson, he grumbled to himself. Smart-ass nigger. Within the apartment, Gene Moore, breathing heavily, placed his bag carefully on the floor. He walked through the apartment, looked out the windows and returned to face Jackson.

"How much?" he asked.

Jackson hadn't expected him to do that. Not just take the first damned empty apartment he showed. What the hell. This has the worst furniture of any apartment in the building. Of course, the nigger couldn't know that. Probably good as anything he'd

38

ever seen. Jackson chewed thoughtfully on his cigar stub.

"I can let y'have it for two-fifty a month," he said at last.

"Two-fifty! You mean two hundred and fifty dollars a month for *this?*" Moore waved his hand to take in the small apartment.

Jackson chuckled and shrugged. "Take it or leave it. Course," he smiled, "I'll need a month's security. And there's also a fifty-dollar security deposit. For breakage and damage, y'know. You look like the wild type. Know what I mean? Throwing parties, that sort of thing. Get yourself some black pussy and some dope and why, before I'd know what was happening, you'd probably wreck the joint."

Gene Moore glared at him. "Man, you are pushing just a little too hard."

Jackson went straight to the point. "I can't turn you down 'cause you're black," he said flatly. "That's what the law says. A lot of commies passed them laws to favor you people. So the law says I gotta show you the place and even rent it. Law says I gotta rent to any nigger son of a bitch just like anyone else."

He savored the sound of the insult. If anything was gonna do it, that would. Unless this son of a bitch was a buster. They came around every now and then and you couldn't insult them no matter *what* you said. They was paid to be insulted. They took all the crap you shoveled to them and they had lawyers and civil rights commissions backing them up and they rented your apartments, all right. And then they got drunk and urinated in the elevators and scared hell out of the good folk in the building so bad they started to move out, and before you knew what was happening you found yourself in the middle of the nigger headquarters for the rest of the block. Then there was no keeping them out. That's how they busted the good neighborhoods, and Jackson was pretty damned sure this was another one of them busters. He started to panic that maybe he hadn't been rough enough to keep this one out. He'd have to do something fast.

"Course," Jackson said carefully, slowing his words

39

to a calculated drawl, "I got a right to know just what my tenants bring in here with them, huh?" The nigger examined his face, trying to fathom what obstacle the white man might be dragging in at this point. Jackson pointed to the bag. "You been hangin' on to that thing mighty careful," he said, lidding his eyes. "Too careful for what's right, eh? Whatcha' got in that bag, boy?" Gene Moore edged his leg closer to the suitcase.

"We were talking about the apartment, Jackson," he said. "If I add up your figures right that's two-fifty for the apartment and two-fifty for a month's security and another fifty for damage security. That's five hundred fifty dollars." He locked eyes with the manager. "I'll take the apartment and pay you now."

Jackson sucked in his breath. "I asked you what you got in that bag."

The Negro didn't answer. Charlie Jackson reached down for the suitcase.

"Don't do that, mister."

Jackson looked up with a smile. "You telling me what to do in my own building?"

"Just keep your hands off that bag."

"Well, shit, boy, I *know* what rights I got as manager here and those rights include knowing what people bring into this place. I'll just take a look and make sure you ain't bringing in dirty movies or dope or—"

A black vise clamped onto his wrist as he extended his reach. Jackson tried not to show his pain but he couldn't prevent wincing. Jesus, but the nigger had a hell of a grip! "Don't touch me, you black son of a bitch," he hissed.

"I said leave the bag alone." Moore eased the pressure and Jackson jerked away his hand, rubbing his wrist. His eyes narrowed to angry slits.

"That was a mistake, nigger. Biggest goddamned mistake you ever made." Jackson smiled coldly. "Now I got a case of assault. Open and shut. You black bastards ought to keep your hands in your pockets. You're a hell of a lot better off playing with yourself than putting hands on your betters."

Moore laughed harshly. "All right," he said. "You win. I don't need this apartment that bad. I won't be

40

staining your precious goddamned building." He picked up the suitcase and started to leave.

But he failed to reckon with the wounded vanity of the other man. Charlie Jackson positioned himself before the open door. "I ain't through with you yet. You ain't hauling your black ass outta' here until I see what you got in that bag. You're working too hard to hide something, that's for sure. You put your hands on me and that gives me a right to protect me and my tenants. Open that bag, I'm telling you!"

The manager's voice had raised to a half-shout. Gene Moore looked beyond the man, through the open door to the hallway, where several people had gathered. He could almost taste the animosity in the air. Moore took a deep breath. He knew he had to get out of here, fast. He didn't want this to go any further.

"I apologize," he said, choosing his words carefully, making certain he could be heard out in the hall. "I apologize, Mr. Jackson, and now I'm leaving."

Jackson turned to glance at his tenants. Instantly he squared his shoulders, emboldened by their presence, urged by their eyes to stand his ground against the black intruder. "Open that goddamned bag," he growled, "or I'll tear it open myself."

Gene Moore sighed. "I've apologized to you," he said, an air of resignation about him. "I won't do it again. I'm walking out of here, Jackson, and if you're going to stand in my way I'm just going to have to move you." He made one final attempt at conciliation. "I don't want no trouble with you or anyone else. I'll just be going and—"

The need for performance before an audience was too great for Charlie Jackson. The shame of being told off before his own tenants by an upstart nigger was something he knew he could never live down. Only action could suffice. He walked up to Gene Moore and stabbed a thick finger into the Negro's chest. It hurt. He meant it to hurt, and he could see the pain in the man's eyes. He opened his palm and placed it flat against the nigger's chest and shoved.

There was nothing there. Jackson shoved with all his strength and his hand met no resistance. The last thing

41

Jackson remembered hearing were several words, spoken almost in a whisper. "Oh, man, but you have been begging for this." He remembered those words and then he knew he'd picked the wrong nigger, all right, he knew it when he felt the white-hot poker slam into his knee and continue all the way down to his instep. Even as it was happening to him Charlie Jackson recognized the hard shoe scraping skin, and then something heavy crashed into his instep, it all seemed to be slow motion, but his head snapped back and he felt the pain in his eyeballs and only for an instant did he know that something hard and straight thudded against the side of his neck because Charlie Jackson was unconscious long before he hit the floor.

Gene Moore looked down at the crumpled form. He shook his head. "Goddamnit," he said. He picked up the suitcase and started through the door, frightened faces melting away before him. He hadn't taken two steps down the stairway when a woman's piercing scream ripped at him and he knew he was in trouble. He went down the stairs as fast as he could move, the heavy bag slowing him, dragging his motions, and he heard feet pounding after him. He made it to the lobby and went through as quickly as he could, wanting to get to his car parked across the street. Windows opened above him and the same piercing shriek cut through the air with frightened, screamed words. He prayed there wouldn't be any fuzz cruising nearby, because all he needed was thirty seconds to get the hell out from under. That crazy white man! What the hell did he have to do all that for? Gene Moore didn't want to hit him, the last thing in the world he wanted was attention drawn to him, and—he dodged a car, the driver looking at him, startled, and then he was by his own car. He heaved the heavy bag into the back, jerked open the front door and slid behind the wheel. He was smooth and fast and the engine kicked over immediately, he glanced behind him, there was a car but he could cut it off and he jerked into the street and he saw them streaming from the building, fingers pointing, and no sooner did he get into the open street, the way before him clear, the tires squealing as he tramped the accelerator, when he saw the flashing red light start up behind him. Christ, at least there's a car between us, he thought, as he recognized the police car, blocked by another vehicle. Moore tore down the street, worked the brake and accelerator simultaneously as he came to the corner, taking the turn sharp and gunning it when he started to roll out, going for speed; just get away from the Man in that damned police car behind him, and then he knew he was really in trouble because he saw the car slewing around the corner behind him and they were hot on his ass and coming with everything they had.

His only hope was traffic, to weave and twist and put cars between him and his pursuers. He knew if he could break free into the Negro district he had only to get a few blocks ahead, make a break for the first bar and shout the cops were after him and he'd disappear as though the earth had swallowed him whole. But he had to get that distance first and he was frightened he wouldn't make it because he knew, in those early seconds of his flight, that the police car after him was one of those supercharged models that could hit ninety miles an hour within fourteen seconds from a dead start, and—

And the traffic wasn't there. Moore slammed the accelerator down and headed for a bridge, a few blocks beyond the bridge he'd plunge into the traffic he sought, but first he had to make it there and he was almost to the bridge when the rear windshield shattered with a strange popping sound and almost as fast as the front windshield to his right shattered he heard the scream of the bullet. There were more shots as his front tires slammed into the edge of the bridge and he felt the slight shock, but he was on the bridge, the car behind him gaining, and he felt the stabbing pain in his shoulder at the same instant the rear left tire exploded. Gene Moore gasped from the shock of the bullet in his shoulder and the car swerved wildly. In pain and reacting blindly his foot hit the brake, and that was the last conscious mistake he ever made. The car whipped crazily to the right and went through the metal guardrail as if it were tissue paper. Moore felt the sensation of

43

hurtling through the air and the horizon tilting under him and turning stupidly one end over the other. The car rolled from one end to the other as it fell away from the bridge to a concrete retaining wall forty feet below. It struck with the back end and crumpled the fuel tank, and then metal screeched along concrete with a shower of sparks into the spraying fuel and the ball of flame shot upward for a hundred feet as the fuel exploded. The car was still moving, still decelerating as it tumbled and spun, wrapped from one end to the other in bright orange flames, pieces tearing off, ripping away, the car disintegrating and burning. It slid down the concrete wall to where there was a trickle of water in the culvert, and there came another muffled explosion of fuel and more flames. On the bridge the police stared and drivers leaped from their cars, staring and pointing, and suddenly there came a terrible, savage blast as the car exploded again, a blast that tore it into shreds and sent chunks of the car ripping away with insane speed. One watching driver died instantly as a piece of metal tore into his neck and decapitated him. One of the police officers, as he reeled back from the blinding heat and the concussion of the blast, remembered thinking, as he was hurled to the concrete of the bridge, that no car ever exploded like that and there was something in that car, and why was that nigger so all-fired crazy to run from them like that in the first goddamned place?

Bob Vincent cursed quietly. After all these years the damned thing still fooled him. A rueful grin started to his face until he clenched his teeth in self reproval. He found little humor in the idea of his leg hurting him when there hadn't been a limb since a shotgun blast at close range turned his leg into hamburger and splintered bone. He'd been a young and eager FBI agent then, part of a team after a group of men who'd held up a bank and killed three people. They cornered the men, but they tried to escape by shooting it out. Vincent went into a room filled with tear gas. One of the men inside *wasn't* blinded. He lay on the floor with a shotgun in his hands and when Vincent crashed in the gun went off. He was lucky. Instead of taking the blast in his belly where it had been aimed, the full charge smashed into his left leg. The doctors didn't even try to save what was left.

His superiors clucked sympathy, and everyone figured Bob Vincent's budding career as an FBI agent was over. Everyone but Vincent. He gritted his teeth and went into artificial limb rehabilitation with concealed pain and a determination that startled his doctors. It took a year, but when he finished he felt he was as good as new. When he told his superior he was ready to return to duty he received more sympathetic noises, but no agreement with his own convictions. Vincent went directly to Washington; it took three days of impatient waiting to talk personally with the head of the FBI who listened in silence. But he gave Vincent a chance, and when Vincent went through every test, including obstacle courses and hand-to-hand combat, and came out with superior ratings, he went back to work.

Fourteen years without that leg, he thought, and still

I can feel pain where there hasn't been anything there all this time. Then he recognized the feeling for what it was. This time the inner chagrin showed on his face as he realized what he was doing. It was an old game he called Avoiding The Issue. Sometimes he wondered if anyone else might be aware of his self-incrimination. He glanced to his right. Lew Kirby sprawled as comfortably as his seat belt permitted within the confines of his seat. The coach section of the big jetliner didn't offer much in the way of comfort. Lew knew the tricks· no sooner had they eased away from the terminal when he removed the armrest and slipped into his sprawl. Bob Vincent admired the manner in which his assistant extracted maximum comfort from minimum offerings. He slipped down in his seat, tightened the belt comfortably across his stomach, murmured to Vincent and was immediately asleep. He'd stay that way unless they flew into turbulence or an offbeat sound reached his ears, or even if Vincent called his name softly. It wouldn't take more than that to bring Lew awake. He sleeps like a cat, Vincent thought.

Bob Vincent rubbed his hand absentmindedly along his knee and to the plastic limb beneath. Few people were aware Vincent was an amputee. The leg articulated beautifully. He walked, ran, danced and swam with that leg. And sometimes, he admitted to himself, he used it for a subconscious excuse to evade matters at hand. He glanced again at his assistant. Lew Kirby was a walking tree stump, a short and stocky man who appeared shorter than his five-feet-eight inches because of his enormous shoulders and chest. Certainly, reflected Vincent, Lew didn't appear to be an FBI agent with an extraordinary talent in his work. Lew had achieved championship status in intercollegiate heavyweight boxing and wrestling, and his physical bulk belied the brilliant mind within the heavy, scarred brow. Lew studied organized crime as other men study economics or electronics. He had a rare ability to think "with" those who frequented the shadowy other side of the law. His genius lay in producing a whole from fragmented parts of a situation. Bob Vincent was of the

46

opinion that he might well be forced to lean heavily upon that talent in the days to come.

Vincent ordered his mind into disciplined thinking. He enjoyed a mental filing system within which file drawers opened and closed to display their contents on command. It had taken time to create such order within his skull, but time was an old friend to Vincent. His perfected ability to keep his fingers on the pulsebeat of virtually everything within a case stood him well. As an Assistant Director of the Federal Bureau of Investigation, with his home office in St. Louis, Missouri, Bob Vincent, from his early years with the Bureau, had been tapped for positions of responsibility. At times, he grimaced, such responsibility could be a distinct pain. Most men within the Bureau who commandeered executive desks rarely departed their home offices. The role was much like that of the captain of a large ship. He ran his vessel and its crew from his position of authority. The reins of information, control and command extended from his nucleus authority. While he carried out inspections every so often, he didn't run that vessel from the engine room or the fantail or anywhere else but the bridge.

So it was with Vincent's position as an Assistant Director within the Bureau. He had at his command a small army of intelligent and highly skilled agents and special assistants. They did the work in the field under his guidance and direction, and when decisions of high-level importance had to be made, men such as Bob Vincent made them. No matter how important a particular case, Vincent didn't abandon his desk to command his men on the scene. He coordinated from where he was. Anything else was wasteful of manpower, time, energy and finances, an expenditure the Bureau found both extravagant and stupid. Efficiency of effort was critical to the Bureau. Its operation was that of a well-organized machine, not a series of grandstand plays by a chosen few. This reality held little favor with a public sated on television thrillers, but then, the public taste always left much in question.

These thoughts contributed to the chagrin suffered by Bob Vincent. For the first time since occupying his

47

executive desk, a position held for nearly ten years, Vincent was conforming to the public image of the FBI which he, Vincent, held in much distaste. He found himself still surprised with his orders. There had been no suggestion or even a recommendation couched in official courtesies. The Director, personally, ordered Vincent from his office into the field. Although such gravity was hardly needed, Vincent was told the case on which he had been placed was under the direct scrutiny of the White House. Specifically, by the President. Not even the crackdown against a Soviet spy ring, Vincent recalled, had precipitated a flap of such magnitude.

But then, Vincent reflected, the threat they faced now was infinitely more immediate. Few things that came across his desk raised Vincent's eyebrows. Even so minor a facial expression engendered whispered comments among his secretarial staff. Vincent had been brought to the point of muttered exclamation when he first learned of the case to which he was now assigned, an incident his staff deemed worthy of much discussion during coffee breaks.

The immediate impression of Bob Vincent was of a man who remained, in the face of all problems, unflappable. Reserved, competent, keenly intelligent, Vincent "came on slowly." At forty-seven years of age, imbued with granite self-confidence, he never found the need to convey with words either his ability or his own self-respect for his capabilities. Especially so, Vincent reflected, when he was surrounded with men of equal traits. In his work with the Bureau, results counted. Vincent found reliability more to be desired than flamboyance, knowledge infinitely superior to impressions and conclusions which might contain within them seeds of doubt. Vincent was, as all good Bureau men should be, outwardly average, with no visible characteristics that might link him to a position most Americans were wont to consider glamorous. He and his family—Susan and their three children, two girls and one strapping boy whose destiny was creating mayhem on the gridiron—lived in a suburban development of St. Louis, with Vincent seemingly of the same professional ilk as

48

his neighbors. Their friends held Vincent to be legal counsel for an investment firm, a role the family nurtured with easy effort. Their closer friends were, of course, aware of his position with the Bureau, but by tacit consent and intelligence on their part it received little play in their daily conversation and pleasant gossip.

To the stewardess who passed by their seats during the flight, Robert Vincent was a man difficult to categorize. Stewardesses are expert at this game which they play among themselves, yet Vincent could have been in the insurance, banking, legal or any other profession of which they knew. A man just over six feet in height, a trim 176 pounds, immaculately groomed, his breast pocket handkerchief "just so," he defied casual identification. His hair, once a dark brown and now salt-and-pepper, was combed straight back, almost severely. His eyes were so deeply brown they appeared dark, a strange sharp contrast to a rather lean, pleasant face. Bob Vincent, concluded the stewardess in their section, might also model for executive advertisements. If nothing else, the girl noted as she dismissed Vincent from further speculation, he and his companion were ideal travelers. One slept and the other, the older man, remained deep in thought almost from the time the jetliner left the ground. This last observation was one with which Vincent would have agreed. For he had turned back the hours to a specific point in time, to that moment when the Washington office—Dick Morrow made the call—thrust the burning coal directly into his hands.

"Had the chance yet to study the report?"

Vincent frowned. If he didn't know better he would have thought Morrow was—well, never mind. Perhaps he was just giving him a bit more time to focus his thoughts. "Yes," Vincent replied to the query, "I've gone over it."

"What do you make of it, Bob?"

"Interesting."

"Is that all?"

"*Very* interesting. That better?"

Morrow snorted. "It's all yours. Orders from the top. And you're to field this one personally," he added.

Vincent paused only a moment. "Oh? That also from the top?"

"Uh-huh. The boss is at the White House right now. He'll call you himself soon as he's back." Morrow hesitated, as if he were deciding just how much to tell the other man on the phone. "Uh, Bob, maybe I didn't make my point before. You're to make the scene yourself. Personal charge, report directly to this office, that sort of thing."

"Dick, if I've heard you correctly—"

"You have." Vincent heard Morrow chuckle. "Pack your bags, old friend."

Vincent frowned. "I'll have to know quite a bit more than what I have if I'm going to do any good. I—"

"Have you received word from Kansas City?" Morrow broke in.

"No. Nothing from K.C. has crossed my desk. Not today, anyway," Vincent appended.

"Should be coming through any minute. I'll fill you in. We've got our first break on that missing Air Force job."

Vincent wanted to be positive. "The Lockheed? With the bombs?"

"That's right."

"Where did they—"

"Nothing on the plane itself," Morrow said, anticipating Vincent's question. "This is where Kansas City ties in."

Vincent kept his silence, waiting for the details. "As I said you'll have the report shortly," Morrow went on. "So I'll give you just the highlights. The local authorities had an incident, apparently with racial overtones, involving a Negro trying to rent an apartment in midtown." Vincent almost extended the telephone to arm's reach. He wanted to study it carefully, to be certain he heard Morrow correctly. How did—? He forced himself to listen. "The Negro and the apartment manager had it out," Morrow went on, "and the Negro took off balls out by car. A patrol car pursued and ended up firing several shots. The Negro's car went off a bridge and down a culvert. The car exploded and burned. A few seconds later, we don't have the exact time sequence yet, another explosion. Something in that car detonated. The force of the explosion was excessive by several factors for whatever gasoline was being carried."

Vincent waited. It would soon fit.

"One of the local police went through the wreckage closely. The force of the explosion aroused his suspicions. He found something, all right. He called the local office in K.C. They'd already received notification on the Air Force plane and since there was the possibility of a tie-in—"

Damn Morrow for his dramatic pauses! Bob Vincent remained silent, waiting.

"You there?" Morrow couldn't resist the drama.

"Go on, man," Vincent said quietly.

Morrow sighed audibly at the lack of excitement in Vincent's voice. "The wreckage was torn up," Morrow went on. "But there was some debris not from the vehicle." Again the pause, then the punchline. "A piece of metal had an Air Force serial number, an identification number on it."

"When was this?" Vincent queried.

"Early this morning. K.C. passed it to us and we moved with it."

"Did it fit?"

"It fit, all right," Morrow confirmed.

"It's from one of the missing atom bombs."

And that, Vincent knew, was but the beginning. The rest of it came in during the next several hours. He received full details of the C-130 that apparently had vanished into thin air. Vanished, that is, until he received the detailed report from the Inspector General's office of the Air Force. The conclusions he read in that report matched those he drew himself. The airplane had been forced down (he made a note to get greater detail from the Air Force on that matter), and during its period on the ground the bombs were removed. He knew the C-130 took off again, after which it vanished. He studied the report from the Air Traffic Control

51

Center at San Francisco, and then the terse comments from NORAD and the abortive attempts at interception. He wondered just how reliable might be the link between the missing C-130 and the unknown radar blip tracked on its westward movement. How many blips crossed the coast each day without identification? That needed some clarification. Certainly, whoever knew enough to fly that airplane would know how to turn off a transponder! But did the crew fly it out? And if they did, was that flight of their own volition? He forced a halt to the questions flooding his mind. Take it step by step, he reminded himself.

But it was a giant step from the missing transport to a Negro rebuffed in an attempt to rent an apartment in Kansas City. The link was there, all right, and finding that link would answer many more questions. Instinctively Vincent knew this would be their toughest hurdle. Kansas City filed an exhaustive report on the incident with his office. Vincent hadn't completed his first reading before he silently cursed and condemned witnesses who were blown hither and yon by their emotional response to a situation. By their emotion and their imagination. There had been six eyewitness descriptions from within the apartment house of the Negro. Five agreed he was young, one insisted he was at least ten to fifteen years older than the others claimed. The physical size of the man varied to an extreme of five inches in height and some sixty pounds in weight. The report of the apartment manager, Charles Jackson, would appear to be the most reliable, since he had spent the greatest time in the closest proximity with the man. Even as the thought came to him, Vincent read the interrogating agent's conclusion, appended to the transcript of the interview with Jackson, that the apartment manager almost certainly exaggerated the physical bulk of his assailant. Vincent nodded in silent agreement with that conclusion which was based on obvious psychological appreciation. The manager, Jackson, had been observed by his tenants in a verbal exchange with the Negro. Subsequent to this there was a physical exchange during which the Negro handily dispatched Jackson. To save face with his tenants at having been, um, clobbered seems to be the best word, Vincent mused, Jackson psychologically would build up the Negro to an impressive physical opponent. Vincent studied again the other eyewitness reports and accepted, at least for the moment, the description of a medium-built Negro in his late twenties or early thirties. Of course, Vincent reflected, that sort of identification was about as useful as a conclusion that no more than three to four million Negro males in the country would fit that general description. And it gave him no leads as to—

No, it had been there, he thought, as he mentally turned pages. One woman claimed positive identification. Vincent wondered why he had rejected the claim until he reviewed its details. The woman claimed she had seen the same person on a television-covered riot in New York's Harlem area. There had been several close-ups, she insisted, and she *knew* she observed his face for several seconds. Although Vincent held grave doubts as to the reliability of such identification, they had no choice but to check it out. Here the problem was the sheer weight of what had to be done. Tedium compounded enormously. Could the Negro who had been in the apartment house, the Negro with one of the atomic bombs in his car, be the same person identified on the television screening of a racial disturbance? The odds overwhelmingly said no. But there was always that off-chance. It was also, Vincent thought sourly, their only real lead. The wheels were set in motion at once. Photographs of every known leader and member of the hardcore black militant and civil rights groups in the New York area were being displayed on a closed-circuit television screen from New York, and studied by the woman in Kansas City. When they exhausted the New York file they would transmit from the leading cities other pictures of male Negroes who fitted the general description. No one expected positive identification but the possibilities of an odds-on recognition couldn't be laid aside. The issues were too vital, the stakes too great, the need too urgent.

Now only four atomic bombs were loose in the land.

At least one of the five hijacked bombs had been

53

transported to Kansas City. It was transported either by the Negro alone, or with a group, possibly a mixed color group, or it had been transported to Kansas City and there delivered to the Negro they sought, where he attempted to bring it into the apartment house. Vincent immediately rejected the thesis that a separate group had transported the bomb. God knew they were easy enough to carry since they could fit within a large suitcase. Vincent would not believe the separate transport agreement because of the events subsequent to the bomb arriving in Kansas City. Why would any group be so foolish as to ignore the problems of racial antagonism in an apartment building which had never permitted occupancy except by whites? Any group well informed of the situation would have sent in a white man, at least to rent the apartment for them, before attempting to bring in the bomb. Vincent had to reach certain conclusions in order that he might progress with the scanty information he had. He felt safe in certain assumptions. The attempt to rent the apartment smacked of urgency in the move. Which meant, as well, that little time had been lost between arrival of the bomb in Kansas City and arrival of the man they sought at the apartment building. Could he, Vincent, then conclude this did not involve a black power group with its organization entrenched solidly in the major cities? He could, of course, but he knew he might be leading himself down a primrose path. *If* he accepted the tenuous identification by the woman, he would be forced to conclude that black power or civil rights was in some manner involved. Yet, and here again the road of probabilities and possibilities forked wide, there might well be a black power group in all this, which had made the decision to restrict the knowledge of the terrible weapons now at its disposal to the smallest possible number of conspirators.

Any one of these possibilities remained distressingly open. As did others. The Negro might well be part of a group of both blacks and whites. He might not even be Negro. He could be Cuban, or Puerto Rican. He could even be a Chinese from the northern reaches of that

54

land where dark skin, although not Negroid, was common.

Several things could be accepted as fact. The first, of course, was that a *group* was involved. A group of skilled professionals. They were either skilled in the handling of airplanes and its attendant facilities, themselves, or they had for their use a number of men (and women?) capable of such action. Vincent doubted the existence of one group hiring another. The hijacking of the C-130 was so audacious and skilled a move, timed with the events on the ground, that it smacked of a single homogeneous group. Vincent lacked hard fact with which he might substantiate this conclusion, but he felt, surely and instinctively, he was correct in his thinking.

No question existed but that a bomb—an atomic bomb—was involved, and had, in fact, been in the car that burned and exploded. Vincent shuddered when he thought that the nuclear charge might have gone off during the impact and subsequent flaming explosion of the vehicle. Three hundred thousand tons of high explosives! That would have torn the heart out of the city and— Back to the reality, Vincent, he chided himself. The Air Force hadn't wasted a moment when they received word one of their missing bombs appeared to be in Kansas City. The serial number wasn't enough. A radiological monitoring team rushed from the nearest air base to the site of the accident, already cordoned off by advance Air Force request. Serial numbers can be faked.

Refined plutonium can't. The radiological team confirmed almost at once the presence of plutonium in the crash area and for several hundred feet around. That confirmation came in exhaustive technical terms that dismissed all possibility of doubt.

Vincent, at first blush, felt they had been incredibly fortunate that the atomic bomb itself had failed to explode. He was also aware of his shortcomings in this area. Atomic bomb mechanisms simply weren't his cup of tea, and he put Lew Kirby on the scene immediately. Security disappeared in the urgency of the moment.

"It's the way the weapons are rigged," Kirby explained to Vincent. "The bombs can't be set off accidentally. The fission process, I mean. In order for the bomb to detonate, several arming interlocks must be removed. All in sequence. There's no way to bypass any one of the six separate steps needed to set up the mechanism. So unless this whole sequence is carried out, the final step to set off the bomb can't be activated. This is when the bomb implodes and—"

"Implodes?"

"Right. It's an implosion. The plutonium, the stuff that is fissioned, is kept porous. They've got gold cones and beryllium in the bomb mechanism—"

Vincent waved his hand in protest. "Slower, slower. I don't need a course in how to build an atom bomb, Lew. I assume the gold cones and the, the—"

"Beryllium."

"And the beryllium are involved in the final process before fission takes place?" Kirby nodded. "Just the implosion. What's that all about?"

"Like I said, the plutonium is kept in porous condition. The gold cones have something to do with damping the plutonium, extra insurance that a chain reaction can't start by accident. Anyway, the final step in setting off the bomb is for shaped explosive charges to go off. The explosion goes *in* instead of out. That's the implosion bit. When the plutonium is squeezed into a dense mass the fission takes place. The beryllium has something to do with it. But the point the major made was that unless all these six steps take place in sequence the bomb can't go off."

Vincent scratched his chin. "What was the explosion in the car?"

"Another little safety gadget. The major said there's always the chance that when they try to set one of these things off the mechanism, the sequencing, won't work properly. The bomb simply crashes into the ground. They want to be sure that whoever's on the receiving end can't then pick up the bomb and learn how the whole thing is put together. There's also the matter of the plutonium, which they would rather not get into somebody else's hands. So if the sequencing system

56

doesn't work and the bomb hits the ground there's another explosive charge that—"

"Not the charge for the implosion?"

"Uh-uh. A separate charge that explodes the mechanism outward. Blows it to hell and gone in little pieces. That's what went off in K. C."

"How much of it?"

Kirby grinned. "They must have come up with some dandy new plastic explosives. Three pounds."

"*Only* three pounds?" Vincent showed his skepticism.

"The major said three pounds of that stuff, they call it DMT, would blow a locomotive right off its tracks."

Vincent took several moments to digest what he'd just learned. The information was comforting. At least the things wouldn't go off if they were just dropped, or—

"The major was really quite cheerful about the whole thing," Kirby continued. He laughed at the expression on Vincent's face, pleased he'd gotten through the granite demeanor of his superior. "He said the nukes, as he called them, were the safest weapons ever devised. He told me about a transport that crashed when it was carrying eight hydrogen bombs. He waved some wild figures at me. A total of two hundred and forty megatons, he said."

Vincent didn't want to answer. Kirby shrugged. "I felt the same way as you do now when I heard that. What can you say? What the hell are they doing with a quarter of a billion tons of explosive force in one airplane, anyway? The major said the transport plane crashed and burned and—"

"And obviously," Vincent picked up the thought, "the bombs didn't go off."

"Obviously," Kirby said dryly. "The major added that if they had, then half of South Carolina would have disappeared. Nice, huh?"

At least, Vincent mused, they wouldn't have to worry about the other shoe being dropped accidentally.

I hope, he added to himself.

6

Lew Kirby released the seat belt from across his stomach and stretched. Bob Vincent watched with amusement as Kirby one by one cracked his knuckles. He grunted with satisfaction and removed his shoes. He cracked his toes and wriggled them with obvious self-satisfaction. Vincent winced.

"I know the signs," he said, a half-smile on his face. "You've got hold of something in that thick skull of yours."

"Uh-huh."

"That's all? Just a grunt?"

Kirby grunted again. "Us Neanderthals got our rights. Besides, I'm not awake yet." He reached up to stab the stewardess call button, glancing at Vincent. "Coffee?"

Vincent nodded. "Good idea."

"Yeah," Kirby said. "Helps clear the cobwebs." He started to speak but chewed his lip instead, his hesitation glaring. Finally, he turned to Vincent. His words came out reluctantly, as if he were uncertain of giving them voice.

"I think," he said with a deep breath, "I know who our boys are."

"You're aware, of course," Vincent said with open sarcasm, "that I'm fascinated by your remarks."

Kirby took a final drag on his cigarette and stubbed it out within the empty cup. "I know," he said. He spoke quietly, a certain agitation visible to Vincent. "I'm not playing games, Bob. Just trying to be sure the pieces all fit together."

"Oh, ho. Afraid of putting your foot in your mouth?"

"Could be."

58

Vincent wasn't to be put off any longer. "I'll keep your physical antics a secret. Now," he pushed, "you said you might know who we're looking for."

"Maybe I should have said *what* instead of *who*," Kirby countered. "I mean, I don't know who in terms of giving you names. But I think I may have a lead on them. As a group."

Vincent waited.

"You remember that bank in Georgia?" Kirby led off slowly, unwilling to be rushed.

"Banning?"

"The one and the same."

"I remember it," Vincent confirmed. He was disappointed and showed his feelings. "You believe it's the same group. Well, obviously. You haven't much to go on, Lew," he cautioned. Vincent disliked conversations that led nowhere.

"Maybe it's more than it looks like. I mean, I've been trying to think it out their way," he said in reference to the group that had come under his suspicion. "Sure it's circumstantial as hell. But I've got a feeling. It won't go away. The more I think of it—" Kirby shrugged.

Vincent didn't answer the obvious. Kirby waited until the other man motioned for him to continue.

"Well, let me take this one step at a time. I want you to be with me all the way." He glanced again at Vincent, who nodded his agreement. "All right," Kirby went on. "No group operates without leaving their signature. Somehow, in some way, just what they do, or even what they *don't* do, gives us a sign of some sort. This bunch, whoever they are, have left their handprints all over this thing. They—"

"Are you referring to Georgia or to the—"

"To both," Kirby said quickly. "I mean both the bank robbery and the, well, however they got that airplane with the bombs. The *modus operandi* is the same. It's *got* to be the same," he said with sudden heat, his hands clenching into huge fists, surprising even Vincent with his sudden vehemence. "Look, that bank job was wings all the way. From beginning to end, right?"

59

Vincent didn't answer. He felt he could already see where Kirby was headed, but he preferred not to interfere. Not yet. Time enough for that after Lew spelled out his conclusions. Kirby took his silence for at least speculative agreement.

"There are several ways they could have gotten into the bank without tripping the alarms," Kirby said quickly. "From what we've seen they set up the roof door the day before they hit the vault. They know enough about mechanical and electronic systems to assure they'd have a free hand. They know explosives and chemicals and, what's more important, they were in a position to get their hands on what they needed. This all points to an organization, to a team operation, and it—"

"How did they get into the bank?" Vincent for the first time felt compelled to interrupt the recitation.

Kirby looked carefully at him. "I've already said. Through the roof door."

Vincent sighed. "You don't know that. All you know is they used the roof for their exit, that they jammed the door behind them, even that they worked on the lock mechanism. I'll grant you," Vincent tried to keep the smile from his face, "they knew enough about electronics to do their work well. The master board for checking all doors showed—at least on the panels— that the door was locked. But it doesn't mean they entered the bank through the roof."

"How else could they have gotten in!"

"*You've* got the floor, remember?" Vincent chided Kirby. "As one possibility they could have remained within the bank until they were prepared to make their move."

"They could have, sure," Kirby snorted, "but they didn't. That door was jimmied to open only from the outside. They'd wired the thing so that the lights downstairs would show the door was locked. If they opened it from the inside it would have tripped an alarm. In fact," Kirby threw in the clincher, "that's exactly what did happen when whoever was in the bank left to get back to the roof."

Vincent thought that over. "That's confirmed?"

"Yeah. It's one of the things I checked out. I made sure to check it out because it means they operated from the top down, not from inside."

"All right," Vincent acknowledged. "Now tell me how they reached the roof in the first place."

Kirby's expression went sour. "Any one of a dozen," he said. "They could have stayed on the roof, out of sight. That's easiest but not safest because they couldn't tell if someone would do a security check of the roof." He eased back into his seat and lit another cigarette. "They could have come onto the roof at night by using a rope ladder. They could have been dropped by helicopter and—"

Vincent's expression was quizzical. "You don't believe that, do you?"

"No, but you asked me the different ways they could have gained entrance to the roof and—"

"What's your own opinion?"

"No helicopter, that's for one. Too much noise. The place is lit up well enough to have showed something as big and making as much racket as a chopper." Kirby's expression showed his confidence. "I think the rope ladder is one of the better possibilities. But," he frowned, "I don't like it. The police patrols are on a random pattern. Then the guy would have had to carry too much stuff with him, tossing up a grapnel first and then climbing to the roof. Besides," Kirby finished with conviction, "getting up didn't get him down the same way. I don't think there's any question but that the man we're looking for didn't leave by going over the side of the bank and trying to get away on foot. That's impossible. The place was surrounded almost immediately after the alarms went off."

Vincent pursed his lips, started to speak, then changed his mind. Kirby saw the gesture and the hesitation. It meant that Vincent had an argument he preferred to hold for a better moment. "You come up with all the different ways you can get to that bank, to the roof," Kirby said slowly, "and you eliminate them one by one. First, they weren't in the bank overnight. Second, the rope or the rope ladder is out because of getting away. Third, the helicopter. That's out for the same reasons. Too much noise and action going in, and certainly it wasn't there to get him out. Fourth, he could have come in by plane, a plane flying as slow as it could and—"

"I notice you're using the singular," Vincent said. "Why are you certain it was only one man?"

"Because of getting out with the money," Kirby shot back. "Everything ties to how he managed to get away. More than one man fouls up everything. It complicates the escape so much it compromises it. No, whoever carried out this caper did a solo job at the bank. Besides, I wasn't finished." He grinned at Vincent, who waved him on.

"There's another way." Vincent almost laughed. Kirby's expression was one of a cat about to pounce. "Everything—let me back up for just a moment— everything ties in to making the getaway. No use being a smart-ass getting in if you can't get out. Whoever got in, left the same way. From above."

"Only two things are left," Vincent commented. "Rocket belt or parachute."

Kirby nodded. "Give the boss a cigar. Almost," he added. "Can't be a rocket belt. Aren't that many around and they make more noise than a jet taking off. Besides, they haven't got any range and, well," he gestured impatiently, "that's out."

"Which leaves the parachute."

"Right. There's nothing else. Furthermore, it's not that difficult. Not for a man who's really good at it."

Vincent digested Kirby's words. "I don't know how big that roof—"

"I do," Kirby said. "With some practice I think that even I could have done it." He said his last words with quiet confidence.

"That's right," Vincent nodded. "I'd forgotten you were a paratrooper."

"I also did some skydiving," Kirby said. "Just for the hell of it. But some friends of mine are pros at this stuff. I gave them the bank dimensions, added in wind-age and the rest of it and asked them if they could hack

62

it. At night. They said that with good visual definition they could do it twenty times out of twenty tries."

"Did you pass this on?"

"Uh-huh. It might help us also. Anything they dig up could be a strong lead for us right now."

Vincent agreed. But there was still one more problem, and he put it to Kirby. "All right. I'll buy what you've come up with. Now—how did your friend get out?"

"Balloon."

"What?"

"That's right, a balloon," Kirby repeated, his mouth set in a stubborn line. "Damnit, it's the *only* way."

"Don't wave conclusions at me for confirmation, Mr. Kirby."

Kirby laughed aloud. "All right, so we worked that out, too. I got the lifting capacity figures for helium and hydrogen. It turns out that if our friend used a specific type of chute, which is common with skydivers, you could inflate a balloon within the shroud lines and the canopy. Enough of a balloon to pick up everything he brought down with him, plus his own weight."

"Then what?"

Kirby shifted in his seat. He noticed the warning sign to fasten seat belts. Almost at the same moment the stewardess' voice came over the loudspeakers to announce their descent. Kirby held his words until the belt was once more across his lap.

"All we could do," he said after the pause, "was to work out every possible way they—the man at the bank and those working with him—might have operated. We checked the weather bureau records for the night of the robbery. There was a steady wind that night. If I recall, about fourteen miles an hour. The wind blew in a direction from the front of the bank to the back. In that direction, when you leave the bank, you move over some lakes, then a couple of hills, and open farm country beyond that."

"So you're saying," Vincent came back carefully, "that the man who hit the bank parachuted to the roof in the dark—"

Kirby nodded.

"—and after getting the money, and setting off his devices in the bank, went back to the roof, where the balloon was obviously ready for use, and just lifted into the sky?"

"That's what I'm saying." Kirby folded his arms, quietly challenging Vincent to produce flaws in his conclusions.

"Tell me the rest," Vincent said. "It's a fascinating scenario, to say the least."

Kirby set his jaw. "Fascinating or not," he said, a touch of resentment in his voice, "it's the way I work it out. He had enough wind to drift into open country before full daylight. He could have brought the balloon down by a road. He could have used a second chute to come down after he released the gas in the balloon. A car could have picked him up anywhere. Or even a plane, for all I know. I don't think that matters, for Christ's sake. I—"

"Any reports of a parachute from the countryside that morning?" Vincent's voice was deceptively quiet.

"None," Kirby admitted. "But that doesn't mean a thing. He could have come down before anyone saw him."

Silence drifted between them. Vincent was pleased with Kirby's work to support his theories. He might just be right. Indeed, he had gathered the most plausible set of circumstances to the situation. Circumstantial evidence, even extrapolating a situation, could not be ignored. At times it could be everything, and in this instance it appeared to be. If everything—Vincent put his thoughts to words. "If everything you say, even the generalities of it are true, then you believe there's a link between the bank robbery and the missing airplane?"

"Link? Jesus, Bob, it's a flag waving in the air!"

"Don't be too hasty. After all—"

"I'm not being hasty!" Kirby protested. "I didn't dream this up. I—"

"How do you link the two?"

"The odds are they've got to be one and the same. Two different outfits, each with the same capabilities,

64

the same method of operation, coming in this span of time and being wholly unrelated just doesn't stack up."

"If that circumstantial balloon of yours ever pops, you're in for a long fall," Vincent cautioned.

"You got any better ideas?" Kirby challenged.

"Poor argument," Vincent said with a smile. "You're retorting instead of answering. Any ideas I might have do not bear on your suppositions."

"Ouch."

"You deserved it. Anything else to add?"

"Yes." Kirby set his mouth in a hard line and glared with mock anger at his superior.

"All right, then," Vincent chuckled. "Consider yourself coaxed."

"I think we've got more time than we think."

"Your words are encouraging, to say the least," Vincent said with sarcasm. "Let's have the rest of it."

Kirby sobered. "I've been going over the Kansas City report from beginning to end," he said carefully. "Something doesn't add up."

Vincent motioned impatiently for him to continue. Kirby glanced through his window and turned back to Vincent.

"We have an individual," Kirby said, "who is a young Negro, carrying an atomic bomb in his suitcase and trying to rent an apartment in the middle of Kansas City. Somehow this individual, or his group, miscalculate badly. They try to rent an apartment in a building that's hostile to Negroes. Now, there's that first mistake. Not picking someplace where they wouldn't draw any attention. Why this particular apartment building? Well," he said to answer his own question, "it's near the center of town. If you're going to explode the bomb, it will have the greatest effect on the city. With me so far?"

Vincent nodded.

"Okay, stay with me just a bit more. It's their *thinking* I'm trying to second-guess. Why not just take an apartment in the colored part of town where there wouldn't be any fuss? Because they're trapped by their own limitations," Kirby said with sudden emphasis. "It

65

didn't occur to them that just having the bomb *any-where* in that town was the real danger. But from whatever they know of these things they assumed—and assumed is the key word—that whatever they planned to do would be strengthened by having the bomb where it would do maximum damage to the city. That sort of thinking twisted their plans just enough to give us a break. The manager of the apartment building turned out to be a nigger-hater of the worst sort. In this instance it worked for us by fouling up the plans of this group." Kirby showed a pleased expression on his face. "It also told us they're setting up things carefully instead of moving in a rush, and—"

"You're losing me," Vincent warned.

"Stay with me, boss," Kirby shot back. "Why did they want an apartment in the first place?"

"I think that's obvious."

"Now you're guilty of my mistakes," Kirby growled. "The key in all this is the apartment."

"Go on. I think I'm beginning to see—"

"Yeah. Why did they need an *apartment?*"

"Of course," Vincent said softly. "They could set the bomb off anywhere. From a car or a truck, a trailer, a motel—"

"Anywhere," Kirby added. "But you would use an apartment only if you need *time*. So our friends aren't out just to explode the things. They're setting up a master plan of some sort and they need some time to do all the things they've got in mind. So, maybe," he shrugged, aware of the precarious house of cards he was building with his logic, "we have a little more time than we thought."

"I hope you're right," Vincent said. The grim tone of his voice spoke for them both. Their adversaries had the bombs and were moving according to their own plans. They still had four atomic bombs at their disposal. From the scanty evidence to date, those bombs most likely were going to end up in the hearts of four American cities.

With all they had learned to this moment, however, they groped clumsily.

66

What cities?

And if their invisible opponents still needed time, how much time?

Vincent knew all too well their answer might appear in the form of a blinding flash of an atomic bomb exploding somewhere in America.

7

It was hardly a room, mused Bob Vincent, calculated to bring confidence to a pilot. Or to a passenger, Vincent amended his thoughts as he studied General Sheridan's conference room at Norton Air Force Base. Two sides of the long and high-walled room exhibited gruesome photographs of crashed, wrecked and gutted airplanes. The third wall had been prepared for this meeting with photographs of C-130 transports, pictures of the missing crew, details of the nuclear weapons, and flight charts of the route scheduled for the vanished airplane. A combination projector screen and blackboard made up the fourth wall. General Sheridan had prepared expansively for the conference, for which Vincent was grateful. He was even more pleased with Sheridan's quiet acceptance of the White House ruling that the final authority in the investigation would be the FBI. But Vincent had been in his business long enough to recognize that there were occasions when such authority had an undesired effect. It removed individual impetus to get the job done. Vincent wanted little to do with such authority; he would wield it when necessary, but he was more interested in meaningful cooperation. This was a devilishly complicated job they had on their hands, and time scrambled about beneath their feet like a spilled basket of kittens. Besides, Sheridan was even more anxious than the FBI to bring this mess to final solution.

"General," Vincent told Sheridan, "no one knows the military side of this operation better than you or your people. The White House has decided the Bureau will run this investigation. I'm not sure that was the best move."

Sheridan made a careful study of Vincent. "How so?" he parried.

68

"I don't want to do anything that will interfere with your methods," Vincent replied smoothly. He was getting surer of his ground. "I'd like you to proceed in whatever manner you and your people are accustomed to working. I'll stay off your back. I'll help you and I'll expect the same from you."

Sheridan returned the candor. "You've got it," he snapped. "We're already in a dogfight with a few agencies from Washington. And frankly, Mr. Vincent, I'm damned glad to hear your words. Maybe *you* can get them the hell off our necks."

Vincent nodded slowly. "All right," he said. "And we'll keep this conversation, ah, between ourselves?"

Sheridan chuckled. "You can count on it."

Now, in the conference room, Vincent was receiving the full measure of the general's words. Colonel Beyersdorf glared angrily across the conference table at Ria Carlisle from the National Security Agency. "Miss Carlisle," Beyersdorf said in harsh tones, "if I hear you even repeat those words, I will forget you're supposed to be a woman and I'll have you removed forcibly from this base. Is that clear?"

The dark-faced woman's eyes flashed dangerously. It was obvious to Vincent that Ria Carlisle was accustomed to dishing out authority rather than being lashed by it. The colonel with thick glasses had taken her aback with his sudden outburst. Only for the moment. Ria Carlisle took a deep breath.

"Colonel," she said icily, "you're out of line. I only—"

"You only impugned that an Air Force crew knuckled under to piracy without resistance on their part!" Beyersdorf roared. "Your prissy-mouthed accusations have no place in this room or anywhere else unless you can substantiate them. And you can't do any such damned thing! You're insulting six men who may be dead. You're not fooling anyone, *Miss* Carlisle. What you're trying to do is clear enough. You want full NSA control of this whole affair, don't you? But I won't have any more of it and you'd better understand that. You may ask questions. You may make recommendations. But you will, by God, do so with a decent tongue in your head!"

Beyersdorf slipped back suddenly into his chair. The others at the conference table were as astonished as was Ria Carlisle. Until this moment Lieutenant Colonel Paul Beyersdorf had occupied a quiet back seat to the others. No longer. Immediately obvious to Bob Vincent was that Beyersdorf had spent the early minutes evaluating just where the meeting would go. Vincent berated himself for not seeing what had been so clear to Beyersdorf. And to Sheridan, for that matter. Damn Washington, Vincent thought, glancing at Lew Kirby as if his assistant were privy to his thoughts. I've almost forgotten the competition and the infighting for top seat. Obviously, he thought dryly, this young officer hadn't done any such thing. There's a man who knows how to support his boss. Vincent almost chuckled as he looked again at Kirby. The FBI man was studying Beyersdorf with clinical interest, taking lessons, as it were.

Beyersdorf pointed a finger at Ria Carlisle as if to admonish a child. "Let's get something straight in this room," the colonel snapped. He glanced briefly about the large table. "*We* do not consider this a grab-bag opportunity for claiming, usurping or abusing authority. *Any* authority. Perhaps some of you have forgotten, but the lives of millions of people are gravely endangered. We are missing an aircraft. Six men have vanished. Six of the best men we have in uniform, every one of them handpicked, every one of them a combat veteran, every one of·them checked a thousand times over for their reliability and devotion to duty. We are also missing, again as some of you appear to have forgotten, five nuclear weapons. To find out what's happened to the airplane, the men, and where the bombs may have gone—or at least where four of those bombs may be right now—is going to take our closest cooperation. We *need* all of you," he said, again glancing throughout the room. He paused deliberately and then struck once more at the woman from the National Security Agency. "But there will be no cheap theatrical asides for any one agency to take over from anyone
70

else. This is an Air Force problem that now faces the entire country. Where your responsibility is clear we accept your findings or your decisions. But this is an Air Force matter which you have been asked to help solve. We can't work with you if you insist your own interests are more important than the fact that so many lives are in danger." He ended his tirade with a final piercing look at Ria Carlisle.

Bravo, thought Vincent. He wondered idly if General Sheridan had discussed his private conversation with himself, then decided the general had kept his silence. Vincent made another mental note to keep an eye on Beyersdorf. He felt compelled to step in quickly and end the unhappy chord already struck in the meeting, but hesitated. He wanted to see where else this would go.

Ria Carlisle had already turned for assistance to her superior from the National Security Agency. John Hoving, by her side, smiled thinly. Vincent knew that Hoving was evaluating the exchange, weighing his position in the room. It could hardly be more obvious that General Sheridan hadn't so much as twitched to interrupt Beyersdorf for what was a blatant breach of interagency protocol. Vincent studied Hoving as he shifted position in his chair and painted a pleasant smile on his face.

"Now, Colonel," he said in a syrupy tone, "I don't think it's a matter of anyone trying to usurp anything. I—"

Vincent almost laughed aloud. Beyersdorf wasn't having any ingratiating phrases and he cut the NSA man off at the pass.

"Mr. Hoving," he broke in at once, his gaze riveted on the other man, "we are not going to get into a discussion of agency protocol. I'm not interested in your gentlemanly defense of Miss Carlisle or her indefensible remarks. Shall we get to the issues at hand?"

Bob Vincent exchanged glances with General Arthur Sheridan, and Vincent felt they both shared the same thoughts. Beyersdorf had done them both—Sheridan, as well as Vincent—a swift and effective favor. He had brought to a head what might have simmered for hours or days, neither of which they had in any abundance. Vincent brought to mind what Sheridan had told him of the slender, bespectacled Beyersdorf. "He's one of the world's true authorities in heuristics. You familiar with that? It's the psychological science of hunches applied to cybernetics. To computer systems. Beyersdorf has an uncanny ability to correlate every aspect of a rough situation. He can figure out every aspect of what we face as fast as your wife can do her shopping list. Watch him carefully, Vincent. He'll show you where and how things are going."

Vincent nodded to himself. Beyersdorf had cut to the quick of what was happening—an interagency struggle to take over, in effect, the emergency program to find the missing atomic bombs. Vincent needed some fast computing of his own. His gaze went slowly around the table. In the sudden silence people were leaning back, trying to collect their own thoughts.

Well, there's no problem with the Air Force, Vincent knew. He had already made up his mind to let Sheridan and Beyersdorf, as much as was possible, run this whole show while he, Vincent, worked with them as an equal partner. Sheridan knew where the authority lay, and Vincent found no need to demonstrate the gavel passed on to him by the White House.

But Vincent was less than sanguine about John Hoving and that irritable woman with him from the National Security Agency. Vincent had crossed swords before with their group. NSA believed its giant computers buried deep beneath the Virginia countryside held the panacea to just about every major threat arrayed against the country. Electronic folderol! This was a problem of people, and it must be solved on those terms, not by consulting some underground computerized oracle. Yet Vincent knew he must tolerate their presence despite his suspicions of their value to this situation. Hoving, Vincent had been quick to notice, had sat back with an enigmatic smile while the woman with him did her best to disrupt the conferees. Ria Carlisle appeared quarrelsome, but she was also brilliant, and if a querulous demeanor would help, then Vincent was prepared to accept the sting of the nettle. Beyersdorf, obviously, thought otherwise, and Vincent felt himself inclined to go along with the colonel.

Would John Hoving, pondered Vincent, also prove more trouble than help? It all depended, Vincent knew, on how he tries to support that female barracuda with him. Vincent made a mental note to reserve judgment on which way Hoving would move. For the moment he knew he could leave the matter of Ria Carlisle in the hands of Beyersdorf.

There was another unknown fly stirring the ointment. A ponderous man with a large red, round face topped by a shock of unruly white hair. The public had never heard of Neil Cooke. But within the Intelligence community, and throughout the FBI, he was regarded as half-devil and half-god. The one man in the top echelon of CIA who had managed to escape the lash of official censure, for the simple reason he had managed to avoid the terribly wrong decisions for which CIA had oftentimes been responsible. Bob Vincent knew from his own experience that avoiding errors was not quite the same as making the right decisions, and Neil Cooke might possibly be a superb fence straddler feathering his own nest in CIA. Vincent could only wait and see.

Vincent continued his study of the others at the table. The next two men within his gaze were capable professionals; Fred Elliott of the FAA and Bill Thorp from the CAB's Washington office. They had no axes to grind, no holy grail of stolen authority to seek. They came as honest professionals prepared to do everything they could to solve the situation with which Vincent and Sheridan grappled. In a pre-meeting conversation during which Sheridan expounded his thoughts, Fred Elliott summed it up neatly. "You may be right, General," he'd said. "You'd *better* be right, and fast, or you're going to be the wrongest man alive." Vincent appreciated Sheridan's dilemma. The general might be proven accurate in every judgment he made, but if an atomic bomb killed a few million people then sure as God made green apples he *would* be "the wrongest man alive."

Beyond the FAA and CAB representatives sat Colonel Harold Kimball from Army security. Vincent's initial response to Kimball was that too many bodies were cluttering up the search for the missing bombs. His resentment vanished in a flurry of common sense. They might have immediate need of Army assistance, and having their representative here would cut bureaucratic interference to its minimum. The stiffly formal Kimball, tall and spare, brought to the table only an open mind. His aloofness (and noninterference) left Vincent somewhat in a better mood regarding his presence, a feeling enhanced by Kimball's attending the meeting as an observer for the Department of Defense. By wearing three hats—Army, Navy and DOD—he actually reduced by two the number of people at the emergency conference. He had yet to say his first word to the others.

Alongside Kimball slouched a suit-rumpled scientist who appeared bemused by the entire affair. Vincent wondered if he were so jaded by his work that he remained unimpressed by the calamity hanging over all of them. Dr. David Scheinken of the Atomic Energy Commission. Nuclear weapons scientist. The man who had personally assembled and then exploded one hundred and forty-three nuclear thermonuclear devices. The man who consorted with Satanic violence, who manipulated the mechanisms of nuclear weaponry with the same practiced ease and comfortable skill one found in an expert watchmaker. Dr. Scheinken wore a comfortable sports jacket and slacks, affected a thick-haired turtleneck, and might have been straight off a campus lawn. But he wasn't. He was nursemaid to Hell, and he was at the meeting to answer any questions that might arise concerning the missing bombs.

He had said little more than Colonel Kimball. What Dr. Scheinken did say produced scant comfort. Ria Carlisle had thrown the question at him. Hoping to achieve some discredit of the others by making the danger seem to be exaggerated, she queried the AEC scientist on bomb mechanisms. "From what I understand, Dr. Scheinken," she said briskly, "these devices have built-in safety factors. Don't they?" Scheinken nodded, and she swept on. "Well, how can we expect a
74

band of criminals to know so much about nuclear weapons they can arrange to set off these bombs whenever they want?"

Scheinken smiled in response to her words. "My dear," he said with good temper, "you are avoiding a fact of life. We have so many bombs today that they must be handled by thousands of people. Ordnance personnel are made up largely of enlisted men, not officers who are specialists in their work. Since most people are in uniform for only a limited time we keep things as simple as possible. Any intelligent high-school student could operate the mechanism on these nuclear devices."

Ria Carlisle didn't answer immediately. Robert Vincent leaned forward and looked carefully at the woman from NSA. "Miss Carlisle." She turned at the sound of his voice.

"Where did you get your information, please?"

"What? I don't understand what you mean, Mr. Vincent." Not querying. Sharp, irritable.

Vincent gestured lightly. "I'll make it clearer," he said slowly. "I would like to know why you are so positive the bombs are in possession of, um, you said, and I quote, 'a band of criminals.' How did you ascertain this?"

"It's *obvious*, Mr. Vincent," she reprimanded.

"Remarkable," Vincent said smoothly. "I must have missed that somewhere. Would you fill me in, please?"

"Who else would have pirated a military aircraft with nuclear weapons!"

"*Shit.*"

As one person they turned. Neil Cooke sucked noisily on a large calabash and looked around the table. "That's the only word for it," he said in a deep, throaty voice. "Shit. Nothing else describes blind guesswork. She has no more *proof* than anyone else, which is none at all, as to who may have the bombs." The pipestem stabbed in Sheridan's direction. "General, I suggest you go on with the meeting." Neil Cooke turned to look directly at Bob Vincent. "My apologies," he murmured in a final aside at the infuriated Carlisle.

Two other chairs were filled. Jim Krider, an old

acquaintance of Lew Kirby's, was the number two man on the security staff of the White House. Lew insisted on Krider's presence. "Krider's sharp and he's fast," he explained. "If we go more than a few more hours without finding those bombs then the President himself is in danger and you may have to order him out of Washington. Krider's the straight-line contact for that. Get his ass here fast as you can."

Krider flew out on the first jet. Lew Kirby was right. If the roof even threatened to cave in—

Vincent tried not to keep his eyes on the last man around the table. Lloyd Packard. One of the toughest Department troubleshooters. His presence reflected the sensitive line between Air Force and State. Several incidents with nuclear devices had contributed to the interagency estrangement. Hydrogen bombs scattered along a Spanish village. A downed B-52 in Greenland and the horrified word leaking out that within the huge bays was a single weapon of eighty-five megatons. Enough incidents to keep State scurrying wildly with Air Force operational failures. Lloyd Packard was the man from State riding shotgun on the Air Force. Now, Vincent thought sourly, he had his best case. Five bombs missing. Vanished.

It didn't matter that one bomb had turned up in Kansas City. No one knew where the others had gone. They all had their ideas but they didn't *know*. They didn't know where in the world they might have been taken. That was the gist of it. The bombs could be anywhere in the world. Lloyd Packard was a statue of disapproval. Tall, smooth, impeccable; pale-blue eyes that shouted accusations of bumbling inefficiency. A man who collected scalps.

Heads turned as the captain pushed into the conference room and went directly to General Sheridan. He placed the teletype message in the general's hand and left. The others at the table watched Sheridan's face tighten. A shudder went through his frame as he passed the message form to Vincent.

"They've found the C-one-thirty." Sheridan paused for the murmured exclamations. "Maybe I shouldn't
76

have put it that way," he said. His voice was strangely cold. The sounds died instantly. "They found some wreckage approximately fourteen hundred miles west of San Francisco. A ship is in the area now. They've recovered one body."

The words rapped at them in staccato bursts. "They haven't found the others. Just the one man. The copilot. Captain Ben Michaels. They found *part* of him." Sheridan spoke in a toneless voice. "The upper torso and head. His legs were missing."

"Well, then," cried Ria Carlisle. "I'm sure we all feel very sorry for the crew but this *does* solve our problem, doesn't it!" She peered about the table, her eyes darting and her voice shrill. John Hoving kept his eyes on General Sheridan and he gripped the woman's arm to stem the babble. She turned to him in anger.

"John, what are you—"

"Shut up," he hissed.

She saw the naked disgust in the general's expression.

"Yes, Miss Carlisle. Just shut up," Sheridan rasped. "You see, the captain's hands were *tied with wire behind his back*."

"We haven't any choice. We start accepting circumstantial evidence and move from there. Time's running out. Any comments?"

No one interrupted. "All right, I'll make a fast runthrough," Bob Vincent said quickly. "You know the details leading to the disappearance of the aircraft. Mr. Kirby's given you a complete report of how the navigation facilities were knocked out on the ground. You've heard the report from the Air Force, with corroboration from FAA and CAB, of what most likely happened at the abandoned airfield where the C-one-thirty was forced down. The bombs were removed from the C-one-thirty, loaded onto the twin-engine aircraft, then flown to some unknown point. We know that one bomb found its way into Kansas City and is no longer a threat. Four bombs are still in the hands of the group we're trying to identify. For the record, no identification has been made of the Negro who had the bomb in his possession."

Vincent nodded to Paul Beyersdorf to pick it up.

"We accept the radar track at San Francisco as that of the C-one-thirty," Beyersdorf said. "It's academic now, but I don't want to leave anything lying around. The C-one-thirty, as you know, went down some fourteen hundred miles west of San Francisco. I don't think there's any question of what happened, and the FAA and CAB agree with us. We found three spent rifle cartridges at the desert airfield. There may have been more. We surmise that at least one P-fifty-one, or another aircraft of this performance, circled overhead after the C-one-thirty landed. When the crew exited the aircraft they were fired upon by the, we'll call them hijackers for want of better identification. Sergeant Kelly, the guard, was armed with an automatic weapon, and I'm assuming until proven wrong that he was killed at once. It wouldn't have been difficult to do with a thirty-thirty rifle and a telescopic sight. We don't know how many more of the crew were shot down or if they tried to destroy the aircraft. All we know is that persons unknown seized the aircraft and its cargo and they—"

John Hoving motioned with his hand and Beyersdorf nodded. "Do you have any idea, Colonel, how they could have gotten that airplane into the air again and flown it so far away before it crashed?"

General Sheridan took the question. "Again it's assumption, but there are only one or two ways this could happen, Mr. Hoving. My bet is that some or all of the crew were killed, most likely after they were tied with the wire found on Captain Michaels' body. After the bombs were off-loaded the crew members were returned to the aircraft. Someone who knew how to fly a C-one-thirty then took the airplane into the air. It's quite possible for one man to do this. They may have used two pilots but that doesn't matter. They took the airplane off the ground and flew it back over the airstrip. At that point they set up cruise power settings and turned on the automatic pilot. Once the airplane was on course and climbing steadily they bailed out. As soon as they were on the ground they boarded the twin-engine plane waiting for them. The C-one-thirty flew out to sea until its fuel was exhausted, after which it crashed."

"I'm inclined to agree with Mr. Kirby's theory," Beyersdorf said, picking up the review. "He's told us the details of a bank robbery in Georgia, and everything points to a group skilled in this business. The *modus operandi,* as he explained, is extraordinarily similar, right down to the use of parachutes. That may be a lead. I hope so. We'll have to lean on Mr. Vincent's office for help in that direction."

"You're aware we haven't made any identification in that area," Vincent cautioned.

"Yes, sir," Beyersdorf said. "However, I'm hoping that the Bureau, working with FAA, may come up with something. It's the best lead we have so far." Beyersdorf turned to Fred Elliott. "You had a call a short while ago," the colonel said. "Anything to add?"

The FAA man shook his head. "Not really," he replied, showing his disappointment. "I'd hoped we might have come up with something about the P-fifty-ones. There are still several hundred of these fighters active in civilian use. We've already run spot checks, with the assistance of the FBI, for additional manpower but we haven't come up with a thing. The airplanes could have flown to the desert on a carefully timed rendezvous with the C-one-thirty or they could have been stashed away for weeks at any one of a hundred fields. No one would ever see them. Without a long search it's impossible to get anything solid." Elliott shrugged. "We could always stumble on something to identify the pilots. But right now we have nothing." Elliott ended his report abruptly. Like the others he felt helpless, without anything further to add.

Bill Thorp from the Civil Aeronautics Board shook his head. "I haven't anything to add to what Fred just said," he told them.

Colonel Harold Kimball declined to comment. Lloyd Packard joined him in frigid silence.

Dr. David Scheinken fell asleep. No one had reason to rouse the scientist from his slumber.

John Hoving of the National Security Agency

stepped into the awkward breach. "I've ordered an intensive computer evaluation of every possibility," Hoving said. His tone was brisk, his demeanor the expert cooperating fully. Which included ordering Ria Carlisle to confine her remarks to him only. "Certain possibilities may not be apparent to us here," Hoving said, as if addressing a corporate board of directors. "We need information or leads to the identity of the group involved. The computer checks *every* possibility, no matter how slight, a million times faster than we could do so. Furthermore, I—"

"Mr. Hoving?"

"Sir?" Hoving looked at Lew Kirby.

"Mr. Hoving, how long will it take your people to program the computers with all the information you have available? I mean, so that there could be meaningful results."

Hoving showed his surprise at the query. "Why, ah, if it's full priority, and I assure you, this is," he said, "about two days to cover every contingency."

"Two days, sir?"

"Yes."

"We don't have two days, Mr. Hoving. I don't think we can waste two *hours*." Kirby rested his hamlike fists on the table. "With all due respect, when you complete your computer, um, studies, where are we? What can those studies possibly tell us we can't determine right here and now?"

Vincent looked sharply at his assistant. Kirby was on to something and he was driving nails home in the NSA coffin. Vincent glanced at Hoving, who had the appearance of a man squirming beneath a tightening screw.

"Well, now, Mr. Kirby, with all due respect to *your* side of things," Hoving said, the coolness barely discernible, "you're hardly qualified to judge NSA's capabilities with—"

"Please, Mr. Hoving." The quiet tones from the thick, muscular body were unsettling. "I'm not arguing," Kirby said. "I asked you a question. I'm interested in saving time. Would you please give me an answer?"

80

"I'm not certain I can answer you on your terms, Kirby."

The FBI agent shrugged, a massive-shouldered rejection of Hoving's reply as so much nonsense. Kirby looked around the table. "What Mr. Hoving proposes is interesting," Kirby said. His tone was a spectacularly effective disposal of the National Security Agency. "I'd like to read it sometime. *After* this is all over. A computer study is an exercise in gaming theory. This isn't a game." Kirby sat up straight. "This is police work." Kirby paused, the subject of close attention. "We're spinning our wheels. Computers won't get us out of anything. The big question is what do we do now. *Now*," he grunted.

A pipe rapping sharply on the table returned their attention to Neil Cooke. The CIA man surveyed the ashes he'd scattered. He addressed no one in particular. "Bravo, Mr. Kirby," he said heavily. "We might yet get something done here." He smiled at the hostile glares from Hoving and Carlisle. "But you won't unless you make up your minds as to who or what is responsible for all this. And if you can't agree on that I suggest you put it aside. Our good general is now reduced to, as Mr. Kirby has said so eloquently, spinning his wheels." The CIA man studied his pipe carefully. "He is *not* finding the bombs."

The reference to Sheridan threw the problem squarely to him. But Neil Cooke didn't rattle the general. If anything, Sheridan coveted Cooke's needling. He had an unsettling effect on the group, all the more pronounced because of his accurate thrusts.

"I agree, Mr. Cooke," Sheridan said, his expression blank. "I'd also appreciate conclusions you may have drawn regarding the identity of—"

"I don't know, you don't know and nobody knows," Cooke broke in. "Let's admit we're all guessing. At least we'll take off the rose-colored glasses that way."

"I've never had them on," Sheridan said brusquely. "Let's have your ideas and get on with it."

"All things being equal, General, we may have a direct link here with a Communist operation controlled from out of the country."

"Oh, for Christ's sake, Cooke, you'd find a Communist under your mother's bathtub! Can't you keep an open—"

The CIA man turned with a cold mask on his face. John Hoving's shouted interruption died away under that frigid fury. For a long moment Cooke held his tongue. Finally he left no doubts. "Shut your mouth, Hoving. Try to use that thick skull of yours for thinking. Don't fight with me, man. *Think*. When you've got something constructive to say open your mouth. Otherwise just keep it shut."

Bob Vincent shook his head, dismayed with the bitterness showing nakedly between the two men. They were here to work together and ... Yet, Vincent saw, Neil Cooke hadn't wasted one word of his conversation, had hewed to the problem at hand. Could Hoving really be that stupid? He had no more time to dwell on the subject as Sheridan's voice cut between Hoving and Cooke.

"Drop it," the general cracked. With his command went the unspoken warning that his patience was wearing thin. Sheridan locked eyes with the CIA representative. "Go on," he urged.

Cooke didn't beat around the subject. "We've got to know who or what is behind getting the bombs. If we've discovered one bomb in a city, the odds are the same action will be repeated elsewhere. You haven't any choice but to assume the worst and *I* haven't any doubt that you're going to do exactly that." Cooke shifted in his chair to face Sheridan directly. "Now, as to who or what. Are they clever men who haven't yet played their full hand? One of the lead possibilities is that we're dealing with a criminal act. If so, then Bob Vincent's your man to get you out of your hole and I'll step into the background. Is this a black militant group? And if it is, how is it controlled? Strictly from within the country? Or is there outside funding? Because this caper's required a lot of money, and maybe that's where the bank robbery in Georgia fits in." Cooke nodded briefly at Lew Kirby and then turned back to Sheridan.

"There's every chance this thing is Communist inspired, financed and controlled," he went on. "If that's so, then Kirby's sniffing down the wrong trail and the bank heist is strictly coincidence. None of us know yet and we're stuck with entertaining both theories. Now—"

Vincent leaned forward, his fingers formed into a steeple before him. "Why would the Communists want to plant a bomb in Kansas City, Mr. Cooke?"

Cooke grunted and reached for his tobacco pouch. "You're getting ahead of yourself, Vincent," he replied quickly. "You don't *know* they were planting the bomb in K.C. Only that this unidentified Negro was trying to rent an apartment in the center of town and that he had one of the bombs with him. He, or they, might well have intended the bomb to be used elsewhere and K.C. was just a stop-off point. But even if he did intend to set off the thing in the city, what's the point of your question?"

Vincent thought over Cooke's words. At least they were through clumping around the bushes. "If there's Communistic control of all this," Sheridan broke in, "doesn't it seem sensible they'd go after worthwhile targets instead of just a city where there isn't a military target? I'd expect them to hit NORAD in Colorado. One bomb, if they could get it close enough, could knock out our air defense control network and our nerve center for space tracking. *That* seems a target worth all this trouble. Or the Pentagon, or the Panama Canal, or any other one of a hundred critical targets. But a city?" Sheridan shrugged. "Just to kill people doesn't seem like the answer."

Cooke didn't waste a moment. "That's from *your* side of the fence, General Sheridan. It's not necessarily reflective of the manner in which Communist planning operates. There's a lot of noise made about ideologies and how different they are. That isn't just propaganda. It's true, and being true means it's almost impossible for the average thinking American to think as they do. I don't want to climb on any soapbox, but it may very well be their goal to set off the bombs in several cities, kill millions of people, and raise sufficient havoc and hell to disrupt our everyday life. One more thing, General Sheridan. Bombs going off in this manner without positive identification of their source would undermine, to a terrific extent, public trust in that uniform you're wearing."

Sheridan didn't buy it. He shook his head. "I don't see it that way. In fact I'm almost convinced the Russians aren't involved."

Cooke smiled at him through a cloud of smoke. "Don't let me stop you, General," he said.

"By getting the bombs by forcing down the C-one-thirty," Sheridan said carefully, "they've focused attention on themselves. Whoever 'they' are, of course. But the Russians wouldn't do that. They wouldn't want to be caught in an open act of terror and murder. It would destroy whatever chances there were for coexistence or whatever they're calling the cold war right now. It's easy enough for them to bring an atomic bomb into this country any time they wanted. There are a thousand ways they—"

"I never said the Russians were involved."

Vincent drew up short. Cooke had nailed the general neatly. He'd never said *Russians*. He had said Communists. Vincent motioned for Cooke to continue.

"It could be the Russians, of course," the CIA man said. "Or the Chinese Communists. Or Castro's people. It could be any of them. What I want to get across to you is that it's vital for us to find out. We're looking, let me assure you of that, and in the same breath I'll confess we haven't a thing to go on I consider concrete. Only possibilities. Let me show you the flaw in your thinking. Everything you've said so far about the Communists not drawing attention to themselves by snatching the bombs the way they did is true. Except," the pipe stabbed in Sheridan's direction, "for one thing. Without this hijacking, if several nuclear explosions took place we'd know, just about positively, that the bombs originated from out of the country. I think Dr. Scheinken will support me in saying there might even be scientific ways of detecting the origin of the bomb by evaluating its characteristics. But *this* way, with our *knowing* the bombs are *ours*, we couldn't prove a thing. Not if the Communists," Cooke smiled
84

at his own caution, "if they're involved, cover their tracks so well we'd never get the details."

"I'll admit I hadn't thought of it quite like that," the general said candidly.

Cooke laughed. "I didn't expect you to. Someone who's spent as much time in SAC as you hardly thinks like a Communist." Neil Cooke looked at the others in the room, then relaxed in his chair. His movements made it clear he had nothing further to say.

Neither, for the moment, did anyone else. They were no closer to positive action than when they'd come into the room.

They were still in their coffee break when the CID officer sent word to Colonel Beyersdorf the information for which he'd been waiting had come in. Beyersdorf excused himself and walked quickly to the office of Major Ron Hess, Criminal Investigation Division. He'd ordered Hess to put a tight blanket on his request and to keep the report for his eyes only. Beyersdorf went directly to the major's inner office. Hess waited for him with the report on his desk.

"It looks as if you might be right, Paul," the major said.

"Was he?" Beyersdorf asked.

"Right under our noses all the time."

"Hell, it's not the sort of thing you look for, Ron."

Major Hess shrugged diffidently. "I suppose not," he admitted, "but it hasn't made the security boys any happier, either. It's the sort of thing we're supposed to know *before* we let them near the nukes."

Beyersdorf dropped heavily into a chair to study the secret report on Captain Myron Smith, USAF. Flight engineer. *Former* flight engineer. Where was he now? If Smith were clean then he was at the bottom of the Pacific in little pieces. If the good captain were to justify Beyersdorf's suspicions then he might just be hale and sound.

And a traitor.

Beyersdorf scanned the report. It was all there. When you knew when and where to look, that is. Captain Myron Smith. Married, four children. An ex-

85

emplary record. Combat in Vietnam with the Ranch Hand group. An outstanding combat record without ever firing a shot. Another straw in the wind when you knew what to look for.

Beyersdorf tapped his finger against the papers. The man whose existence reflected in the report was a pillar of his community. Any community to which he was assigned. A towering pillar of the church. A lay preacher. A devoted student of the Bible. Devoted student, hell, Beyersdorf thought darkly. A fanatic.

Beyersdorf played the hunch. They found the Bibles in his home and his locker, the passages which might be interpreted a dozen ways heavily underscored. The passages warning of man's interfering with the works of God. The passages warning the end of the world would come in fire.

If you were troubled and you believed deeply enough and, somehow, you believed you might even have been chosen, well ... Beyersdorf sighed and closed the report. Their religious pillar belonged, quite secretly, to several protest organizations railing against the bomb. He had devoted time and energy, never through his position as an Air Force officer but always as a civilian, to rallies that sought the end of all nuclear weapons testing. Myron Smith was a souped-up holy-rolling devotee to disarmament. Now, mused Beyersdorf, put all that together. Place that on-your-knees fanatic in a position where several nuclear weapons were within his immediate reach. Let his Bible-whipped conscience run just a bit more amuck than it had before, let there come the thought that a demonstration of the sulphurous Hell awaiting all God's children might just avoid the final fire. *Place the atomic bombs to do this within his reach.* Let him tell his associates. Here was their chance. Was it not preordained? God-damnit, Beyersdorf thought, it all fitted. He didn't know, of course. Well, none of them knew. Neil Cooke had ideas, but he didn't know. John Hoving had disappointed them all with his bumbling. That colonel from Army security was about as useful as a bump on a log, but at least he knew it. Lloyd Packard crouched at the far end of the table, a nemesis from State Department

86

biding his time, waiting to claw at the general. And Scheinken couldn't have cared less. He had enough to worry about with delicate mechanisms and projected yield. One day, if he were wrong, the good scientist would disappear in a wisp of disassociated nuclear particles. Why should he bother himself with the silly problems of idiots who couldn't take care of their own bombs?

Beyersdorf wished that Bob Vincent and that other fellow with him, Kirby, had had more to say at the conference. He wanted to know just how far they'd go in this mess, how closely they'd work with and support the general. Getting the information on the missing flight engineer might have been easier and more complete had he used the FBI for that purpose, but General Sheridan would have gone through the roof had Beyersdorf aired his suspicions to the Bureau that there might have been traitors aboard the C-130. Every man had his Achilles' heel and Sheridan harbored a deep inner rejection of men in uniform as traitors. Especially so when the word "traitor" lay couched in religious belief. Some men would consider Myron Smith to be pure patriot.

A conversation with Colonel Hank Reider of TAC security had sparked Beyersdorf's suspicions. The key lay in obtaining the precise flight plan of the C-130 with its load of nuclear bombs. Even knowing the nukes were aboard demanded someone in position to reach deep into the heart of classified operations by Tactical Air Command Headquarters. No one within the FAA or the CAB could have known of the bombs in the cargo hold of the transport. Not even Alaskan Air Command was sent the specific details of a delivery mission; they were told only the weapons might be expected on a certain date. So the leak had to come from within TAC Headquarters.

Captain Myron Smith was assigned to TAC Headquarters. As flight engineer Smith would know about the bombs. He'd flown many nuclear delivery missions before. No one would have even the slightest suspicion of such information being in his hands. He had the highest security clearance, he was a combat veteran, an outstanding officer, a family man, deeply religious. He—

Beyersdorf looked up to see Major Hess with a telephone in his hand. "Paul, they're asking you to return right away to the meeting."

Beyersdorf nodded. Damn! He was right on the edge of something. It lay just beyond his reach. He stood up and dropped the secret report on the major's desk.

"Stick around for a while, will you, Ron? I want to get back to this as soon as I can."

"Don't you understand? I don't *care* who's behind this. That's none of my affair." Jim Krider tugged his jacket back into place after gesticulating vigorously. A moment later it hung awkwardly on him again as his arm swept through the air to encompass the others in the room.

"I want all of you to get that straight. Who, what, why, when; I don't give a damn. That's what all you professionals are here for. That's what you're paid to do. I've been listening to you for hours. I haven't a thing to contribute to your problem or its solution, but I damned well have a problem of my own to take care of. I think all of you are aware just what that is." Krider fished in his pocket for a cigarette and lit up, inhaling deeply. He gestured toward the head of the table.

"General Sheridan." Krider's voice made the name a proclamation. "You know more about this affair right now than anyone else. With all respect to the others present I must place my question before you. I must have your answer immediately."

Krider paused and the room remained silent.

"Is the President's life in danger?"

Arthur Sheridan didn't hesitate.

"*Yes.*"

Jim Krider sighed, as if knowing the answer were inevitable. He kept his eyes on the general. "Sir, would it be your recommendation that we evacuate President Dowling from Washington?"

Sheridan replied immediately. "Jim, not only the President, but the government as well."

"You can't be serious!" John Hoving stood before

the table, astonishment distorting his features. "General Sheridan, you don't know what you're saying! Do you have any idea of the monstrous complications such a move would entail? Why, you'd throw the entire country into a panic! Government would virtually come to a standstill! You *can't* mean what you say!"

Jim Krider's entire life revolved about the safety and the security of the President of the United States. "Mr. Hoving, I haven't put this matter up for discussion. I'm not here to thrash this out with anyone. Just to get answers to my questions. I hope I make myself—"

"It's not that simple, Krider!" Hoving shouted at him. "This isn't the matter of just one man. Good Lord, you're talking about the internal affairs of an entire nation! You're—"

"*You're* talking about an entire nation, Hoving, not me. I'm responsible for one man. Period. When I want your opinion—and I *do* want it in due time—I'll ask you for it." Krider turned back to Sheridan.

"General," Krider said formally, "you are recommending that we evacuate the President at once from Washington?"

Arthur Sheridan stood ramrod straight. "That's correct. With all possible speed."

"Thank you, General."

Jim Krider left the room immediately. Behind him, all down the hallway, he heard the bedlam of opposing opinion. He heard it and dismissed it from his mind. If Ironpants Sheridan said get the President the hell out of Washington, then that's exactly what he was going to recommend to his boss.

They met an hour later in the general's office. Arthur Sheridan, Bob Vincent, Lloyd Packard and Jim Krider. Krider, the last man to reach the office, came in white-faced and shaken. He went straight to the issue at hand.

"President Dowling's refused to leave Washington."

They stared at him. Even Packard, aloof and disapproving, had agreed wholeheartedly with the general in recommending the evacuation of the President.

"The President—I spoke with him personally—told

89

me he's about to start a conference in the White House that's critical. There are some twenty or thirty top representatives of foreign governments who'll be there and he said no matter what the danger, short of war, he couldn't leave now."

They looked at one another in silence, broken finally by Bob Vincent. "I hope you all realize what that means," he said gravely. "They might just get the President and everyone else at the same time."

8

"You have a reservation, sir?"

The thin, stooped man nodded slowly. "Silber," he said. "Dav—" He broke off in a spasm of coughing. Finally he wiped his mouth and took a slow, careful breath. When he looked up again his eyes glistened with moisture. "David E. Silber." His voice carried painfully across the desk. "I made, uh, the reservation a few days ago. I phoned it in."

"Yes, sir. Just a moment, sir, while I check." The desk clerk disappeared beyond a wall partition and nudged a friend. "Jesus! Did you get a look at that guy? Like he just got out of a TB ward. I thought he'd croak right in front of me."

Which described accurately the man waiting at the desk. Beneath Dave Silber's shirt, yellowed skin stretched tightly against his ribs. Long ago he had weighed a husky 180 pounds. Now he was seventy pounds lighter and his clothes draped awkwardly from his spare frame. His cadaverous face might have come from Buchenwald, the hollows beneath high cheekbones accenting the sunken, gaunt eyes. Thin hair lay carelessly over a parchment scalp. Dave Silber was a walking ghost in a flesh-and-blood world.

Fragile fingers guided the pen through a shaky signature across the registration card.

"How long will you be with us, Mr. Silber?"

"Hard to tell," Silber coughed. "At least overnight. I might be a few days longer."

"Yes, sir. What rate would you like?"

"Something large. Plenty of air." He looked at the clerk. "The cost doesn't matter."

"Right, Mr. Silber." The clerk banged his hand enthusiastically on the desk bell. Silber wondered if he were pleased with renting a suite or was just glad to be rid of the walking corpse before him. Dave Silber had come to recognize the signs, the flinching from his presence. At first he'd been bitter. What did they think he was? A leper? He might just as well have been for the reactions of people around him. Except for Alice and the kids. They were too hungry to fear his appearance. They feared for him, knew he couldn't continue to waste away like this. Soon he'd be only a shadow without substance.

Silber sighed as he walked after the bellhop with his one bag. He lacked the strength to carry it himself. In the suite he told the bellhop to open the windows. He was suddenly desperate for a breeze through the room. From the eighteenth floor of the Mark Hopkins he held a rewarding view of the city spread out before him. San Francisco harbor reflected brightly in the afternoon sun. Silber watched sea gulls wheeling in the air. He wanted to feel the sky.

"I'll turn on the air conditioning, sir." The bellhop was brightly condescending. He irritated Silber as he turned on the air conditioning switch.

"Turn it off, please."

"It'll cool the room off in no time, sir. The hotel's got—"

"I said turn it off. Open the windows."

The quiet insistence demanded bidding. The bellhop hesitated but a moment. "Yes, sir." His face registered surprise at the five-dollar bill Silber presented him. "Why, thank you, sir!" Silber just wanted him to go away.

When the door closed Silber stared through the window. He breathed as deeply as he dared. Not too much. When he sucked in air with a rush, his lungs turned to fire with the terrible coughing. He'd brought up blood too many times for that. I'm running out of time too fast, he thought. I can't come apart now. Not until this is done. It's the only thing I've got to give Alice and the children. He forced himself from the window, opened his bag and took his toilet kit to the bathroom. He poured a glass of water and extracted two bright red pills from a plastic bottle. They went down with difficulty. He had trouble getting anything into his stomach. The pills and water went off like a small bomb, coursing white fire through his gut. Silber leaned for support against the sink, cursing the dizziness that came with the pain. He moved slowly to the bed and stretched out, his eyes closed. Finally he reached for the telephone. He glanced at his watch. Almost three. "Please wake me at four this afternoon," he told the operator. "Ring until I answer. It may take a little while. Thank you." He returned the phone to its cradle. Almost instantly he was fast asleep.

He shaved slowly, enjoying the blade moving smoothly over his skin. The hour's nap had refreshed him, let him think more clearly. He got so damned tired so easily now. The police station was ten or fifteen minutes from the hotel by cab. He wished he could walk but he knew he could never maneuver his frail body on the steep hills. He washed the lather from his face, rubbed aftershave lotion into his skin and returned to the bedroom to dress. He made certain the envelope was in his jacket pocket and left the room. In the cab he settled back for the ride to police headquarters. Funny, he mused. I have no idea what's in this envelope and I really don't care. It's life for them. Enough money for Alice to live out of the country with the children. Live decently, with enough food for them all. He wondered if she'd marry again. He was surprised to find himself hoping fiercely she would. This close to death made it terribly clear how important it was to live every moment available to you. He didn't want Alice and the kids cut off from what a complete family could offer to— The cab pulled up before the stone building. Dave Silber paid the driver and stepped onto the sidewalk. Eighteen steps, he thought, counting them. Take it slowly, don't rush.

Even with caution he saw spots dancing before his eyes. He stood for a while, breathing carefully, dismayed as always with the terrible crash of his heart within his chest. Several policemen left the building, nodding to him. He smiled thinly in return. Finally he could breathe normally and his heart returned to less than frenzied pumping. He turned to enter the build-

93

ing, walking slowly to the high desk. A sergeant looked down at him.

"Can I help you, sir?"

Silber nodded. He withdrew the sealed envelope from his pocket, holding it in both hands. "I have, uh, instructions to deliver this." He hesitated. "I'm supposed to give this to a responsible official in the police."

The sergeant cocked a professional eyebrow at him. "What's it about, Mr.—"

"Dave Silber."

"What's it about, Mr. Silber?"

"I haven't any idea."

"Oh." A pencil tapped tightly on the desk. "You're a messenger, then?"

"I suppose you could call it that."

"Who's the letter from, Mr. Silber?"

"I don't know that, either." Silber leaned forward and held out the letter.

"Mind if I open it?" The sergeant smiled.

"No, of course not."

The sergeant kept his face a mask. Several times he lowered the pages in his hands and looked sharply at the sickly man standing before his desk. Finally he gestured with the papers. "You know what this letter says?"

Silber smiled and shook his head. "I told you, I haven't any idea. I've never seen it. I'm just carrying out instructions." Silber looked around. "Sergeant, would you mind if I sat down? I'm not very well."

"Oh. Sure you can. Right over there."

Silber took the chair gratefully. He watched the police officer and waited. He had nothing else to do. Deliver the letter on the twenty-eighth of June. Those were his instructions. On the late afternoon of the twenty-eighth, deliver the letter personally to police headquarters in San Francisco. Have someone open the letter in front of you, where you can see him do it. Then, wait.

"Is this some sort of joke, Mr. Silber?"

"What?" His mind was wandering. "Oh, I'm sorry.

No, Sergeant. I don't think it's a joke. None that I'm aware of."

No one would play a joke like this. The first envelope he'd received had his letter of instructions. With the letter were one hundred hundred-dollar bills. Ten thousand dollars. In cash. He'd already sent his family out of the country. They—whoever sent him the instructions and the money—had told him what to do. He'd looked at the money and cried. Food, clothing, medicine . . . all of it held in his hand. Whatever they, whoever they were, wanted him to do he would do. As he was now. Following his instructions explicitly.

"You know what this letter says?" The sergeant's pleasant demeanor became more distant with every new flourish of the papers in his gesturing hand. "For Christ's sake, Silber, or whoever you are, this is a *ransom* note!"

Dave Silber refused to think. He nodded. "If you say so," he murmured.

" A ransom note for ten cities. *Cities*, for God's sake! Now I've heard them—" The sergeant cut himself off and sighed deeply. "All right, Silber," he said with overwhelming patience. "What's the game you're playing?"

"I told you. I'm following orders. I was told to—"

The sergeant waved his hand furiously. "No," he snapped. "No more. You're a blind messenger boy for someone you don't know who's told you to deliver a letter here, right? Uh-huh. *Then* what're you supposed to do, Silber?"

The frail man shrugged lightly. "That's up to you, Sergeant."

"Up to *me*?" Wide eyes looked down at Silber. The sergeant glanced beyond the waiting man. Others had come into the room, were looking on with growing interest. "Oh, Jeez. Just wait right there, Mr. Silber. I want Detective Bowman to talk with you."

"Now look, Mr. Silber, I don't want to be difficult, or make it seem as if I don't want to cooperate, or help you in whatever way I can, or you need me to, but this is really, well, it's really most unusual. This letter—you still insist you've never seen it before?—this letter has a list of ten cities. It starts off with Los Angeles, then Phoenix, Oklahoma City, Chicago, Miami, New York, Washington, D.C., Philadelphia, Kansas City and, for last, Nashville."

Detective Bowman made a careful study of the man before him. Bowman was an old hand at interrogating prisoners and witnesses. He couldn't reach Silber. Not a spark of interest flickered in those gray eyes. The man simply didn't care what was in the letter or else he was the best actor Bowman had ever seen in twenty-two years in the business. But the letter—!

"Mr. Silber, you're *certain* you don't know ..." Bowman gestured with the letter.

Dave Silber smiled politely. "Really, it's just as I told the sergeant. I'm carrying out directions. I don't wish to seem difficult, Mr. Bowman, but I—"

"Okay, never mind." Bowman's voice took on professional hardness. To Silber's sensitive feelings, long adjusted to others reacting to his emaciated appearance, Bowman's shift in mood was as recognizable as a traffic light. "No matter what your story may be, Silber," Bowman said coldly, "you can't go around delivering threatening letters. I—"

"Threatening?"

"I forgot." The sarcasm lay exposed. "I forgot you don't know what's in here. This letter, *Mr.* Silber, states that of the ten cities listed here, there are atomic bombs contained in five of those cities, and unless certain ransom conditions are met, then one by one those cities are going to be blown up. Now, look," Bowman said with an ingratiating smile, "we'd like to accommodate you, but *atomic* bombs? Do you really expect us to believe this, this thing?" He rattled the pages under Silber's nose.

Silber shrugged. Bowman recognized massive indifference when it stared him in the face. He couldn't understand it. Silber didn't act like an escapee from the fairy farm, and yet ... The letter was errant nonsense of the worst sort. But why do I feel something's wrong, wondered Bowman. I can't shake the feeling this guy is sincere. He glanced again at the letter.

"What do you know about the securities demanded in here?"

Silber's soft smile came to his face. "Nothing." He remained unruffled in his own waters.

"According to this letter we're supposed to contact federal authorities and arrange for one hundred million dollars—*one hundred million*, mind you—worth of negotiable bonds and securities and cashiers' checks, and have these delivered to you. Very neat," acknowledged Bowman. "No cash. Nothing to be traced until long after it's been cashed or presented for payment." Detective Bowman chewed on a dead cigar. "I know something about these things, Silber, and I want to congratulate you. Beautiful, that's what it is. Almost fool-proof, I'd say." He looked sharply at the pale, thin man. "Silber, what kind of a nut are you?"

Silber's face remained blank.

Bowman went to a different tack. "Silber, you realize I could lock you up for bringing this letter here?"

"If you say so."

"That's all? If I say so?" Bowman showed his glowing irritation. "Don't you care if we throw you in a cell?"

"I couldn't stop you if you wanted to do that, could I?"

Bowman glared at Silber. He'd met plenty of kooks who'd do almost anything to get *into* jail. Immediately he thought of Silber in this vein and dismissed the thought. "You know this is attempted extortion, don't you?"

"I don't know anything, Mr. Bowman. Just that I was told to bring this letter here."

"I forgot. And then you're supposed to wait, was that it?"

"That's right," Silber said with a slow nod.

"What are we supposed to do?"

"I don't know."

"Who sent you here, Silber?"

"I don't know that, either."

"Were you paid for this?"

"Yes."

"Mind telling me how much?"

Silber thought of ten thousand dollars in cash—of the forty thousand more he was promised for completing his assignment. "You wouldn't believe me, Mr. Bowman."

"Try me. Right now I'd believe anything, I think."

Silber smiled. "I'm sorry."

"How did you get your instructions?"

"By mail." He'd tell them anything that wouldn't be harmful.

"Where did the letter come from?"

"I don't know," he lied. He'd seen the postmark on the envelope. From Atlanta, Georgia. There wasn't any use telling that to the detective.

"Silber, if I had any sense I'd throw you in a cell and then forget where I put the key."

Silence. Silber wanted desperately to return to his room and go to sleep. The flight from Chicago had exhausted him. It always took two or three days to regain what little strength he had after a trip.

Bowman sighed heavily and climbed to his feet. "Mr. Silber, I'd like you to do something for me."

"If I can. Of course."

"Go away and don't ever come back."

Silber looked blankly at the other man.

"Just go away," Bowman grunted. "I promise I'll forget I ever saw you."

"All right."

Bowman showed his relief.

"Oh, there's one more thing, Mr. Bowman."

"Say it and get out, Silber. I'm a busy man."

"You'll want to know where you can reach me."

"Will I, now?" Bowman laughed harshly.

"Yes, I'm at the Mark Hopkins. Thank you for your time, Mr. Bowman."

"Sure, sure. Think nothing of it."

"The Mark Hopkins. Don't forget."

"It's burned into my mind forever. Good-bye, Mr. Silber."

"Mr. Mayor, I think you should read this right away."

Mayor John Creighton looked up and raised his

bushy eyebrows. "Sounds like a genuine emergency, Helen," he smiled at his secretary.

She didn't return the smile. "Well, *if* this letter is what it says it—I mean, if what's in here is true, then you've got the biggest emergency you've ever known in your life."

Mayor Creighton leaned back in his seat, measuring the expression on his secretary's face. He'd started to reach for the letter then changed his mind. Whatever emergency Helen fancied couldn't be *that* bad. Real emergencies came in the form of delegations clamoring in his hallway. Irate citizens, legal process, outraged constituents. Emergencies worth their salt didn't come by ordinary mail.

"Tell me about it, Helen."

She glanced at him angrily and shook the letter at him. "According to this, *Mr.* Smartypants Mayor, someone's got an atomic bomb in this city and they're threatening to—"

"*What?*"

She set her lips and refused to say another word.

"Are you serious, Helen? An *atomic bomb?* Here? In Oklahoma City?"

"*I'm* serious. I only hope this letter isn't. Apparently we're one of ten cities that have been sent—"

"Give me that thing."

. . . beyond any question. The nuclear weapons emplaced within five of the ten cities listed are tactical devices weighing approximately sixty pounds each, with a single-weapon yield of three hundred kilotons. The serial numbers of these weapons are USAF-NW-T-527-933, 527949, 622188, 636004 and 721553. You will, of course, ascertain through your own good offices the validity of these statements and the fact that these are the serial numbers of five nuclear weapons that have been removed from USAF inventory. When these facts are validated you will be aware of the gravity of the situation you face.

The documents to be delivered in the form of certain negotiable bonds, stocks, securities and cashiers' checks have been described in full. Your city is responsible for ten million dollars' worth of such payment. If this payment, as listed here, is not made within seventy-two hours of your receipt of this letter, the first bomb will be detonated. Every twenty-four hours afterward, another bomb will explode. You have no way of knowing if there is a bomb in your city. As you can see, however, the odds are one in two, and the responsibility for the lives of your citizens and the safety of your community lies entirely in your hands.

The documents listed are to be delivered to the Mark Hopkins Hotel in San Francisco, to the person of a Mr. David E. Silber.

The effects of a single nuclear weapon with a yield of three hundred thousand tons of high explosives will, we are assured, make evident the need for . . .

Seven mayors in seven cities threw away the letters.

Three mayors notified the FBI immediately.

At ten minutes past eight o'clock the night of June twenty-eighth, agents of the FBI and police officers of the city of San Francisco took David E. Silber into custody.

At fourteen minutes past eight o'clock that same evening, the FBI office in San Francisco notified Robert Vincent of the arrest of David E. Silber.

Approximately at nine o'clock that evening, Brigadier General Arthur Sheridan, Lieutenant Colonel Paul Beyersdorf, Robert Vincent and Lew Kirby boarded an Air Force jet at Norton Air Force Base for the short, swift flight to San Francisco.

9

"I *told* you, I—" He felt the sharp pain and closed his eyes. Breathe deeply. Calm. Stay calm. Take it slow. *Very* slow. Don't die now, for Christ's sake. Silber forced open his eyes and looked across the table. The two men in uniform. Two others seated with them. More in the room, in shadow. The bright lights hurt his eyes.

He raised his arm to protect himself. "Turn the lights out, please." His voice came to them as a rasping whisper. He wasn't afraid. They knew that and he was aware they knew. He saw the older man in civilian clothes glance at someone in the shadows. Then the man before him, what was his name, Vincent? He saw him nod and the lights went out. He heard himself gasp with relief. Wearily he rubbed his eyes, watched the colors dance crazily. With new focus he saw the faces before him.

"Thank you," he said weakly. He sipped from the glass they'd put before him, felt the cool water trickle down his throat. He'd need the pills. They'd taken them away. A doctor would have examined them by now. When he asked for them they'd be there. They didn't want him to die any more than he did.

"I told you," he said, picking up the thread of his reply. "I've told you a hundred times. I don't *know* who sent me the letter and my instructions. It arrived in the mail. That's all."

"And with it there was money, wasn't there?"

He nodded. Despite his resistance they were wearing him down.

"How much, Silber?"

He knew they could make something from the amount but it no longer seemed important. "Ten thousand dollars," he admitted.

101

There came a long pause. He knew they were evaluating the figure he gave them. The questions started again.

"How? In cash, a check, what?"

"Cash. Hundred-dollar bills."

"That's a lot of money just to carry a message, isn't it, Silber?"

He recognized the other voice. The stocky one. The man who drove questions like pounding a thick wooden stake into your body. Silber looked into eyes that stared unblinking at him. Cobra eyes that hypnotized you. Silber shrugged. Maybe once he thought it was a lot of money. Not now. Unnumbered years ahead for Alice and the kids. Not even fifty thousand was a lot of money anymore. But it was enough to give them new life, and that's all that mattered. So he looked into the cobra eyes, unafraid, and he shrugged.

"I said that's a lot of money to play messenger boy, isn't it?"

He shrugged again. "If you say so."

Another voice came at him. "What happens now that you're under arrest, Silber?"

He couldn't help the smile. "You know better than I do," he said quietly.

"You're going to jail, you know."

"All right."

"You may laugh it off now, Silber, but—"

He did laugh. A gentle sound, without malice, that confused them. "Don't threaten me," he said, still smiling. "You don't know how foolish it sounds."

"It'll sound even more foolish when you're behind bars."

He tried to see the voice. They shifted from one man to another so rapidly he lost track of who was talking. It didn't give him a chance to hold his thread of thought. But then, he smiled to himself, he really didn't care. He just wanted to go to sleep. Every so often his heart crashed within his chest, frightening him. Maybe that's what they saw in his eyes. The fear. He wanted to shout with laughter at that. Did they think he feared *them*? God knew he didn't. He feared no man, no calamity, no disaster. He feared only time. He wanted

102

time, begged for it in his soul. Enough time to do what needed to be done.

"You won't keep me behind bars for very long."

He could almost feel them stiffen. His words sounded like a retort to their threat. They didn't know—!

"Why? You expecting someone to spring you?"

"What?"

"To bail you out?"

"You haven't told me what the charges are, have you?"

"You know, Silber. Extortion, for one."

"I haven't done anything to anyone."

"Just carried a letter that threatens to kill millions of people, that's all!" The voice, Silber noted, was properly indignant.

"I wouldn't know. I never saw the letter."

"That's what *you* say."

"That's what I say."

"We don't believe you, Silber."

"Don't then."

"What do you expect to accomplish by all this?"

"I don't know. I'm supposed to wait for you to do something."

"Such as?"

He shrugged. The pain was there again, this time squeezing the heart beating so sharply. He closed his eyes, bit his lip. They saw his face whiten and the questions stopped. He heard movement. It sounded far away. Like trying to listen to a distant sound through a heavy rainfall and the rain muffles what you want to hear and— He felt the needle in his arm and opened his eyes. A different face. He hadn't seen it before. His shirt was open and he felt the coolness of metal. A comforting thought lodged in his mind. A doctor. They were taking care of him. Of course. They had to. He wasn't any use to them dead. The tension fled with the realization. He was going to sleep. They'd be waiting for him when he opened his eyes again. That's all right, he thought. Alice is going to be fine. The kids . . .

"You're pretty sure about all this, aren't you?"

"I'm not sure of anything. I'm too tired."

"Who are your friends in this, Silber?"

He started to say he didn't have any friends. But he did. Unknown, invisible, by mail only. "I'd like to know myself," he said, his answer surprising them. "I'd like to shake their hands."

"Wouldn't you. One big den of murderers."

"I haven't murdered anyone."

"Your friends have. That makes you as guilty as they are."

He didn't answer.

"Where did you get your instructions?"

Wearily: "By mail. Through the post office."

"We know that, Silber. Where was the letter from? Where'd the package come from?"

"I don't know."

"What did the return address say?"

"There wasn't any."

"So you told us. But you could read the postmark. You did read the postmark, didn't you? Nobody gets ten thousand dollars in the mail without at least trying to find out where it came from. What did the postmark say?"

"I don't know," he lied.

"Didn't you try to find out?"

"No."

"No?"

"No."

"Why are you lying to us, Silber? If what you say is true, if you're only a messenger, you haven't a thing to worry about. Why don't you tell us the truth and make it easy on yourself?"

"I have. Told you the truth, I mean."

"Where's the letter with the instructions you say you received?"

"I burned it."

"Why?"

"Those were part of my instructions."

"Where's the paper from the package?"

"I burned that, too."

"Why?"

"I told you."

"Do you always follow instructions so carefully?"

"Under these circumstances, yes."

"What circumstances, Silber?"

"When that kind of money comes with the package and all I have to do is to follow orders, when I'm not hurting any—"

"You're not, huh?" Harsh, angry. Disbelieving.

"No, I'm not."

"If your pals pull off what they're threatening to do they're going to kill millions of innocent people. You call *that* not hurting anyone?"

"I have nothing to do with that."

"The hell you don't! They're threatening to blow up atomic bombs, Silber! And you're part of the whole operation!" They were shouting again.

"I'm not part of anything."

"Why do you have those airline tickets, Silber?"

"Those were my instructions."

"Where are you supposed to go, Silber?"

There wasn't any harm in saying. "Lisbon."

"Lisbon, Portugal?"

"Yes."

"When are you supposed to make that flight, Silber?"

"When you give me the papers the letter describes."

"We're supposed to hand you over a hundred million dollars in securities and let you walk out that door a free man?" A fist pounded against the table. Gentle, then rough. Rough, then gentle. Gentle, then ... "Silber, you'll be in prison for a hundred years."

"I told you not to threaten me. It's stupid."

Silence. They must know.

"You can't threaten me. You can't hurt me."

"You said that before, Silber. Why not? What makes you so special?"

"You can't hurt a dead man."

Silence. The meaningful glances between them.

"If I'm lucky I'll live six months. Heart disease. Cancer. Both of them. Advanced, impossible to stop now. Six months if I'm lucky. Two to three months is more like it. What are *you* going to do to me?"

"He's right. We can't touch him. We can't even shake him." Lew Kirby showed his frustration. "What he says is true. The doctor confirmed it. He's a walking corpse."

General Sheridan's face remained unreadable as it had throughout the interrogation. Neither he nor Colonel Beyersdorf had asked a single question. This wasn't their affair. The FBI were experts at this game. Yet it had been difficult to keep his silence. He'd wanted to grab Silber by the neck and shake him like a terrier mauls a rat. But he couldn't do that. Not because of moral scruples. If tearing Silber limb from limb would have gotten him the information they needed he'd have done it personally. Being gentle with one man and permitting millions to die was insanity. But he couldn't do a thing. Silber was right; you don't threaten a dead man.

Bob Vincent lit a cigarette and returned the pack with exaggerated care to his pocket. "For the record, Lew. I want these gentlemen to have anything we might have turned up."

Kirby shrugged. "It's an open book," he grunted. "Even if I wanted to burn him alive to make him talk I couldn't do it." Sheridan wondered if Kirby had read his thoughts. "If Silber were to fall down dead, then for all we know the answer might be an atom bomb going off somewhere."

Beyersdorf leaned forward with his eyes riveted to Kirby's face. "Do you think he knows about the C-one-thirty? How the crew was killed?"

Kirby shook his head. "No, I don't. He really is in the dark about all this. I believe him when he says he had no idea what was in that letter."

"He's about as perfect a contact and delivery man as you could ask for," Bob Vincent added. "Our biggest problem is time. Somewhere in his background there had to be a contact between Silber and the men who sent him the instructions and the money. The same men, or at least they're associated with them, who got your airplane and the bombs. Somehow they managed to pick up where Dave Silber was and they learned about his health. As Lew said," Vincent motioned to

106

Kirby, "Silber's a walking corpse. He won't live more than a few months. We've checked him out as far and fast as we could in the time we've had so far. No criminal record. Nothing. His family left the country three days ago. They were living in Chicago. We've already run a solid screen on their neighborhood, people they knew, that sort of thing. They were almost destitute. If neighbors hadn't helped them, one of their children would have died a few months ago. It's the sort of story that comes out of the slums. No money, no doctor, no—" Vincent shrugged. "Anyway, whoever knew Silber in the past, for one reason or another, must have run into him again. Or, more likely, found out about his physical condition and that he and his family were destitute. If they knew the kind of man Silber was, then he was perfect for them. Silber's totally unselfish about this whole thing. He's bitter about the manner in which he can't provide for his family. We learned his insurance was cancelled a year or more ago. He's going to die and all he's got to leave his wife and children are some bitter memories."

Vincent thought of his own family. It made it easier to think of what went on inside Silber's mind. "And then along comes a package with a letter of instructions, a sealed envelope he's told to deliver at a certain time to the police in San Francisco, and ten thousand dollars. I don't doubt but that's the figure. What he received, I mean. I'm convinced there's additional money waiting for his family in Europe."

For the first time in nearly an hour General Sheridan broke his self-imposed silence. "Do you know where his family went?"

"Not yet. They had to travel with her passport, of course. We know they flew Air France to Paris. Mrs. Silber had a French car waiting for her in the city. Citroën. That's all we know. The French authorities have an alert out for her, but we haven't heard anything yet. I don't believe it would be of any help if we did."

"Why not?" Beyersdorf asked.

Kirby picked up the question. "Dave Silber's doing

107

what he can for his family. I don't believe he plans ever to see them again."

"It does make it difficult," Vincent said, "to put the pressure on him. He's not only going to die but he's completely selfless in his motives."

"I'm touched," Sheridan said, almost with a snarl. "I can give you a sob story about six widows whose husbands were in that C-one-thirty."

Vincent looked at him coolly. "I didn't mean it that way, General."

"I know that," Sheridan said quickly. "I apologize." He didn't dwell on the matter. "If these people we're looking for had some contact with Silber in his earlier years, that means there's a chance Silber was in the flying game. There may have been some association that way. Anything there?"

Vincent nodded. "It's there, all right. Back in nineteen forty-three Dave Silber was an air cadet. Trained at Kelly Field, near San—"

"I know where it is. Can we help in any way?"

Vincent glanced at Beyersdorf. "The colonel's been on it with some of our people. There's nothing more we can do except wait for Hoving's office—"

"That jackass!"

"That may be so, General, but he's right when it comes to NSA's computers. They've got the best system in the world. Despite the manner in which Hoving conducted himself at the conference, which," Vincent threw in as an aside, "was most unusual for the man, he knows how to carry on when the chips are down. He did order their main computer cleared for this particular emergency, and his best programmers were put on twenty-four hour alert. They're sleeping in a dormitory at the computer banks. Or they were until we got the fingerprint lead that Silber once was in the old Army Air Forces."

Vincent shifted in his chair. "Nothing can beat the NSA setup for this," he said. "It would take us months to check out the hundreds of leads that are involved. And they become numbered in the tens of thousands when you add all the years. Dead men don't show up in the cadet classes that existed at that time and we've got

108

to run checks all the way through. The computers will do that in minutes—or they can do it in minutes once the programmers set up the computer runs. We've got to track down every single person from the day Silber first wore his uniform, and then we've got to run a follow-through on every person we can. It's a process of elimination and the speed of the computer isn't all we'd like it to be."

Beyersdorf nodded slowly. "I know that only too well, Mr. Vincent. It's the programmers. It takes physical steps, physical movement, and bulk of material to feed the cybernetics system. That's the block, the time problem."

Kirby raised one eyebrow. "You sound right at home there, Colonel."

Beyersdorf said it simply. "I am. For the record, I'm glad Hoving's on this. No matter what I had to say to him yesterday, he's very good."

"What about the President?" Arthur Sheridan couldn't shake from his mind the nuclear shock wave smashing into the White House. "Has Krider been able to persuade him to—"

"No luck," Vincent interrupted. "I've spoken to Krider several times today. They're considering taking the President out of Washington. Against his wishes. Even by force, if necessary. The Secret Service can do that if they're convinced his life is in grave danger."

"Which, apparently, the President is *not* convinced about," Sheridan retorted. "Not so long as Hoving's computers tell him the danger isn't yet critical and Hoving tells that to President Dowling."

"He may be right, you know," Vincent said quietly.

"I hope to God *you're* right," Sheridan snapped. "Have you ever seen one of those things go off?"

"An atomic bomb?"

"Yes."

Vincent shook his head. "No, I haven't." His smile was fleeting. "And I hope I never do."

"So do I," Sheridan came back without a pause. "But *I* have, Bob." He was lost in reflection for the moment. Vincent and Kirby exchanged glances. Sheridan didn't realize he'd used Vincent's first name. To

Vincent and Kirby that represented a significant mark in their relationship with the two officers from the Air Inspector's office. It was a minor but vital detail. The general, without his saying so, had accepted completely their help and their superior knowledge in attempting to track down Silber's background. After the furious exchanges at the conference, there'd been some question in Vincent's mind whether or not this would happen. But it had, and it would make things easier. God knew they needed all the help they could get.

"I've dropped—personally—sixteen atomic bombs and four hydrogen bombs," Sheridan was saying. "Tests in Nevada and in the Pacific. And I've seen a few more go off while I was on ships and on the ground. I don't ever want to see another one. When I think of the President in the same city with one of those things, and it may go off without any warning . . . " He shook his head. "Goddamnit, we've got to get that man out for his own protection. How the hell can Hoving go against *that*?"

Vincent tried to stay on middle ground. "There's more to it than just the President's safety," the FBI man explained. "There's the Congress. And those in the Pentagon. And other public officials, and foreign diplomats, and, well, it's quite a list. The President told Krider he was in the midst of an international conference. If he were to disappear without reason, damned good reason, that could withstand the scrutiny of the most suspicious people this world has ever known, it could precipitate a terrible panic. The rumors that would result from such a move would in themselves trigger an avalanche of reaction. Please remember, General, that up to this moment not a word of what's happened has leaked out to the public. This has been a White House decision." Vincent's expression revealed his own inner turmoil about the point. "I don't know if it's right or wrong and I'm relieved I don't have to make that kind of decision. Because no matter what that decision is, it's going to be wrong."

"How can—"

Vincent's gesture held off the reaction. "General Sheridan, the fact is we haven't the faintest idea where

110

those bombs may be. All we have to go on is conjecture. We don't—"

"I know, I know," Sheridan broke in again. "That letter could mean everything and it might not mean a damned thing, except to lead us down some primrose path. I know what you're going to say and I wish I could argue with you, but I can't. The bombs could be anywhere, in any one of a couple of hundred cities. They could have put one in London and another in Tokyo and one in Mexico City and . . ." His voice trailed off for the moment. "Anywhere," he said bleakly.

Kirby rose to his feet and stretched. "I—" He stopped short as the office intercom buzzed. Kirby reached over to the switch. "Kirby here."

"Is Mr. Vincent with you, Lew?"

"Yeah. He's listening. Shoot."

"It's Silber. He insists on seeing Mr. Vincent. Immediately. Says it's vital."

Kirby glanced at Vincent. He was already on his way to the door.

"What time is it now, Mr. Vincent?"

Vincent studied Silber carefully. For the first time their only lead to the location of the atomic bombs appeared agitated. When Vincent failed to answer immediately Silber gestured with impatience.

"I slept longer than I expected," he said. "The drugs —I was supposed to give you a message at eleven o'clock tonight."

Vincent glanced at his watch. "You're ten minutes late, then. Is this part of your instructions?"

"Yes, yes."

"All right, Mr. Silber." Vincent spoke in a calm, unruffled voice. He didn't like the flush on Silber's face. "What's the message?"

"You're supposed to look at the mountain."

Vincent forced himself to remain without expression. "Would you repeat that, please?"

Silber's hands fluttered nervously. He seemed strangely birdlike, helpless. "You're supposed to look at the mountain. At midnight." He gasped for air. "That's it. At midnight."

There was something dreadfully important here. Vincent studied Silber through narrowed eyes. It was time to change his tone.

"*What* mountain?" he snapped.

Silber took a deep breath, closed his eyes for a long moment. "The name is Gorgonio," he said slowly.

"Gorgonio!" General Sheridan barked the name and Vincent motioned him to silence.

"Is that Mt. Gorgonio?"

"Uh, yes. That's right."

Vincent noticed that Beyersdorf was gone. He kept his attention on Silber. "Can you tell us why, Mr. Silber?" Again his voice was pleasant.

Silber shook his head slowly. "No. I don't know anything else. My instructions were to tell you at eleven o'clock tonight that you're supposed to look at the mountain, at Gorgonio, at midnight. Really, that's all I know." He stared blankly at them.

In the adjoining room Colonel Beyersdorf was already putting through an emergency call to Norton Air Force Base and shouting at another man to get Jim Krider at the White House on the other phone. It was coming to a head. There was only one reason why they would be told to look toward Mt. Gorgonio at midnight.

Someone was going to set off an atomic bomb.

He looked at his watch.

In exactly forty-three minutes.

10

General Arthur Sheridan burst into the room and saw the telephone in his aide's hand. "Cooper?" Sheridan barked.

Beyersdorf nodded. "Priority call," he answered quickly. "I'll let you know the moment I—"

"What about Krider?"

"Other phone," Beyersdorf said, gesturing. "He's trying to get the White House right now. We'll—hold on, General." Beyersdorf listened intently to the telephone. "Listen," he snapped in a cold voice, "this is Red Priority. Got that? *Red* Priority. I don't care where General Cooper is or what he's doing. Get him—he's landing now? All right, you have a vehicle on that runway and you get him into base ops at once. General Sheridan is waiting right here to talk with him. *No,* goddamnit! Don't even put that phone down. Keep this line open and stick that phone in General Cooper's face the instant he comes through that door. Now get with it!"

Beyersdorf cupped his hand over the speaker and turned to Sheridan. "You heard it, General."

"Right." Sheridan turned to the FBI agent on the other telephone. "How's that call to the White House?"

"They're trying to get him now, sir."

Sheridan turned as Bob Vincent and Lew Kirby came up to him. "I'll have Marcus Cooper at Norton on the phone any minute. Your agent is trying to get Krider on the other horn. Can you get—Kirby, would you get a priority call through to the Pentagon? Chief of Staff, Air Force. Use Code Red Wing Six. It'll get you right through no matter where he is or what he's doing. Don't worry about the Joint Chiefs. The Code is automatic for them to be rung in."

Vincent waited with visible impatience. "General, where's this Gorgonio mountain?"

"It's San Gorgonio," Sheridan replied. "Big peak, over eleven thousand feet. In the San Bernardino Range."

It was Vincent's moment to snap the questions. "Exactly where?" he demanded.

"About twenty miles east from San Bernardino. Maybe eighty or ninety miles east of Los Angeles. The city itself."

Vincent's expression was grim. "Flat out, General. Do you think—"

Sheridan was anticipating the question. "What the hell is there to think! They've set this up. *I* don't know if they've got one of those bombs up there, but what the hell can we do? We've got to accept the bomb is there. We've got to try to find the damn thing in just about thirty minutes." Sheridan slammed a fist into his hand. "Christ! There's a whole bunch of small communities all around there. If that thing goes off at midnight, and I'm damned sure it's up there set to blow— We've got to get out a warning. Can your people take care of that? Good. Every radio and television station in the area. They're still all hooked up on the emergency net. We can go through NORAD if necessary. They've got permanent emergency lines to major areas and they can fan out the word. Make it short and snappy. Everyone inside and stay inside. There'll be just time enough for that. Tell 'em a plane carrying a bomb has crashed on San Gorgonio and it's burning and there's some danger its bombs may go off. That'll stop any panic about an attack. When you get NORAD —I'll get on the horn as fast as I can to them—tell 'em enough so *they* won't go pushing any red buttons."

Vincent turned to several men who had followed him into the room. "You heard?" They nodded. "Get on it immediately." He dismissed them from his mind and turned back to Sheridan.

"You said something about finding the bomb. Can you?"

"How much?"

"There's a chance."

114

"I don't know. It depends on—" Sheridan cut short his answer as Beyersdorf signaled him to the phone. "Bob, grab the extension. I want you in on this." He jerked the telephone from Beyersdorf. "General Cooper? Yes, Art Sheridan here. Just a moment. Bob Vincent of the FBI's coming on the other line. He'll be listening in and may have something to say." Vincent nodded to Sheridan as he came on the extension.

"General, there isn't any time to lose. Just stay with me," Sheridan said, speaking swiftly and clearly.

Vincent heard Major General Marcus Cooper draw in his breath. He'd just landed a jet fighter, the phone had literally been thrust in his face as he was rushed to base operations, and now a lower-grade officer was snapping at him with drill-sergeant fire in his voice. Marcus Cooper knew Arthur Sheridan. They shared the same base and he knew the brigadier general's reputation. It was the old story. When the other man is in the know and you're made aware that something hellish is underway, don't stand on your rank. Go with it. If the other man is wrong you've got all the time in the world to put your personal brand on his ass.

"Go ahead, Art."

"You know about the missing C-one-thirty with the five nukes it carried, right?"

"Yes. I'm up on it. Has there—"

"No questions yet, sir. There isn't time to break it all down now but we have very good reason to believe one of those bombs has been emplaced atop San Gorgonio. In just about thirty-five minutes or so that bomb is scheduled to explode. It's a three-hundred kiloton weapon and you know what'll happen if it goes off."

For a moment the conversation lay between hard, fast thinking. Marcus Cooper was running through his mind what had already been made clear to Arthur Sheridan. San Gorgonio lay twenty miles from Norton Air Force Base where Marcus Cooper was commanding general. Under that command were three squadrons of helicopters. One for air-sea rescue, another for specialized operations and the third a training organization. Each squadron had six powerful Sikor-sky choppers. Of the eighteen machines on the base at least twelve to fifteen would be in commission, and of that number at least four were always kept on alert status. That meant that four fast helicopters could be airborne in minutes. Another two to six could be put in the air soon afterward, but they couldn't help. Every minute now was critical. It was only thirty-four minutes before midnight.

Thirty-four minutes to what would be the moment of detonation for three-hundred-thousand tons of hell.

Both men ran the same thoughts through their minds. Then agreement separated. "General Cooper, it's imperative we get helicopters to Gorgonio to find that bomb. We've got to——"

"I'm aware of that, Arthur," Cooper said briskly. "I haven't wasted any time. Since we still have several things to work out that will require a few more minutes I've already dispatched the alert aircraft. They're on their way now. But it'll take them a while. It's not just twenty miles as you know. For the benefit of Mr. Vincent—you there, sir?"

"I'm listening, General."

"All right, then, it's not just a matter of twenty miles. Those helicopters have to climb to eleven-thousand feet in order to look for anything. We've got to have a plane over them to drop flares. We'll use everything we have. Flares, searchlights and even matches if that's necessary. While we're talking, my crews are being informed by radio of the situation. We'll take care of everything else that has to be done. We're hotlining FAA to divert all commercial flights from the area, and we'll notify the California governor and other officials. All that's being done right now. But I don't think you realize how impossible it is to find something on that peak in the middle of n——"

"What about your radiation control teams?" Vincent broke in.

"Hah! Worthless, Mr. Vincent. There's no radiation leakage from those things. A counter could be sitting right under one of those bombs and it wouldn't tell you what was on top of it. You've—we have to find that thing physically and then hope we can disarm it." General Cooper paused. "That's a problem there, Sher-

116

idan. There won't be time to disarm the damned thing without an expert around. Got any bright ideas?"

Sheridan swore. There wasn't time to go asking around for expert help.

"Only two things," Sheridan replied, trying to avoid a sinking feeling. "They carry automatic weapons on the alert choppers, don't they?"

"Yes. Two weapons per aircraft."

"If they find the bomb they've got to fire at the weapon from point-blank range."

"What?"

"That's right," Sheridan insisted. "It'll blow apart the mechanism and prevent the nuclear device from activating."

"What about the safety explosives?"

"They'll have to take the risk. The only other thing would be to pick up the bomb and drop the damned thing into something like Death Valley, but there won't be enough time for that. Our only hope," Sheridan threw all the emphasis he could into his voice, "is to find it and wreck the nuclear mechanism. If we don't," he stressed anew, "that thing goes off at midnight."

"General Cooper, Vincent here. What's the mountain like?"

"It couldn't be worse," Cooper snapped. "High, rugged, desolate—the lot. There aren't any lights. We've got to use flares and chopper lights. That isn't all, mister." Cooper found himself defending the task on which his men had been sent. "The choppers will be working in thin air and their performance will be lousy. Just to make things worse the weather is rotten. Broken clouds and high winds. Some rain, if the weatherman's right. With the weather, the distance and the climb to altitude they won't have more than five or ten minutes at the most to carry out that search." They heard Marcus Cooper suck in air. "I'm going to level with the both of you," he said. "We haven't got more than a snowball's chance in hell of finding that bomb."

"General Cooper, we've *got* to try!"

"Why the hell do you think I sent out those choppers, Vincent?"

"My apologies, General. We're on the short edge of it here and—"

"No sweat." Cooper's voice was brusque. "I'm getting off this thing. I want to talk directly with my crews."

"Can we keep an open line with you?"

"Of course. Major Wilkins will stay on this end."

The major's voice came through the telephones. "Standing by, sir," didn't tell them very much.

"We're looking for a *what?*"

"You heard the man, Ace. An atomic bomb."

"You're playing with yourself. You've *got* to be. Or else someone's put LSD into the water supply." Captain "Ace" Diamond swore to himself as turbulent winds smacked at the big helicopter. The higher they went the worse it got. Goddamned crazy nonsense going out like this. If they were on the deck it would have been fine. But the big Sikorsky labored for altitude with complaints registered all across the engine gauges. Their orders were to push the machines right to the redlines and to hell with chewing up equipment, just so long as they flew.

The world vanished as they punched into a cloud. Diamond wished he knew how big, how high the damned thing was. But he didn't and neither did the three choppers in loose formation with him. He stayed glued to the instruments with both hands and feet alive on the controls. "Jack," he shouted to his copilot, "tell the others to fan out. Number Two more to the left and Three to the right and tell Ass-End Charlie to drop back some more. There's no telling where we all are in this stuff." Before they plunged into the clouds at least he could see something. A faint horizon, some stars. Now it was flying strictly on the gauges. He listened to Jack warning the other pilots.

The realization that they hadn't any navigational references worth their salt hit him with sudden impact. He swore again. "Jack, get home plate. Tell them we've got to have radar steer all the way in. We're in the soup and unless we can climb away from it in just about one minute I'm aborting. All we're gonna do," Diamond grumbled, "is make scratch marks on some rock up here." The copilot doublechecked the radar transponder as he called in his request to Norton Air Force Base radar control. Radar came back that they had a clear signal and would vector the helicopter flight. So far they were in good shape. "If," Diamond muttered, "you can call mountains you can't see good news." But at least they had radar protection. For a moment they were silent, the powerful clattering roar of the Sikorsky muted by their headsets. The machine rocked intermittently, vibrating all the time, every now and then shuddering her length from sharp blows. Diamond knew they were taking the wind streaming off the mountain, tumbling wildly as it ripped down the slopes, churning the air about them. Diamond jabbed down on his intercom button, calling his radioman.

"Chuck, give me that story again. No, wait. Do the others have it?"

The radioman didn't have time to answer. "Sir, it's General Cooper. He's coming in direct. Open frequency to all of us."

Diamond nodded. "Tell the others to be sure they're tuned in to the Old Man."

He winced as rain smashed against the plexiglas before them. Goddamnit. His copilot flicked switches in automatic response. Wipers, pitot heat, defrosters . . . one by one Jack stabbed and pushed to meet the situation. One part of Diamond's mind flew his craft. The other listened to the voice crackling through his earphones.

". . . Cooper here. I'll give it to you fast and straight. We have every reason to believe that a nuclear device has been placed somewhere on the peak of San Gorgonio. That's as close as I can give it to you. You're to try to find that device. The odds are—it'll be like looking for the needle in the haystack. It's a three-hundred-kiloton weapon. It's no bigger than a small suitcase and for all we know it may be buried or concealed in some manner. But I want you all to try. The information I have is the device is set to detonate exactly at midnight. That's twenty-four hundred hours straight up. Use everything you have to find that thing. I know what

119

you're going through but I can't stress too highly the importance of your mission. You should have an aircraft orbiting the peak just about now. It will be dropping flares steadily to give you as much light as it can." They heard the general take a deep breath and at the same moment they emerged from the rain shower. Diamond's copilot pointed dead ahead of them. In the distance the first flares were going off, intense, tiny points of light. They floated slowly downward, twinkling in the mists ahead of them, already showing the severe winds off the mountain by drifting rapidly leeward.

Cooper's voice came to them again. "If you have reason to believe you've sighted your target—and your best bet may be an antenna of some type—it won't do any good to pick up the weapon directly. Your orders are to use your automatic weapons directly against the nuclear device. I repeat, if you have reason to believe you have sighted the device, you are to use your automatic weapons against it. Be alert for an explosion. There's a chemical explosive that's part of the nuclear system and that's what we want you to try to set off. It's three pounds, I repeat, three pounds of plastic explosives, so stand off a bit if it's possible to do so. There's no danger of your setting off the nuclear device with your weapons." Again there came a pause. The flares ahead of them were brighter as the helicopters labored under full power to reach the peak. If anything, the turbulence was even more severe and Diamond knew his control of the big Sikorsky was being jeopardized. He wondered just how much time he'd give it. The thought came to him that if they waited just a bit too long they might be within the— He turned off his thoughts on the atomic bomb exploding. Later, later, he swore to himself. He glanced at the clock on the instrument panel. Sixteen minutes to midnight. Jesus Christ. He wanted to be the hell gone and away from that damned peak *before* midnight. If there—

God bless Cooper; his next thought came with the general's continuing words. "Now listen to me carefully. We'll stay open contact with you all the time. If for any reason you lose radio contact, then at twenty-three fifty-five, at five minutes to midnight, you troops get the hell out. You understand that? At five minutes to twelve get going. You go to full power and you take those choppers out of there, diving all the way, and you do it at redline. I want voice confirmation immediately on this. Red Wing One, sound off."

"Red Wing One, affirmative."

They barked out their call signs.

"Red Two, affirmative."

"Red Wing Three, gotcha."

"Red Four, affirmative."

"Mike One, did you read?"

The transport circling above San Gorgonio came on the radio. "Roger, sir. Mike One, loud and clear. Affirmative."

"Good luck, all of you."

General Marcus Cooper went off the radio. The controller came on to maintain open contact. They knew the Old Man was right there alongside the microphone. His final orders made them all feel somewhat better.

They reached the peak area with just over nine minutes of search time. And then that was cut even further—

"Red Three to Red Leader. *Mayday, Mayday, Mayday.*"

In the air and on the ground, men stiffened. A chopper in trouble in rough air, at night, more than two miles high—

"Leader to Three! Go ahead!"

The helicopter pilot's voice was extraordinarily calm for what he reported. "We've got fire in the engine. We're pulling away downwind. It's spreading pretty fast. I think we may have to bail. Over."

"What about your bottles?" Diamond barked. "Can you get it out?"

"Negative, Red Leader. We—"

Norton Control broke in. "Red Three from Control. Try to stay in that thing as long as you can and continue downwind. Do you read?"

"Yeah, Control." Red Three was extraordinarily laconic about his blazing machine. The other pilots saw

121

the deep red glow spreading from the descending helicopter. "Don't know how long we can stay up here. Getting pretty hot." Pause. "Oh, oh. No joy, Control. We're starting to come apart. We've got to leave this thing n—"

They saw three dull flashes of white as parachutes opened beneath the flares. Then an angry pulse of orange flame as the helicopter exploded.

"Anybody see any more chutes?" No one had seen more than three canopies blossom beneath the flares.

"We got only three, Leader."

"Three." Pause. "That's all, Leader."

Another silent whisper of flame. The Sikorsky impacting against a slope.

Five men were in that crew.

Only three chutes. Someone forgot he was on open radio line and swore viciously.

Captain Diamond wasn't thinking about that. He couldn't help the two men who were in the chopper when it blew apart. Three men had bailed out. In high winds and darkness and on a cruel slope, against tumbled rock. Time had grabbed at all of them. If that bomb went at midnight those three men, *if* they were all still alive, would be within the searing touch of the nuclear blast . . .

"Red Leader to Two and Four. Close up, close up. Let's find that mother."

The mountain rose before them.

"Has the President been notified?"

Vincent cupped his hand over the telephone mouthpiece and nodded to Sheridan. "He's got the word. We're keeping an open line to his office. He's standing by." Vincent paused for a moment, deep in thought. "What about the local areas?"

"We've done everything we can right now," Sheridan said. "All military fields, the works. Full notification. We're alerting every medical facility we can. If that thing blows we're going to have our hands full getting emergency teams in here. Oh, yes. If you're still talking with the White House . . . good. Let them know that we're already moving to take care of fallout problems downwind. We've got monitoring aircraft in the air. They're on their way here from Nevada. And—just tell them we're on top of it."

Vincent appeared troubled. "I hadn't thought that much about fallout, General. Is it going to be severe?"

"It is."

Sheridan's brief reply was more eloquent than any speech. Vincent turned back to the telephone.

Sheridan and Beyersdorf had already held a brief conference with Norton Air Force Base on the tremendous deposit of intense radioactive fallout downwind of the bomb. Thank God the winds blew along a path that was sparsely inhabited. But the winds could shift. They were almost unpredictable except for the general easterly flow. The bomb would go off against the surface of the mountain. It would tear away the entire peak and . . . Sheridan visualized a fireball two thousand feet in diameter, caressing the earth and then leaping upward with tens of thousands of tons of radioactive debris, most of it to fall soon after the explosion. If it rained, and rained hard, they'd be better off because it would localize the effect, and— He forced himself off the subject. The experts were in control now, were already making their frenzied preparations, and—

"I think I can make out something!"

"Damnit, what—"

"I can't tell, Ace. It looks like a whip antenna of some sort. Bring the light a bit more to the left and— There! See it? you can see the light reflecting off—"

"To hell with what it may be! It's the only thing we've seen so far. Moriarty! Baxter! You two see it?"

The two gunners peered through the open side doors, their waist belts securing them to the lurching helicopter. "Yessir! We got it! You want us to give it a burst?"

"Damn right," Diamond grated. "I'll hold this thing steady as I can. Hold on," he said hurriedly. "Red Two and Four from Leader. Did you read that?"

"Roger, Leader. Four reads. We're backing off."

"This is Two. All clear."

"Gunners, open fire," Diamond barked.

The big Sikorsky vibrated through her frame as the gunners blasted away.

"Sheridan? You there?"

"Go ahead, General."

"Is Vincent listening?"

"I'm on, General Cooper."

"All right," Marcus Cooper snapped into the telephone. "We've bought it. Run out of time. I'm ordering my helicopters away from the peak. I—"

"But, General—"

"They can hardly stay up in the air!" Cooper roared. "We've done everything we can. There's only four minutes to midnight, damnit, and I'm not going to kill those men. One of the choppers picked up one of my people who bailed out but we can't even find out where the other two landed. If they leave now at full speed they'll just stay ahead of the shock wave. That's it." In the background they heard the helicopter pilots confirming their orders to pull out at maximum speed.

"For your information," Cooper went on, "they did everything humanly possible. They saw something and Red Leader went in as close as they dared. The gunners shot it up but it looks as if all we did was to tear up a remote weather station. I'm sorry, but there's nothing else to do. Vincent?"

"Yes."

"If you still have that open line to the White House you'd better notify the President of the situation."

"Yes, of course. Thank you."

Vincent's arms felt leaden as he took the other telephone. Just before the President came on he glanced at the wall clock.

Two minutes to midnight.

San Gorgonio lay a straight-line distance of four hundred and twenty miles from San Francisco. He was still on the telephone when he glanced through the window.

He knew midnight had come.

11

Allan Clarke watched the radiance of Los Angeles Valley streaming multi-hued and glittering through broken clouds. The distant sky beyond seemed clearer. Clarke turned to his wife at his side and leaned back so his two passengers in the rear seats of the small plane could hear him. "Looks good up ahead," he said above the engine roar. "Phoenix Weather said the front would end along the San Gabriel Mountains. They called it pretty good."

His wife failed to share his good humor about improving weather. "It'll be the first time in three weeks they've been right about anything," she said cautiously. "It doesn't look that good *yet*."

He patted her knee. "Of course not. The front's still another hundred miles ahead of us. But look for yourself, honey. It's getting better every minute." Mrs. Clarke, ever pessimistic about weather forecasts, sniffed her disapproval.

Clarke's friend behind him tapped his shoulder. "Allan, how high are we?"

Clarke gestured at the altimeter. "Twelve thousand five. Why?"

The man gestured self-consciously. "Isn't there a pretty high mountain around here?"

Allan Clarke laughed. "Spoken like a true backseat driver," he chuckled. "There sure is. San Gorgonio."

"Well, shouldn't we be—"

"Look out the left window and you'll see that peak you're so worried about, Fred. It's about a half-mile away and a thousand feet *below* us." Clarke laughed with good humor. He glanced at his watch. "Just about twelve," he said. "I'll give Los Angeles Radio a call and we'll see what's up at Santa Barbara."

He dialed in the radio frequency for the flight station

and turned his transmitter to 122.1 megacycles. "Los Angeles Radio, Comanche Niner Six-Six-Eight-Poppa. Over."

They were on the ball tonight, answering immediately. "Comanche Six-Eight-Poppa, Los Angeles Radio. Give me a position report immediately, please. Over."

No response.

"Six-Eight-Poppa, go ahead, please."

Allan Clarke didn't answer.

His eyes had been burned out.

The four people in the small plane were the first to know of the three-hundred-kiloton weapon exploding against the peak of San Gorgonio Mountain. They were first to know, and they knew nothing. Pure, naked light ripped out the retinas of their eyes. In the instant Allan Clarke's throat started the muscular spasm to cry out the tremendous heat pulse engulfed the airplane. Still in that same instant, paint, metal skin, plexiglas and the human skin exposed to that light exploded in flame.

It happened too swiftly for even one pitiful shriek against the unknown terror. Before this could happen the fireball flashed a half-mile in diameter. The shock wave erupting from the savage nuclear flame engulfed the small machine in its tidal wave of raw energy.

A giant hand squeezed.

What appeared to be crumpled tissue paper spun wildly in the aftermath of the blast that was already far beyond.

Precisely at three seconds past midnight of the twenty-ninth of June, at the summit of San Gorgonio Mountain, a suitcase-sized container stirred with electrical impulses. Lens-shaped plastic explosives became fiercely glowing gases under enormous pressure. There was an *inward* explosion squeezing together a porous mass of heavy metal. As the plutonium condensed it received a withering flood of neutrons. In time measuring millionths of a second, unnumbered plutonium atoms split apart.

The tactical nuclear weapon vanished. In its place raged a tiny star with a temperature of one hundred million degrees, far hotter than even the interior of the

126

sun. The pulsations erupting outward—visible light, infrared and hard radiations—were seen only as that terrible blinding flash.

San Gorgonio's peak lay just under three miles from where Jane Thomas, in a home of stone and wood, lived in scenic isolation. Jane Thomas stepped outside for a breath of fresh air, to look at the few stars shining through broken clouds. She never *saw* the explosion. The light shattered the fragile jelly of her eyes and exploded her clothes and body in flame.

She was dead before the shock wave flung itself down the mountain to hurl the lifeless rag doll through the air.

Three hundred and thirty miles to the east, flying at an altitude of forty-one thousand feet, the pilot of an American Airlines jetliner stared with mouth agape. Later, the shaken man said:

"It was just like the, well, like the sun exploding. All of southern California looked like it was on fire. I didn't know what was happening and I thought, I really thought, my God, the sun's exploded. From our altitude the sky was absolutely clear over the southwest corner of the country. I could see the light reflected off mountains beneath us. We were flying north at the time, so I saw the light to my left and at the same instant, I mean right then with absolutely no time lapse I saw the mountains ahead of us and below us and even far to the right, way out to the east, reflecting that light. I turned back to my left and my eyes felt as if someone had stabbed them with an icepick, but I could still see, and then, Holy Jesus, I saw this huge thing, growing and getting redder, pushing its way into the sky, until finally it faded from sight. I think it hung there in the sky, looming over the horizon, for maybe fifteen or twenty seconds. It was a frightening thing, really terrifying, and then I knew the truth. It was an atomic bomb. None of us knew what the hell to do then ..."

Twelve miles from San Gorgonio's peak, on a small road winding between huge boulders, Police Officer

Stan Powers saw the night vanish in a brilliant flash. At the moment of detonation a wall of rock lay between him and the summit of San Gorgonio. Stan Powers stared in disbelief as his lightstunned eyes saw a negative print of reality. By the time reaction seeped back into his brain the car went into a ditch and rolled over on its side. Powers thought someone had set off a dynamite explosion and he started for his gun. Then he realized he hadn't heard a sound. At that instant of comprehension the shock wave engulfed the small mountain pass in which he was standing, churning the ground beneath him and to every side with rolling dust. Powers threw up his arms instinctively as pebbles and stones tore at his body with painful impact. It was then he became aware of the sustained tornadic roar. Officer Powers came out of his crouch with blood trickling down his face. He squinted in the dust whirling about him, then remembered his flashlight. He switched it on and ran toward an open area. He still heard the celestial kettledrums rolling forth their thunder.

He pushed his way past a rock outcropping and stopped, his heart frozen. He was unaware of his hand moving in a cross before him. Twelve miles away a creature hunched over the broken summit of San Gorgonio, flinging great chunks of Hell into the sky. A monstrous genie clawed upward from the bowels of the planet, fuming and writhing, belching forth deep-red flame, curling within its substance, growing horribly, spilling its terrible drum-roll out over the world. Blazing colors stabbed and shredded the boiling smoke as the monster cried into the heavens. The baleful eye of the fireball waned, issued forth a final explosion and withdrew into the bloody darkness of the upward surging cloud. It boiled upward with incredible speed, its dazzling colors gone, now deep red, and then a blackened hue, and purple and brown and gray. New fire spat angrily from within, lightning bolts from the electrically saturated air. As Powers watched, the cloud heaved within itself and invaded the stratosphere.

Officer Powers realized he was watching Hell from his knees.

"I was at the opening night of the Red Door, the new night club in Redlands, which is about twenty miles south of San Gorgonio, although until last night I never thought of it quite that way." Newsman Dick Slater lit another cigarette and moved his fingers back to his typewriter. "I remember glancing at my watch and noting it was midnight. That's when it happened. I had my back to the window where I was sitting and it was as if a million flashbulbs had all gone off together. Just this eerie white light, so brilliant you couldn't see a thing. Like the greatest strobe light the world's ever known, in one huge flash that stops everything where it is. It freezes them in position and it's as if time just comes to a dead stop. I didn't know then, of course, that the light had come from twenty miles away, from the top of San Gorgonio. I knew instinctively something was crazy. There just shouldn't have been a light like *that*. I turned around and looked through the window and the light was still there in the sky, like God had decided he didn't want the night anymore.

"I recall distinctly I saw everything outside the window etched in light. There was the Pelican Cafe, the clear red color of a car outside, the pumps at the Mobilgas station across the street, the hills all around us, rapidly turning to purple as the light faded out. I remember dashing outside. Dozens of people were with me. Someone shouted and we all turned to look to the northeast.

"There, high above the hills between us and San Gorgonio, over the mountain itself, a terrible ball of red fire whirled into view. That's the only word for it. It whirled upward from the mountain, or rather from the boiling mass we could still see flowing all around the peak. We knew it was Gorgonio; it's the only thing that big in that direction. Purple gathered along the edges of the flaming red and started spreading within. We gaped like kids who have just seen some terrible nightmare coming to life. I think someone cried out. 'My God, it's an atom bomb!' I don't know who said it. Maybe it was even myself.

"Later—we found out it was about three minutes after we first saw the flash—we were hit with this

129

tremendous blast of sound. It wasn't like anything I'd ever heard. It reverberated all about us. It seemed to come from all sides and it hit our eardrums like physical blows, and we heard it booming and echoing throughout the hills. A couple of people nearly jumped out of their shoes from fright.

"Then it was quiet again. We could just make out what looked like a white plume with lightning flashes coming from inside it. It grew and grew and I knew I was looking at a mushroom cloud, the kind I'd seen in so many pictures and films. It really hit me then. It had to be, it could only be, the atomic war. And I remember thinking 'You bastards, you dirty bastards . . .' "

John and Helen Kowalsky looked up from their television set. "Did you see that?" he asked his wife.

"It looked just like—John, was that a flash from a camera?"

John Kowalsky was on his feet. At their floor-to-ceiling picture window he jerked aside the drapes. "My God! Helen, come quickly!"

She rushed to his side. San Gorgonio reared into the night sky twenty-three miles from their home. During the day they had a beautiful view of the mountain, framed as it was between high rock walls. But they never saw it at night unless the moon was full, and even then it was little more than a shape on the horizon.

They saw San Gorgonio now. The entire top of the mountain was aflame. Something huge and shot through with red and yellow and orange and blue flames was boiling into the sky, lighting up the world beneath the leaping conflagration.

"Is it—" She couldn't say the words. Instead her hand flew to her mouth, the knuckles against her teeth.

They stood in silence for several minutes. John Kowalsky should have remembered about shock waves. A long time ago he'd read something about the subject. He'd forgotten it. A shock wave rushes down valleys and through canyons and along constricting passes, sometimes gathering strength in its mindless plunge. John Kowalsky had forgotten that a natural passageway

130

between high walls ran outward from his home straight toward San Gorgonio.

A steel fist of air rammed into the picture window. The window bulged, then gave way. The jagged shards erupted into the room, preceding the blast which for a fraction of a second hesitated against the exterior of the house. The glass tore inward with blinding speed to lacerate the young couple into pulpy gore.

The children slipped and stumbled as they ran crying to their mutilated parents.

"We were thirty-five miles away, maybe closer to forty. You know where Twenty-Nine Palms is? All right, forty, then. Oh, yes, we saw the whole thing. We were in the kitchen when the light flashed. Just like that the whole world was dazzling white. Someone screamed and by the time I gathered my wits around me the light was already fading to yellow. The only sound we heard was that scream. We ran outside and looked toward Los Angeles. I remember thinking that it was an atom bomb. An attack, you know. Against Los Angeles, I thought. The moment I looked toward the city I knew something terrible had happened. I started to cry. From one end of the horizon to the other the world was still yellow and then it changed. The light became luminescent as if the edge of the world was glowing. It was, well, an incredible green that kept shifting and flashing and then became violet. Right after that it got dark again. But we could still see something that glowed by itself. It was terrible.

"A ball. A shining black and red ball. I don't know how I could see something black at night but I could. I still don't understand it. Every now and then white and blue light flickered. Like watching heat lightning, you know? It kept going higher and higher. Then maybe four or five minutes after we first saw the light it felt like the sky split in half. I've never heard a sound like it before. I belong to a rifle club and I'm used to noise. But this . . . it was like rifles blazing away only magnified a thousand times. Like someone ripping the sky right in half. That happened twice. Two giant, double-

131

sounding cracks, and all the time there was this muffled roar.

"The noise died away. My friend was standing beside me and she was crying. 'It's Hiroshima,' she said. 'It's Hiroshima come home.' I was never so scared in my life . . ."

He'd been expecting it. He felt the terrible weariness flood his mind. Brigadier General Arthur Sheridan had seen that light before. The light he'd prayed he would never see again. From San Francisco, hundreds of miles to the north, Sheridan and Robert Vincent watched the gleaming light flash through the heavens. It dulled swiftly into a shifting, iridescent green, then it pulsed, once, twice more, a throbbing flicker that left them with a sense of horror.

Sheridan snatched the telephone from Vincent.

"Krider? Goddamnit, man, answer me! Krider!"

"I'm here, General. What is it? You sound—"

"Never mind how I sound!" Sheridan snarled. "Listen to me good and get your ass in high gear. *They weren't kidding.* An atomic bomb has just exploded to the south of us and it's probably right where they promised it would be. San Gorgonio. That's right. They just blew the damned thing."

Sheridan flicked his gaze to Vincent. *"Get the President out of Washington.* Get him out *now.* His life is in grave danger. Before you do anything else get those helicopters there and get him out and don't waste a damned minute. You got it? With what's just happened you've got full authority. Get him out whether or not he wants to go."

Sheridan tossed the telephone to Vincent and turned to his aide. "Is that line open to the Pentagon? Let me have the phone." He turned again to Vincent.

"You know what happens now? From here on, it's hell to pay for everyone. That list of cities will be on every radio and television station within the hour. You're going to see the damndest panic you've ever known in your life."

"What are you going to do?" Vincent asked the

132

question quietly. For this moment it was Sheridan's ball game and he had to do the running.

"I don't know if they'll agree with me," Sheridan said, his tone flat and grim, "but I'm going to try. I'm asking the Joint Chiefs of staff to talk with the President. They can reach him in the evacuation chopper by radio. I'm going to ask them to declare martial law, because all hell's about to break. More people are going to be killed through panic than—"

Sheridan turned to the phone. He didn't need to end his sentence. It didn't take much imagination to see the picture.

One hundred million human beings were going to run.

In panic.

God help anyone who got in their way.

"Mr. McManus?" Ed Gubitz kicked himself mentally. "Sorry, sir. This way, please, Mr. President."

Press Secretary Gubitz led President Charles Dowling through the corridor. At the far end of the hallway newsmen and technicians prepared for an unscheduled broadcast. They had no idea what might be in the wind; best bet was some new outbreak of "limited war" almost anywhere in the world. It was odd the President should broadcast at this hour—it was just after 3:00 A.M. EST—but a videotape made now and repeated during the day would leave him free just when his time would be most needed.

Several men glanced up to see Gubitz preceding the President down the corridor. At the same time, Dowling was joined by a half-dozen men in uniform; the President held an impromptu conference in the hallway. The group looked up as a clattering roar invaded the White House. Three fast Marine helicopters pounded down from the night sky. The newsmen heard shouted voices over the idling rotor blades. The President and those with him looked on with interest as the men departing the helicopters met with a group expecting their arrival. The disturbance lasted but a minute, and the helicopters crashed their way back into the night. The news group bent to their tasks.

In the corridor Tom Saunders, the President's aide, joined Dowling. "Time, sir. We'd best be ready." President Dowling nodded and with his entourage moved to join the waiting newsmen.

In the broadcast room President Dowling took the seat behind his desk. He waited patiently for last-minute adjustments with lighting and camera positions. They were ready with sixteen minutes to spare. The President looked up at his aide and nodded. Tom Saunders spoke briefly with two Secret Service men in the corridor and then closed the door. The newsmen looked at each other with mild surprise. They'd never *closed* the door before.

The press secretary coughed for attention. "Are the cameras and microphones off?" Someone nodded. "They're off, Ed." Gubitz thought a moment and made a sudden decision. "Kill the power leads," he told them. He waited out the exclamations and repeated his words. "Kill the power leads, please. The President has something to say to you personally." Puzzled, they carried out Gubitz's bidding and turned to the man behind the desk.

President Dowling joined his fingers together and leaned forward. He studied each face before him and the newsmen shifted uncomfortably. The President always prepared for a broadcast with personal banter between him and the press regulars. No one could recall Dowling subjecting every face to such careful scrutiny.

"I have something to ask of you," President Dowling said without preamble. "It may require some compromise with your professional ethics, but I assure you it will be for only a brief period, and the cause is worthy of such action on your part." They couldn't help staring a him. "If it is impossible for any of you to meet my request, please let me know right now and you will be escorted from this room." Dowling glanced up at the clock and brought his eyes back to theirs. "There is very little time, gentlemen," he prompted.

They looked at one another. "Okay by me." "Sure." "Of course." "We'll go along with you, sir."

"Good. What we discuss in this room must remain secure in later hours. You'll see why as quickly as you learn what I tell you." They nodded, their earlier confusion replaced by a wait-and-see attitude.

"First, during the last hour an atomic bomb has exploded in the United States. It was not a test. By the same token the bomb has nothing to do with an attack. It exploded about one hundred miles from Los Angeles, and while we don't have time to go further into the

135

matter right now, we expect to take some casualties from that explosion."

No one made a sound.

"That's the purpose of this broadcast. It's necessary for the President to speak directly with the people throughout the country. The video and sound tapes will be repeated through the night and tomorrow morning. You gentlemen still with me?"

They nodded, overwhelmed, attentive.

"Second, we have reason to believe there may be an atomic bomb somewhere in the capital." Dowling again glanced at the clock. "Time's running out. We may all be in grave danger," he said quickly, speeding up his words. "I don't know any more than what I've told you right now." He paused and took a deep breath.

"And third, gentlemen, I am not the President." He didn't wait for their reaction. "The President was evacuated from the White House a short time ago and is now in a secret redoubt some distance from here. He is prepared to make this broadcast—himself—in just a few minutes. Everything is ready for him in a room duplicating this one. Outside of those involved no one else knows of this arrangement. Or," Fred McManus observed, "his emergency evacuation. I must also tell you the President left the White House against his wishes. His safety, however, is paramount, and we were left with no other decision."

One newsman couldn't contain himself. "Sir," he blurted, "this isn't some kind of joke, is it? I'd swear you were, you *are* President Dowling."

Fred McManus thought of the months of diligent observation he had made of Charles Dowling, the long studies of films and the sound of the President's voice on tape, repeated over and over while he practiced every gesture, every movement, the voice and its wide range of inflection. He thought of the mild plastic surgery that brought him to an exact double of Dowling, how no one had ever thought they'd need all those exacting preparations. Now they did. It was that simple. The public would be told soon enough that President Dowling was safe. But not yet. The immediate word of a precipitous evacuation of the President could have a nasty reaction. It was preferred that he be seen and heard from, as far as the world knew, the White House.

"The President," Fred McManus said with a smile, "will be on your television monitors at any moment. "You'll see for yourself. As you've already worked out, I'm sure, we'll transmit the video-sound from, ah, where he is right now into the White House and feed from here. I see that the time's up and—"

President Dowling's face flashed on the screen.

President Charles Dowling was annoyed with his whirlwind rush from the White House. Until this moment he'd managed to avoid such nonsense but there was no putting off those eager beavers any more. Confound them. Even the Secret Service agreed with the Pentagon this time, and that was a minor miracle in itself. Dowling's thoughts moved swiftly through the many facets of the emergency thrust upon them. If there *was* a nuclear weapon somewhere in Washington then they'd have to evacuate a great many more people than himself. They would have to— He turned to his military aide. "Steve, get someone to notify the top embassies, start with the Russians, that I'm going on the air with an unscheduled broadcast and they're to be certain they monitor what I have to say. Tell them they'll understand immediately and that we're prepared to offer them full cooperation in evacuating by helicopter any key personnel they want to get out of Washington." Dowling concentrated on what demanded his priority attention. "Use the hotline for a call direct to Moscow. I won't be able to talk with the Premier for a while, but be certain his people get the facts on that bomb explosion. I'm sure they know about it already, but I don't want them drawing any wrong conclusions that we're trigger happy in their direction. And be certain they understand there might be several more bombs going off, and—you know how to handle it."

President Dowling lapsed deep into thought for the broadcast. He disliked being away from the White House. Part of his job was taking the same risk as any soldier on the battlefield, but those responsible for his

137

safety obviously didn't share his thoughts on that matter. Even as he wrestled with his ideas for the talk he would make he knew what must be said. The truth. Anything else could burst explosively among the nation with even more impact than a nuclear blast in a city. Panic was the single biggest problem they faced and he was relieved to know immediate steps had already been taken to absorb what must certainly come in the daylight hours. Mass evacuation of tens of millions of people. He hoped the words he would use in the next several minutes would reassure— He cut off his own thoughts with an angry gesture. The truth of the situation hit him with full impact.

For the first time in history an entire nation was hostage for ransom.

"The sons of bitches! The no-good, rotten mothers!" Lew Kirby clenched and unclenched his powerful hands, wanting to tear someone limb from limb. His face showed barely controlled fury. "If I ever get them within reach, I'll—I'll—" He ground his teeth in rage as Bob Vincent and General Arthur Sheridan looked at him with astonishment.

"If you're all through raving," Vincent said calmly, "I'd like to know what hit you."

"It's that son of a bitch Hoving, that's what!" Kirby shouted.

Vincent sighed. "I can hear you, Lew."

Kirby took a deep breath for control, his muscles rigid. "All right. Sorry." Vincent smiled to himself with the snarled apology. "You know the computer-run NSA was making on Silber's background, right? The thing about his being an air cadet in nineteen forty-three, or whenever. Okay. This has been our only break, our only lead to whoever might be behind all this. Well," Kirby said with venom, "the shits just blew the whole thing. They were well into the computer checks when they did another little survey of their own. Goddamn them." Vincent's expression compelled Kirby to get with it. "When they got to thinking about the bombs they programmed one of their electronic mothers to check out *their* safety. They gave it the works.

138

Probability A, B and so on down the line. One of their probabilty curves shot the hell way out and off the chart if any one bomb went off. So now the bomb's a reality, and they took another quick look at their probability curve and you know what the hell it told them?"

Kirby's face showed his disgust. "According to their oracle *they're* one of the prime targets in the country! How's *that* grab you, huh? The computer said they were right on the top of the list, and with the bomb maybe being in Washington, *they're* all endangered and they consider the programmers almost impossible to replace, a national asset and that sort of jazz, and, well, the long and short of it is that NSA's pulled most of it's people out of the computer center."

There it was. Vincent could well understand Kirby's reaction of outrage. He felt the same way himself. He looked helplessly at Arthur Sheridan. The general and he had worked hand-in-glove and the Air Force had made certain not to interfere either with FBI authority or procedures. It had been a mutual arrangement. Secretly Vincent had great hopes for the NSA computer study of Dave Silber's background, for the electronic process of elimination that might give them some tangible leads to his associates, or to whoever might have set him up as their contact man. That Silber had been chosen by coincidence was too much of a coincidence in itself to be true. The computers could help tremendously—*would* have helped, he thought with a sudden growing anger of his own. Not now, with Hoving and the others pulling the rug out from under their only substantial hope for identifying the people they sought.

Vincent felt a leaden weight settle within his stomach. Their only real hope now lay in combing every city on the list. The target list, he'd come to think of it. That process was already underway, had been ever since this whole mess was dropped into his lap. Old-fashioned police work. Prosaic, pavement-beating, stair-climbing, door-opening, question-asking police work. Every agent they could put onto the job. Every police officer the departments in every city could spare. Additional help brought in from the outside. Checking every motel, every newly rented apartment, every mysterious truck or auto left somewhere in a city street, for any long period in a garage or— The helplessness of it all nearly crushed him. Just the thought of a truck or a station wagon being left in dead storage in any one of a thousand garages or parking lots was enough to make him throw up his hands. Yet there wasn't any other way. This was the *only* way they might succeed. They'd do everything within their power to break down Silber and . . . It wouldn't work, Vincent realized with even more futility than he'd known before. Silber made it clear enough.

You can't kill a dead man.

He was right.

Time was their enemy. For some there had been no time. The thermal impulse and crashing shock wave snuffed out the lives of the first victims.

Now there would be walking dead.

Victims of the seething radiation tumbling downwind of the bomb, sweeping before the strong winds blowing from the Pacific. The explosion ripped away the summit of Gorgonio to hurl millions of tons of debris in all directions. The howling fireball that shot upward sucked into its ascending maw a thick, roiling pillar of radioactive dust and particles. Now, that debris was returning to earth in a long irregular pattern of death.

The radiation teams rushed by the Air Force and Army along the predicted downwind pattern faced a twofold immediate emergency. Far from the drifting, settling cloud there was still time to warn those who lived where the terrible dust would settle. Some could be evacuated immediately. Others had time only to rush to thick-walled or underground shelters. Still others, for whom there was no time to flee, could remain indoors for whatever protection lay within their grasp. When all this had been done, the radio and television warnings, the screaming sirens and the flights of loud-speaker-equipped helicopters, there remained those already caught in the heaviest fallout.

The formula was simple enough. Within fifty to one hundred miles downwind of San Gorgonio, in a pear-shaped pattern twenty to seventy miles across, almost no one would survive. The radiation levels measured in many thousands of roentgens per hour. Six hundred roentgens kills ninety-eight percent of those exposed to its invisible, deep lacerations of the human body.

By great fortune the men who detonated the nuclear weapon to serve their warning, exposing the terrible light to the teeming millions of the Los Angeles Valley, had also selected a point of explosion that minimized greatly the most severe effects of fallout. By far the worst radiation heaved to earth across the wide expanse of the Joshua Tree National Monument where it decimated the animal population. But the spread was wide enough to condemn those communities in the immediate area. The explosion had ripped Palm Springs to the southeast with winds that shattered windows and stripped buildings of their exterior protuberances. Most buildings took no further damage and the people of Palm Springs believed themselves out of danger. It was a cruel respite. Soon afterward the thick rain of solid particles descended across the fabled desert resort. Within an hour of midnight Palm Springs was a ghost town.

Its people yet walked and made frightened sounds to one another. Those who could, fled the pattering rubble, yet they were condemned equally with those who remained. Many racing away in their autos doubled over with severe cramps and vomited uncontrollably. Few would survive the coming day. Their bodies would be found along the nearby roads and for many miles beyond. Theirs was an evacuation of terrified futility with the end inevitable in the hours ahead.

Banning, Indio, Cathedral City, Coachella, Mecca . . . these were the cities and towns that became tombstone epitaphs for their people. This was to the southeast. To the north and northwest more communities were struck with seething radioactivity. The invisible killer laid its lethal blanket over Fawnskin and Big Bear City and Twenty-Nine Palms and many more smaller hamlets and towns.

The San Bernardino Mountains first, and then the Chocolate Mountains still farther to the southeast,

141

diverted and captured a major portion of the heaviest fallout. Capricious winds sweeping along the western flanks of both ranges sent a particularly heavy pocket across the Salton Sea to inundate Brawley, Imperial, Seeley, Holtville and El Centro. Silent murder showered Mexicali to send the terrified Mexicans in blind panic to the hills.

Its intensity fading steadily, yet still wicked in its effects, the thinning cloud sped before the prevailing winds. Phoenix registered one hundred roentgens as the cloud swirled across the Arizona capital. There came a blank stretch where the deadly particles missed the earth, then settled in a broad sweep over both the American and Mexican communities of Nogales.

No one could tell where the deadly whisper would touch. Swift jets raced back and forth to measure the boundaries with sensitive instruments chirruping details of radioactive decay. California, and Arizona to a lesser extent, received the brunt of fallout. Heavy concentrations would show up across a wide central band of New Mexico, with Gallup and Santa Fe in the northern reaches bearing the worst of the diminishing fallout. There would be other patches, no longer so deadly to the human beings caught in its silken swath, reaching across most of the continent. Those who received only a whisper of the invisible death never knew how fortunate they were. The bomb of San Gorgonio was, after all, a miniscule affair. Just *one* thermonuclear bomb was five hundred times more powerful than the atomic knife that sheared away the top of the California mountain.

Brigadier General Arthur Sheridan had called the events with unerring accuracy. Not even a war could have brought on the explosive reaction of people in the large American cities. To have recommended, even to have urged evacuation would have saved thousands of lives. But to urge restraint while news stories poured from Washington of emergency evacuation of embassy staffs, of politicians and diplomats, stretched credulity far beyond its breaking point. A nation fed a diet of political chicanery and outright deception was in no mood to ponder a Presidential expression of confidence

142

and a plea for calmness. The words had behind them all good intention, but the intent was diffused by past events and the stark reality of the moment.

The one explosion grew in frenetic news reports to numberless atomic calamities throughout the land. Distant lightning flashes became the far-off glow of nuclear fire. Rumor, fear and then naked panic flashed through the metropolitan centers. The apocalyptic eloquence of past years came in a span of hours to full flower.

By dawn's light the abandoning of official Washington became the story of America's cities. Those who received the word earliest fled before the highways and tunnels and bridges choked with the outpouring swell of terrified humanity. Who could blame the people? President Dowling committed the unforgivable blunder of not stating fully the facts as they were. What he said was true. Yet it was dishonest by omission. It took only one newsman to learn of the letters received by ten mayors of ten cities. Within minutes *that* news flashed nationwide by radio, television and news wire. The people felt a sense of dismay that this could have been kept from them, and the little faith remaining in political pronouncements vanished in outpourings of rage. Blind destruction visited the cities on a scale that paled the worst riots of the long, hot summers. This time there were few police and even less National Guard uniforms to curb the hating violence. Most were in the pummeling, bruising rush to abandon cities.

The exodus, blind, furious, struggling, claimed more lives than the bomb atop San Gorgonio.

For that, feared the people, was only the prelude.

The atomic genie was loose in the land.

13

Never forget. Not for one moment must you forget there are three atomic bombs we don't know about. Three bombs that may be in three cities. Three bombs that spell out the lives of millions of helpless human beings. Don't forget it, Vincent. Not for a second. Think of the worst. Think of lower Manhattan . . . Think of lower Manhattan, hell. Think of St. Louis where your own family lives. Of Susan and the children. But that won't help. They're in the suburbs. Sure, but you don't know where that damn thing is. And I don't know if it's even in St. Louis, he chided himself angrily. *Damnit, stop moping and start thinking! Think of the worst. Think of lower Manhattan . . .*

Robert Vincent drummed his fingers against the desk. How could he forget the figures stabbed into his brain? But it was so important he mustn't forget. He kept hammering the numbers into his skull. Lower Manhattan. He compared it to Hiroshima where the people had jammed together in the seaport. A population density in the concentrated center of town. More than 135,000 people to the square mile. Teeming humanity. Incredible. Yet it was nothing compared to lower Manhattan where the daytime working and living population came to 720,000 human beings to the square mile! Vincent thought of the fireball raging in the midst of lower Manhattan and his blood ran cold. He remembered Lew Kirby's rage at discovering the pullout by John Hoving and his cohorts at the National Security Agency. Vincent felt the same deep anger budding within him, knew he was trying to compensate for his frustration by directing his anger at the one man who might yet help them in finding the three bombs still unaccounted for. His thoughts kept returning to the fireball. Two million people might die from one blast with millions more injured and sickened from radiation. And there were still three bombs. Somewhere out there . . .

His own anger astonished and frightened him. He prided himself on never reacting emotionally to an emergency. It didn't matter how broad the scope or severe the consequences. Yielding to emotion when the strictest objectivity was his only advantage was indescribably stupid. He had found a momumental rage growing toward David Silber, and in a moment of enforced calmness he realized that if he might react so strongly then others would do the same. Or worse. David Silber remained in a room with only one cot and two chairs. Silber sat or lay on the cot. Two of Vincent's most reliable agents, both wearers of the black belt in karate and aikido, sat in the room with Silber. Neither man carried a weapon. They were lethal weapons in themselves and they were present to guard Silber against any intruder and to be certain, for whatever reason there might be, that Silber didn't try to take his own life. The man was detached only by the thinnest of lines from the horror infecting everyone else to be left alone even for a moment. If he succeeded in a suicide attempt the final payment might come in the fireball they dreaded. If—

"Mr. Vincent?"

He looked up.

"Silber's asked to talk with you, sir. He says it's urgent."

For a moment Vincent stared dumbly at the agent. The last time Silber asked for him it was with the message to look at the mountain.

What in the name of God did he have this time?

"You don't believe that shit, do you? You can't believe it! No sane black man ever believe it! Look for yourself! See for yourself! Look at whitey runnin' to save his ass! Look at them roads! Look the way the cops protecting whitey, getting the hell out and gone, getting away from the bombs! This what they been planning all the time!" The speaker screamed into the microphones and they screamed electronically with him

145

through the loudspeakers in the city square and the sound racketed with earsplitting clamor through the streets and between the high buildings. *"This what they been planning! You knows it, I knows it, they knows it! This how them mother-fuckers gonna take care us? This how they got their final solution to the black problem! They get all the whites hell outta the cities and they gonna blow that goddamned atom bomb right here! Where we are! Where they get us in bunches! I say don't let them mother-fuckers get away with it! Let's tear down their goldamned city first!"* His eyes rolled wildly and he threw out his arms and pointed toward the main avenues. *"Let's get ours now! Go, Go! Let's tear down this goddamned city so bad they won't need that bomb do their dirty work!"*

Twelve thousand people died in Cleveland. The fires would rage for a week.

There was no bomb in the city.

Except the human time bomb that finally went off.

"All right, Mr. Silber," Vincent said. He kept his voice free of emotion. "What is it this time?" The instant Silber started to answer Vincent began talking again. He had to get Silber off balance. He doubted it would work but he had nothing else to try except the cat-and-mouse game. He slipped in the needle. "How much time do we have before you and your playmates decide to kill a few million *more* people?"

Dave Silber stared at him. Vincent would have gambled his entire career that the man before him had absolutely no idea of what he was talking about. Comprehension of Vincent's words came slowly. The words failed to register. Then Silber's eyes widened and his lips parted. Vincent knew the processes through which Silber moved. He'd been told the contents of the letter. He knew the people who'd paid him to deliver the letter and the subsequent messages at specified intervals had threatened the authorities with atomic bombs hidden in cities. This man and the others claimed that whoever worked behind the scenes had killed the men of an Air Force transport plane, but—right there, Vincent knew,

146

David Silber slammed into a psychological stone wall. It was too much for him to digest all at once. A letter wasn't reality. Being told six men were dead didn't make them dead. He knew something overwhelming was under way all about him. He had memorized his instructions and he knew what to do and at what time. The six men might even be dead, for all he knew, but he had nothing to do with that and— He forced himself off that line of thinking. It had to be a lie about the atomic bombs! Where would anyone get five atomic bombs? It was, was—ridiculous. Impossible! He refused to believe a word of it.

Vincent studied the gamut of emotion. First the eyes widening, then the lips parted. Finally Silber's tongue moved slowly over his lips, wetting them, pink against cadaverous white. Vincent studied his prey. First the shock. Then confusion. Now rejection.

"I don't know what you're talking about," Silber said. He forced the words to his lips. *Kill* millions of people? His head swam. It couldn't be true! They were lying to him!

Vincent's voice was harsh, scornful.

"All right, Judas, what's your message?"

Judas?

"Cat got your tongue?"

"N—no. I just . . ." *Judas?*

"I'm busy, Silber. We're all very busy. We've got several million dead people to worry about. And the millions more who are going to die because of you and your ghoulish friends. If you've got something to say, *Judas,* spit it out now."

"I—I was told there was going to be a, I don't know exactly, some sort of demonstration. At midnight, I mean." Beads of perspiration showed on his brow and his upper lip.

Is he going to crack? Vincent dared not entertain false hope.

No one said a word. Silber shifted uncomfortably in his chair. He whitened suddenly. The pain. Not severe this time, but it was there. It could be a warning. The final squeezing of his heart. His thoughts flashed the spectrum of the past and of tomorrow in a single

147

bound. He was dying. A weak heart. Cancer. Two months, maybe three. Who knew? Alice. The children. Hungry. Clothes in rags. Stinking, dirty tenement. No future, no future. Goddamn them all!

Vincent groaned to himself. From somewhere David Silber found a hidden strength. It showed in his eyes. Damnit! He had him on the run and somehow he'd bounced back, had grasped something in his mind. The pitiful shoulders squared, he sat straighter and his lips pressed firmly together.

"I was told there would be a demonstration at midnight," he said, new strength in his voice. He met Vincent's gaze squarely. "I presume this happened."

No answer.

"My instructions were to tell you to look at the mountain, at Gorgonio, at midnight. After that, I'm supposed to tell you that you're to send me on my way out of the country within twenty-four hours. With the papers listed in the letter."

Now, Vincent knew.

"And if we don't decide to play ball?" Vincent barked. "What then?"

Silber didn't answer.

"What happens next?" Vincent roared at him.

"I—I . . ."

The words wouldn't come. Not then. Before he spoke he remembered his instructions. The message to give them.

"The next demonstration will be closer to home." That was the message. Closer to home. Could this man be telling the truth? Could he?

"Speak up, *Judas!*"

"They—they said there would be another . . . another demonstration . . . I . . ."

"Damn you, spill the rest of your filth!"

He had the look of a frightened, cornered animal.

"Where, Silber, *where?*"

"They didn't s-say. I don't know. Closer to home. That was the message, to tell you it would be closer to home. I don't know what, I mean—"

"I'll tell you where, you *traitor!*" Could there be something left in that diseased shell of a man? Some

148

spark that went back to when Silber stood proudly before a flag and took the oath to defend his country? Some vestige of some church? Which would win? Country or family? Which remained strongest within this sickly creature? Hatred for the past or conscience? Vincent motioned angrily and a secretary brought a newspaper. It had taken heaven and earth to get the newsroom of the San Franscico *Chronicle* to print that front page.

Vincent threw the paper at Dave Silber.

Screaming red headlines burst against his eyes.

THREE MILLION DEAD! ATOM BOMB DESTROYS LOS ANGELES!

Dave Silber whimpered.

Now, now, Vincent knew. Time for the final thrust. Get him alone. Let his own mind work on him. We can't reach him. We can't hurt him. The only man who can reach Dave Silber is Silber himself.

Vincent moved around his desk quickly and jerked the paper from Silber's hand. He gestured angrily to the guards.

"Take this animal out of my sight."

"Are we merely cattle? Pawns to be used in some monstrous game of political pride? Why are there no answers to these questions? Why does the President remain concealed if there is truth in the words of confidence he sends to us? Why hasn't the ransom been paid? Why? Why? Is American life so cheap, are we all so unimportant, that our government can afford to refuse to pay the one hundred million dollars asked so our cities may be safe for us to return? Before this crisis passes there will be a day of reckoning in Washington. This reporter, and many others, will do everything in his power to impeach President Dowling. All of you should, must, do the same. This man has chosen not to assure our safety. He tells us he will not knuckle under to blackmailers. He, who is safe in some deep cavern of steel and concrete, he tells us not to lose faith, not to yield to panic. He tells us this while he himself is protected and the people are left naked to the atom.

"This man, who spends one hundred million dollars

149

every single day in Asia, would not, will not, spend only one of those days for the good people of these United States. This man, who will spend billions to bring home rocks from the moon. God protect us! tells us blackmail is insidious and we must not yield!

"Has there ever been such hypocrisy? Have American lives ever been forefeited so cheaply? The day is upon us . . ."

"Damnit, I say use the drugs!"

Robert Vincent studied the agitated features of his assistant. The pressure was beginning to tell on even the indomitable Kirby. Like the others he was reaching for any straw within his grasp. There were ways to make Dave Silber talk. They didn't need to use force on the man. No beatings, no torture, although Kirby was almost at the point where he might have considered *any* means to extract from Silber the information that could save millions of people. He felt angry with himself even for thinking in such a manner, and his self-scorn was hardly alleviated by the knowledge that Silber would fail to survive even a single hard blow. Lew Kirby dreaded to think of what he might have done. But, goddamnit, they had to do something!

There were other ways. Neil Cooke from the CIA showed up unexpectedly. He didn't waste time on courtesies. He asked for, and Lew Kirby gave him, the details up to the moment. Cooke nodded slowly and asked to see Vincent. He laid it on the line.

"You see this attaché case? I brought it here because you need what's inside." Vincent raised his brows for an unspoken question.

"Drugs," Neil Cooke snapped. "The best we have. The stuff we use and never admit we use. Don't start giving me any holy nonsense and protests about ethics or morals or any of that shit. You run your operation your way and we run ours the way we have to. I'm not here to split hairs or to discuss our professional theology. I'm here to help all of us out of the worst fix we've been in for a long time. And for the record I'm not here officially. This is strictly my own idea. No one else knows about it. No one else will ever know about it."

Silence settled between them. Finally Vincent sighed. He knew he had no right—millions of lives might be counted on his moves—summarily to dismiss Cooke or his offer of the drugs.

"What have you got in there?" he asked, gesturing at the attaché case.

"I didn't bring anything lethal, if that's what you mean," Cooke snapped.

"I never said you did," Vincent reminded him. "Please, just tell me what you have."

"To start with, a new serum. Truth serum, if that's what will do the job. He won't be able to lie. Nothing on this earth could keep him from spilling everything after one injection of this—"

"That's not the problem, Cooke," Vincent said quietly. "He's not lying to us."

"But the stuff will *make* him talk!" Cooke said angrily. "He'll sing like a canary with his ass on a stove. He can't stay quiet with this in him. He's *got* to talk and he can't lie and he won't be able to stay off what you want him to talk about! How the hell can you—"

Vincent gestured to shut off the words. He buzzed for his secretary. "Miss Bennett? Please have Doctor Wells come into my office. Tell him it's most urgent. Yes, thank you."

The doctor arrived within two minutes. Vincent sketched in the situation swiftly, then turned to the CIA man. "Mr. Cooke, please tell—I'm sorry. Do you know the ingredients of that drug?"

"Inside and out," Cooke retorted. He described the drug to the doctor.

Wells shook his head. "Out of the question. We can't use it."

Cooke stared at the doctor in disbelief.

"Why?"

"Simple enough, Mr., ah—yes, Cooke. Because David Silber is only one short step from the grave. Or you might say he's already got one foot in his coffin. This drug you describe would kill him."

"So what?"

Dr. Wells showed his surprise, but Neil Cooke was already ignoring him. "So what if it kills him?" he

151

snapped to Vincent. "He's not doing you a bit of good this way!"

"It's important we keep him alive."

"Dammit, why?"

"Because if he dies our unknown friends won't know if he died of natural causes or if we killed him trying to get information from him. And they might decide to punish us, Cooke. They still have three atomic bombs. Do you want to be responsible for losing a city?"

"Yes, sir, I sure did. Just six days ago. Uh, let's see, that was 9E. That's it, I'm sure. Apartment 9E. It's furnished, and we don't rent many of those."

A twelve-story apartment building at 2295 Roswell Road, S.E., Atlanta, Georgia. One of the many thousands of buildings being searched in every major city in the United States. A tedious, methodical, saturation, vacuum-cleaner sweep. The FBI agents and local police officers were weary to the bone. They had warrants that could gain them legal entry to any domicile, to any office, to anything with four walls. But that wasn't good enough. They needed memory and they needed cooperation, and it was difficult to get these because many building managers and superintendents had fled the cities. Not at 2295 Roswell Road, S.E., anyway. This one, for whatever reasons he had, wanted no part of the mad exodus.

"Seemed like nice people, too," he went on. "What little I seen of them, that is."

"How do you mean that, sir?"

The manager searched his keyring. "Well, they paid in advance for the apartment. Cash. Very polite. Middle-aged couple. They moved in some things. Not too much. Suitcases and stuff like that. I mean, it's a furnished apartment and you don't need much. They moved in and asked for a new lock. Uh, come to think of it, they wanted a double lock. I told them it would cost extra, but they said they didn't mind and paid for it right away."

"When did you last see them?"

"Not after the second day. That's maybe, um, four days ago."

152

"Could they have come in at night or some other time when you wouldn't have known about it?"

"Well, they could, of course, but—" The old man shrugged as he stopped before the apartment with the key in his hand. "You fellas sure this is all right? I mean, going in like this?"

"It's all right, sir. Perfectly legal."

"Umph. Don't care so much for the legal, but if you say it's okay—"

There wasn't time to scour every apartment and motel room. They needed to be fast and thorough. They were.

Agent Carlos Mendez could sniff out a wire with uncanny skill. This wire lay in plain view where few would have noticed it. Ordinary, telephone wire. Freshly painted to match the wallpaper. The wire ran by a window, behind a drape, beneath the carpet and to a linen closet. Carlos Mendez removed a pile of fluffy towels and saw *it*. Instinctively he knew. He warned the others not to touch a thing and retraced the wire back to the window. The wire was a receiving aerial. The bomb was to be set off by radio signal.

The emergency call went through the nearest FBI office to the Pentagon. Every nuclear weapons team in the nation was on standby. A small jet transport raced from Elgin Air Force Base in Florida to Atlanta where helicopters waited to rush the ordnance team to the apartment building. The men dropped to the ground in a school yard four blocks away and completed their trip by police car.

A young captain who had cut his teeth in the care and feeding of atomic bombs studied the metallic object. "It's baby, all right," he grinned to the others. No one grinned back. Most of them went white. Just being this close to an atomic bomb was bad enough. To know this one was *armed* and might—

The captain laughed at them. "Don't hold your breath, gentlemen. If I make a mistake you'll never know it."

Five minutes later he dragged the bomb from the closet.

"Get on the horn," he said with more relief than he showed. "Tell the people we've pulled its fangs. This thing is harmless now."

"Vincent? Ted Sharps, Atlanta. Want some good news for a change?"

"I could use it." Vincent's brain felt numb, his world a narrowing prison of frustration.

"We found the third bomb."

"Jesus." His voice was a whisper.

"Here in Atlanta. Your people were right. A furnished apartment, rented just a week ago. The blue suiters have already pulled its teeth. Completely harmless now."

"Thanks, Ted. It helps."

"Yeah. Two more to go."

"Have you notified—"

"Right down the line. This may help in Washington. The press is screaming for Dowling's head. Served up with an apple in his mouth. Some of the casualties have been pretty bad where the people ran for it. The press is holding the President responsible for—"

"Oh, for Christ's sake!"

"I know, I know, but that's the way it goes." Pause. "Bob, I think we have a lead on the people who rented the apartment."

Vincent held his breath.

"The old man, the manager at the building, has an excellent recall of people he meets. A middle-aged couple are what we're looking for."

"What about the details!"

"We've got 'em. The man has a pockmarked face, a long thin scar quite visible along the left chin. The building manager noted something else. He called it crow's-feet."

"Crow's-feet? I don't understand."

"Ask your friends in the blue suits. They'll know. It's a characteristic of pilots who fly open-cockpit planes. They squint a lot in the sun and wind. Most old-time fighter pilots could be recognized by just that mark."

Vincent's thoughts soared and dropped just as quick-
154

ly. That really didn't help much. But wait a moment . . .

Ted Sharps might have read his thoughts. "And you know who flies today in open cockpits? Crop dusters and stunt fliers. We're already doing everything we can to get an ID. We'll keep you on tap."

Bob Vincent leaned back in his chair. Crow's-feet, by God! Who would have thought it . . . A man has lines at the corners of his eyes. A clear-cut signature of what he's been doing for years.

Crow's-feet!

Vincent didn't need to ask Ted Sharps the procedures they were now following. Once again the hope for success lay in prosaic, unglamorous saturation. The best possible description by the building manager would be transformed by FBI artists into swift, accurate sketches, which the manager himself would correct until it best resembled the man he recalled. And the woman, of course. That description and artist's rendering would be flashed to every agency office, to every police and sheriff's office throughout the country. It would go to the Federal Aviation Administration, to Customs, to every agency of the federal government, of state, county and city governments. It would end up on every desk, on every bulletin board, on every television screen, on every post-office wall.

There were other possiblities to be followed where only saturation effect could help. The State Department threw open its files to the FBI and there began a hurried, intensive scanning of passport photographs. Any photograph that met the general characteristics reported by the building manager was displayed to him. If the man they searched for *was* one of the group they sought, then he must plan to leave the country. And you do that, if you're traveling any distance at all, only with a passport.

It was a long shot. Terribly long. The odds were against any real hope of success.

Crow's-feet!

"FBI. Jenkins."

"Mr. Jenkins, listen carefully. I have a—"

Jenkins signaled frantically for the telephone call trace to start at once.

"—message for you I'll repeat only once. Got it?"

"Just a moment, please. I'll have to get a pencil and—"

"Never mind the games. If Dave Silber isn't on his way out of the country within twelve hours from right *now*, with the necessary papers, you're going to lose a city. There's a ticket in Silber's name on Pan American Flight Ninety-Four. It leaves San Francisco in just twelve hours. Remember, it's Silber on his way or you lose a city."

The phone went dead.

It took six minutes to trace the call through the main switchboard in Grand Rapids, Michigan. By the time the agents reached the phone booth it had been empty a long time.

"God*damn*. Get me Bob Vincent right away. He's in the Frisco office . . ."

Bob Vincent hung up the telephone. They were making certain, all right. Leaving nothing to chance. Making sure that even if we don't listen to Silber we'll listen to them. Vincent felt impaled on the multiple horns of the dilemma he faced. He didn't dare wait too long. He had the instinct that were they to delay Silber's departure—and he *was* booked for Pan Am Ninety-Four—this time the "demonstration" would rip away the heart of a city. He fought his conflicting emotions until he had no way left to turn. It was incumbent upon his judgment to make the recommendation.

They would have to release Silber. But would the government actually pay the one hundred million dollars that—

He didn't need to make the decision, after all. The telephone rang.

"Mr. Vincent?"

"Yes. Go ahead, please."

"Mr. Vincent, the President is calling. One moment, sir."

He held his breath.

"Mr. Vincent, this is President Dowling."

156

"Yes, sir."

"The securities and other documents demanded in the ransom letter are on their way to your office, Mr. Vincent."

"Yes, sir."

"When they arrive you will examine them, with two witnesses, Mr. Vincent." *Yes, sir.* "Be certain they are all there." *Yes, sir.* "When you're sure everything is in order, you will give the papers to that man, Silber." *Yes, sir.* "Release Silber at once." *Yes, sir.* "Don't let the man out of your sight. I want you personally to escort him to the airport and put him aboard that airplane yourself." *Yes, sir.* "Put two of your best people on that plane to protect him. They're to stay with him until he's in the terminal, safe and sound, in Lisbon. Is all this clear, Mr. Vincent?"

"Yes, sir."

"I know what you've been doing, Vincent, and we're grateful to you."

"Thank you, Mr. President."

Yes, sir.

14

For hours they crawled in a bumper-to-bumper nightmare. The compulsion to abandon the city trembled their limbs with anxious fear. Every lane of the Lincoln Tunnel pointing from New York into the Jersey flatlands carried a burden of vehicles without beginning or end, fed from concrete tributaries funneling into the long tubes beneath the Hudson River. They crawled spasmodically, foot by foot, toward a vague promise of haven. The tubes reverberated to racing engines, blaring horns and the strident clamor of frustrated, frightened people. So many vehicles remained in the tubes for so long a time the thundering exhaust fans could no longer effectively withdraw the carbon monoxide and the heat building up beneath the river. Savage headaches and explosive tempers became the sorry lot of most.

Sooner or later it must happen. A woman behind the wheel of her car sat stupefied from exhaust fumes, dulled by oppressive heat and numb from the racketing assault against her ears. Her children pleaded for a bathroom, for something cool to drink. She turned in anger to cuff a wailing child. Cars before her crawled ahead. Blasting horns and shouted curses from behind frightened her. She slammed down the accelerator, and her car shot forward. The child screamed in vexation and pain. The distraught mother jerked her foot from the accelerator to the brake pedal. She missed.

Her car cracked into another. Tightly packed, the long row of vehicles went through an accordion-like squeezing of metal.

A gas tank crumpled from impact.

A car pulled away from another with a tearing screech. Sparks flew.

Flame exploded along oil-soaked concrete, upward into cars.

There was no way out.

Those at the forefront of the fire pounded madly into the vehicles ahead to push the immovable line of cars.

Families climbed in wide-eyed fear to the safety catwalk on the left side of the tunnel. Others already there jammed against the walls, struggling in panic to run. They hurled the weaker ones from them.

Children crumpled against the cars below.

The tunnel lights shorted, blew out. Headlights stabbed thick, choking smoke.

Screaming animals stumbled and crawled over the cars to get out.

Huge balls of flame flashed for hundreds of feet.

The scream that issued forth was from a single demented creature in its final throes of burning alive.

Three thousand human souls died horribly beneath the river.

"Is he ready?"

Lew Kirby nodded. "Yeah. He's ready. But I still don't like—"

Bob Vincent showed hair-trigger temper. "Never mind," he snapped angrily. "I don't want speeches from you, Lew. Just do what's necessary."

Kirby gestured quickly with both hands. "Sorry, sorry," he mumbled.

Vincent ignored the apology. He knew he was unfair to Kirby, but he had all he could do at this point to curb his anger. The actual moment of releasing Dave Silber, *with* one-hundred million dollars in securities, struck him with more impact than he'd anticipated. It had been the mechanics of the thing that got so deeply to him. Receiving the papers, going through them with painstaking care, having their receipt and itemizing witnessed by other agents, knowing all the time he'd failed, knowing the nation was paying the ransom. Knowing that Dave Silber would walk through the doors a free man and—

He heard a cry of sardonic humor deep in his mind. Silber a *free* man? A few months of pain-racked life . . .

159

how in the name of God could Vincent consider that pitiful, diseased wreck to be *free?* Yet, somehow, torn by conscience, Silber had achieved freedom they might never know. He was returned to his room, closely guarded. There he faced himself, the measure of his struggle judged by his tortured face. And then, as Vincent had feared, Dave Silber made peace with himself.

The nation lost to a woman named Alice and her small children. Dave Silber clung to them with all the strength remaining in his frail body. In that clinging he found release. He was not long for this world and he shed whatever other allegiance his conscience might demand.

He refused from that moment on to discuss anything with Bob Vincent. He retreated within the shell he drew tightly around his mind. The machinery of events was in motion and he needed no contribution of his own to complete what he might do for his family. He had only to wait. His was the ultimate faith.

Vincent motioned to his assistant. "Get Silber. Let's get this over with."

During the drive to the airport, seated between Vincent and Kirby, Dave Silber never said a word. They had nothing to say to him.

Pan American Flight Ninety-Four waited at Gate Eleven. Vincent used Presidential authority to assure that the airplane would remain at its ramp no matter how late they might be. He hated to think a flat tire or a traffic tie-up would cause Flight Ninety-Four to leave without Silber.

President Dowling directed Vincent to have two agents with Silber on the flight. Vincent sent three. The same two men who had guarded Silber in his room, and Lew Kirby.

"You stick with him," Vincent said, knowing his words were unnecessary. "Don't let him out of sight. If he has to go to the bathroom you go with him. If he—oh, hell, you know the speech."

Kirby studied his boss. "I know, Bob. Rest easy, I'll deliver him in perfect condition."

"Thanks." Vincent rested his hand on the other

160

man's shoulder. "Sorry about before, Lew. I didn't mean to—"

"Forget it," Kirby said gruffly.

General Sheridan had the right contacts with Pan American. The airline management cancelled all first-class seats on the huge Boeing, reserving the compartment for the FBI agents and their unusual passenger. Pan Am Ninety-Four would fly San Francisco direct to Gander, Newfoundland, for refueling. The airline sent aboard a relief crew to assure that nothing short of mechanical failure would delay the flight to its destination of Lisbon, Portugal.

The Federal Aviation Agency received word from the White House. "Pan American Ninety-Four has number one priority for Air Traffic Control clearance."

Thirteen hours and fourteen minutes later the Boeing landed safely in Lisbon.

Two hours later Dave Silber disappeared.

What I'd like to say, damn you, is that most of your vaunted associates are loud-mouthed, yapping, bickering, spineless sons of bitches who don't know what the devil they're talking about and haven't the gumption to back up what they do say. Look at them out there. I can't blame them. They at least have the guts to stick it out, to face whatever danger there may be. Christ, at least there's some newsmen left with real balls between their legs. After all their screaming and crying for leadership I expected to see this room filled. I'll bet there aren't more than thirty people here and the room holds four hundred. Well, by God, I'll give those who are here a story, all right . . .

President Charles Dowling nodded to Ed Gubitz. His press secretary tapped the microphone for attention.

"The President has a brief statement to make. After that the floor is open for questions."

The remnants of the Washington press corps were surprised to see Gubitz step to the side. Obviously Dowling had told him to get right with it. And from the look on Dowling's face he's in no mood for—

". . . you already know, an atomic bomb was found earlier today in Atlanta, Georgia. Also, to review

161

quickly, that bomb was disarmed and the city is safe from any explosion. We have now accounted for three of the five missing nuclear devices. So there will be no margin for error, two of the five bombs that were lost have not yet been recovered. I am convinced that through the efforts of the FBI and other federal agencies it is only a matter of time, a short time, before we recover these, and any danger to our cities will be over. I have a complete and abiding faith in these agencies to continue the excellent job they are doing."

President Dowling's instincts told him to play it short and to the point. *No* speeches. He nodded to Gubitz who returned to a microphone.

Bill Mahoney of AP was already on his feet. "Mr. President, there's been a rumor that a bomb has been found in Washington, and this accounts for your return to the capital. Could you elaborate on that, sir?"

"First, we don't *know* if there's a bomb here. We have been threatened with the word that Washington *may* contain a bomb. To further answer your question, I have no knowledge of any such device having been recovered and I'm certain that if this were the case I would be so informed immediately." Dowling looked directly into the AP reporter's eyes. "My return to the capital is prompted by the urgent need for the people of this country to understand that their government, their President, has not abandoned them. I left the White House before against my better convictions. The Secret Service, and I do not fault what they believed to be imperative, felt that under the circumstances, as they existed before, I should be evacuated. That," Dowling said firmly, "was a mistake. This is the seat of government. I am here."

"This means, sir, you're still in danger, then?"

"No more, Mr. Mahoney, than are you."

Dowling saw the first warmth from the press he'd experienced in days.

"Mr. President, Jacques Isteau, Canadian Broadcasting. Sir, do you believe your presence here in Washington will alleviate the problems the country now faces? I refer to the panic that's been reported from around the—"

162

"That is one of the reasons I am here, Mr. Isteau."

"Yes, sir. I understand. I meant to—"

"To anticipate your question, I have no questions as to the basic strength of the American people. They have faced, they still face, a threat the like of which was never before existed in human history. And throughout human history, Mr. Isteau, the initial reaction to a threat of such devastation as may be created by a nuclear weapon, is to put as much distance between yourself and what threatens you. If you're a student of history, then you're aware that even the British, when they were first subjected to bombing attack in nineteen forty, abandoned their cities. They came back, of course. Today the American people face a nuclear disaster on their doorsteps. We are eliminating that danger and we are doing it as swiftly as we can. The President belongs where he can be reached by any element of government or the public. I hope my presence here will enable this government to function as smoothly as it is possible for it to do so."

President Dowling glanced at Ed Gubitz. The motion was sufficient to tell Jacques Isteau to shut up and sit down.

But the party wasn't over yet.

". . . are we to understand that the atomic bombs that are supposed to be in our cities—"

"We have already removed such a weapon from Atlanta," Dowling broke in. "We did the same in Kansas City. There is no 'supposed to be' involved here. We are dealing with a situation in reality and not in suppositions."

"Yes, sir. My question was in reference to their source. There have been rumors to the effect that these bombs were brought into the cities by Communist factions and—"

Dowling leaned forward and threw as much sincerity into his voice as he could muster. "There is absolutely no evidence that the Communists are behind these tragic events," Dowling said carefully. "I have been kept informed by the FBI and the other federal agencies whose responsibility it is to be aware of such activities and the facts associated with them. If there is any

163

evidence to the contrary, I assure you the people will know immediately. This country would not for a moment tolerate the blackmail, the injuries, the deaths to its citizens due to the actions of any foreign power."

"Are you saying, sir, that if you uncover such evidence, this country would take immediate action against the foreign power involved?"

Careful, careful, Dowling warned himself. "I have no intention of permitting this conference to become an endless line of 'ifs, ands or buts,' " Dowling said with cold authority. "I have told you no evidence exists to connect this crisis with *any* foreign power. We are dealing, to the best of our knowledge, with ruthless criminals. Those are the facts." A vision of Vietnam, the USS *Pueblo,* of bargaining tables in Paris, of the truce-line mockery in Korea, flashed in a kaleidoscopic whirl through the President's mind. "But to leave absolutely no room for question, if, and I say most carefully, *if,* we find incontestable evidence that the machinations of this criminal group were inspired or controlled in any way by a foreign power, why then, *yes,* we will take immediate action against that power. And it will *not* be a case of another Vietnam!"

"More coffee, sir?"

President Dowling looked up at his aide. Tom Saunders held a wire-service tearsheet in his hand. "Never mind the stalling, Tom. Just give me the bad news straight."

Saunders smiled self-consciously. "Well, sir," he said, drawing in a deep breath, "apparently you shouldn't have come back to Washington after all. It seems you're jeopardizing your safety unnecessarily. World News, ah, they, I—"

"Out with it!"

"They feel you're being," Saunders forced the word from his lips, "theatrical." Saunders swallowed. "Sir."

For a long moment Dowling kept his silence. The expected rage, to Saunders' immense relief, failed to materialize. Then, when he never expected pure irony—

"Tom, I want you to call every paper and wire-service office in this city." Charles Dowling had the
164

smile of a Cheshire cat on his face. "Tell them to send to the White House, immediately, their best newsman. Tell them the sons of bitches will stay here, *in* the White House with me, until this crisis is over." The President looked through his window at the lights of Washington. "It should be interesting copy to read, eh, Tom?"

"I don't understand, sir."

"Why, Tom, I'm surprised at you. If they're here in the White House when we all get blown to hell and gone, they'll have that exclusive story they're always after, won't they?"

"What the hell do you mean he *vanished!*" Bob Vincent found himself shouting into the phone. It didn't help. The connection to the American embassy in Lisbon was poor enough to start with and— He forced his tone back to normal.

"*How* did you lose him? The man hasn't strength enough to run twenty feet! What happened?"

"The moment Silber entered the terminal we had no more jurisdiction over—"

"I know *that,* confound it."

"Yes, sir. He didn't go through Portuguese customs. Someone arranged for him to be taken directly through the terminal building. We were blocked at Customs. That was apparently set up pretty well, too. We couldn't make a move, Mr. Vincent."

Vincent ran the possibilities through his mind. They'd anticipated just that. Which is why they had agents all over that triple-damned airport. Someone paid off Portuguese Customs officials which, considering the strained relations between the two countries, would have been an easy matter. They delayed the FBI agents who accompanied Silber until their quarry was through the terminal building and out of sight. Vincent had called Neil Cooke for help, and the CIA man responded with the enthusiasm of hounds in full cry. Not to leave anything undone, Vincent enlisted the help of the Air Force as well. Military intelligence agents, including criminal investigation teams, many of which were made up of permanent residents in Europe, moved in as requested. They had a cordon so thick a fly couldn't get through.

But Dave Silber got through, all right. As Vincent listened through the crackling hiss of the transatlantic call he knew his mistakes. Damn himself for a fool! They'd forgotten the *modus operandi* of their opponents . . .

". . . left the airport in a black car. Apparently they weren't taking any chances either because they moved in a group of three vehicles, one leading and the other following the car in which Silber was riding. They drove out of the city and into open country. Our people followed as best they could. We even phoned ahead to several contacts. We were able to do that because there were only a few roads they could travel on with any speed. But they'd had this all set up, sir. The cars went through a gate. One that was guarded, I mean. It must have been a large private estate. Our people couldn't get any further. They were just in time to see a small twin-engined plane taking off about a mile away."

Vincent groaned. The rest of it would be cut and dry. It was.

The plane carrying Silber disappeared into low clouds. There wasn't any way to follow. No plane, no radar. Not a damned thing. The plane could have flown across the border to Spain. It could have flown somewhere in France. Almost anywhere. Vincent didn't believe it. The safest bet was for that plane to fly one or two hundred miles and land at a field where it was expected. There another car picked up—

Robert Vincent knew they would never again see Dave Silber.

"No question about it. That's him, all right."

No one showed the sudden tension. Stay calm. Don't rattle the old gentleman. "You're absolutely sure, sir?" More pictures on the table. "It wouldn't be any of these, by any chance? They do look alike, don't they?"

"They look alike, but that's *him*. See that scar line? The way the skin bunches up on his brow between his eyes? That's scar tissue. And, uh, everything else. Nope, no doubt about it. It's him."

166

They read the name on the passport.

Jesse H. Buckhorn. Rural Delivery, Swamp Strip, Devil's Garden, Florida. "Devil's Garden? Where the hell is *that*? While you're looking—Mary, damnit! Get me FAA in Oklahoma City, pilots' records office. Hey, put through a call to Bob Vincent immediately. Right—"

Fingers pointing on the map. "There it is, all right. Devil's Garden. Southwest of Lake Okeechobee. Yes, yes. Highway patrol on the roads and vertical envelopment by Air Force. Yeah. Sheridan's got everyone standing by. Air Commandos, helicopters, the lot. Get *cracking!*"

One by one the pieces fell into place. Buckhorn's records in the Federal Aviation Administration files at Oklahoma City matched his passport folder. Crop duster and stunt pilot for a loose-flying organization operating through the southeast. Long scar on his left chin, scar tissue above the bridge of his nose, pockmarked cheeks . . . Buckhorn was the boy they wanted.

"Vincent? Yeah, we've got 'em, all right. You ready to copy? Okay. Leader of the group is Mike Jeffries. Ex-Air Force. Damn right. From what we understand he flew in Vietnam and flipped his lid there. Told his superior to shove the war up his ass. Got a DD out of it, but until a few years ago he was still wearing the suit. He spent two years at TAC Headquarters, so *that* fits in. Jeffries isn't married but lives with his girl. Common-law marriage. Her name is Hughes, Pat Hughes. Yes, she's also a pilot. Every one of these people is. Jesse Buckhorn and his wife—got their names? Uh-huh, they've been with Jeffries since they started their outfit in Florida. There's a hotrock pilot with them called Maglioni. Salvatore Maglioni, goes by the name of Tony. FAA has several flying violations listed against his name.

"You ready for the clincher? There's two more in the group that we know of. Man named Gene Moore, and his girl, Leslie Hall. *Gene Moore's a Negro . . .*"

Kansas City fell into place.

FBI Agent Jerry Simmons dropped the telephone back on the cradle. His face was white and he paused only long enough to take a deep breath. Then, quickly, he punched out the standby number at Andrews Air Force Base.

"Major Haggerty," a voice said.

"Code Able, Code Able," Simmons barked. "This is Simmons, FBI, Washington. You ready to copy?"

"Yes, sir. Go ahead," the major's voice snapped.

"We've just taken an anonymous call," Simmons said. "I don't think this one is a crank. The caller said the bomb may be in the Potomac Yacht Basin. In a forty-footer with the name of *Mary Jane*. Get your men moving at once, Major. I'll call ahead for you to reach the yacht basin. Got it?"

"Yes, sir. Forty-footer, *Mary Jane*, Potomac Yacht Basin. I'll have two choppers with the nuclear teams on the way by the time I hang up." In the background Simmons heard a siren screaming. The phone went dead.

Simmons punched a series of number codes that connected him with the Washington alert headquarters of the Coast Guard, District of Columbia police, the Army, the National Security Agency and the CIA, and a special office in the White House.

"This is Simmons, FBI, Code Able," he said crisply. "I'm about to play back a recording of a phone call just received. Two helicopters from Andrews Air Force Base with nuclear teams already on their way. The taped message follows." He punched the tape machine.

". . . *not going to repeat this message, so listen close. Call off your dogs. Silber's gone, man. I mean you'll never see him again. That pretty package you're looking for is in the Potomac Yacht Basin. Right there in the river. Look for a forty-footer called Mary Jane . . .*"

Thirty-eight minutes later they got the word from the yacht basin. The team had just disarmed the atomic bomb.

"Vincent! In here, right away! We've got contact—"

Bob Vincent rushed into the adjoining office where

General Arthur Sheridan studied a ten-inch television monitor. Cables snaked across the floor. Air Force technicians manned mobile electronic control panels connected to a hastily erected antenna on the building roof. Vincent could hardly believe the setup, but the television monitor showed him and Sheridan, the raid on Swamp Strip in Florida *as it was happening*. Sheridan had only time enough to provide Vincent the most cursory description. "Short and sweet," Sheridan said hurriedly, "the TV transmitter in the chopper boosts its signal into space. We've got sixty satellites in synchronous orbit in our defense communications system. The signal goes from the chopper in Florida straight-line to one of those satellites, and it boosts it back down here. The antenna on your roof is phased in only to that frequency and using straight-line we can—"

He cut short his words as audio came in with the picture. Trees flashed in a blur before them as the attack helicopters came in fast and low, spreading out in a huge circle to encompass the landing strip and the buildings they could see on the monitor.

"Foxtrot Six to Groundhog. How's the flick and sound?"

A technician answered immediately. "Roger, Fox Six. Groundhog reads and sees five-by. Go ahead." Vincent marveled at the scene. The two men, one in California and the other in Florida, talked with the clarity of a telephone call from next door.

"Okay, Groundhog. No sign of life. We've deployed troops and they're moving through the area. Couple of planes around and some more in the hangars, but it looks as if no one's been here for a week at the least. We're checking out the buildings now."

The camera operator went to telephoto and moved his lens slowly through the airstrip area. Vincent and Sheridan watched in silence as Air Commandos with automatic weapons at the ready fanned out through the field. The men kicked open doors, raced through buildings.

"We've got somebody." The voice came in from off-camera and the scene blurred as the operator swung

169

the transmitter. They saw a man with his hands above his head.

Sheridan reached for the microphone. "Groundhog to Foxtrot Six. This is General Sheridan. Move in. We want a camera closeup on that man and we'd like some audio on him."

"Righto, sir." Again a blurred, shaky movement as the helicopter moved forward swiftly. The scene expanded in a rush and came to a stop, the camera showing two FBI agents from the lead attack-helicopter questioning the man on the screen.

". . . don't know what you're talking about. I'm the caretaker here and I—"

"Where's Jeffries and the rest of the pilots? Quick!"

"Can I put my hands down? Jeffries? He and the whole bunch been gone two, three weeks."

"Where?"

"I dunno. They never tell me. Like I say, I get paid to look after the place and—"

"Did they say when they'd be back?"

"Uh-uh."

Vincent motioned for the microphone. "Foxtrot Six from, uh, Groundhog. This is Vincent. Can you get my agents to hear me directly?"

"Yes, sir. We've got radio hookup. Stand by, please. Foxtrot One from Six."

"Go ahead, Six."

"I'm direct link to General Sheridan and Mr. Vincent, and they've got some questions they want asked. Over."

"Right, Six. Groundhog, this is Foxtrot One. Go ahead, sir."

"Ask that man if Jeffries and the others have been flying any P-fifty-one fighters in the last few weeks."

The caretaker heard the question directly. He looked around, baffled at the voice, until an FBI agent prompted him to answer.

"Yes, sir, they sure have. Three of 'em. Prettiest things I ever—"

That was the final confirmation.

They knew *who* to look for.

The big question was *where*.

"... at a standstill. It's the same almost everywhere. Until that last bomb is found people refuse to return to the cities. Most airline flights into major airports are still cancelled. Business is at a standstill and the economic loss is running into hundreds of millions of dollars daily. During the last twenty-four hours there have been riots and looting in the big cities, but volunteer forces of National Guard and police have put down most of the dissidents. The news that a bomb was recovered in Washington cheered the nation. President Dowling's courageous stand in refusing to leave the city ..."

Arthur Sheridan yawned. "Jesus, I'm tired," he groaned.

"I don't see why." Bob Vincent smiled. "You've only been on your feet for something like sixty hours straight."

Sheridan rubbed the stubble on his chin. "It feels more like sixty days." He dropped into a seat and stared at the other man. "It's pretty much your show now, Bob. What happens next?"

Vincent sighed. "Much of the same, only more," he said. "The dragnet. Fine-tooth comb and all that. Jeffries and his crows won't be able to move without our knowing about it. *I hope,*" he added quickly. "That bunch has had some pretty cute tricks up their sleeves. But now that we know who they are I think we'll be able to drop the blanket on them. You know the flying business better than I do, Arthur. Somewhere, somehow, they've got to leave a sign of movement. Someone will have seen them—"

"I thought you already had some leads."

"Sure. But they're the sort we expect. We also expect most of them not to pay off. Every nut in the country is seeing Jeffries and the rest. A great many honest people too, trying to help. I don't doubt we've had, in all our offices, more than ten thousand calls absolutely identifying the people we're looking for. We've got to weed out every one of them."

Sheridan nodded slowly. "There's nothing I can do right now?"

"Christ, man, you can get some sleep. I wish I could *order* you to—why don't you sack out in the other office? If anything breaks, I'll let you know immediately."

"I'll take you up on that. At this rate I won't be much use to anybody before long." Sheridan rose painfully to his feet. "One more thing, Bob."

"Shoot."

"Where do you think they've got that last bomb?"

"That's a great question for a quiz show," Vincent said sourly.

Sheridan grunted. "Maybe I didn't use the right words."

"Oh?"

"I don't think the bomb is set up anywhere in a city."

"You sound as if you have a pet theory."

Sheridan nodded. "Yeah. I hope I'm wrong."

Vincent waited.

"They *can't* give up the bomb," Sheridan went on. It's as simple as that. Who throws away their ace in the hole?"

15

The two men in stevedore clothing moved slowly to the freighter deck. In the soft glow of fog-shrouded lights they looked about them casually. They showed none of the professional care with which they examined the vessel. A tugboat hooted dismally, unseen, from somewhere in the misty harbor. Nothing out of the ordinary showed. The *Manuel Hacente* was of Panamanian registry and a familiar sight along the docks of Seattle. In the warm summer night the freighter creaked and muttered through her plates, waiting the final cargo loading before she put to sea. Her prow would cut the Pacific for many days ahead until finally she dropped anchor in Hong Kong.

A seaman approached the two shadowy figures standing by the rail. "Need any help, mates?"

One man took a last drag on his cigarette and flipped the butt over the rail. They heard the momentary hiss as it struck water.

"Right. Like to speak to the Old Man. Is he—"

The seaman jerked a thumb above and behind him. "In his cabin." He looked more closely at the two figures. "He expecting you?"

"Right, mate."

"Well, that's the way."

"Thanks."

"Make sure you knock first. He's a touchy one, he is."

They climbed to the next deck, stepped through a hatchway and worked their way forward to the captain's cabin. They knew this vessel inside and out, knew her every line, every bulkhead and ladder. It was their business to know such things.

One stevedore knocked three times at the captain's door.

"Just don't stand there! Come in!"

The two men glanced at one another. The first opened the cabin door. He stepped in, waited until the door closed behind him.

The captain rose to his feet. He was a huge man, a Scandinavian. "Where's your friend?" he demanded. "You said two of you would come." Captain Hans Boehme squinted in study of his visitor. "Which one are you, eh?"

A slim wallet opened before the captain's face. "Regan, eh? What's the first—"

"Kenneth Regan." The wallet disappeared into a pocket. "My friend's outside, Captain. He'll see we're not disturbed."

"Ho, now! Cloak-and-dagger and all that. Ho!" Captain Boehme turned his back to his visitor. A clink of glasses and Boehme poured two drinks. "To our business, eh?" he cried. "Drink up!"

Ken Regan started to refuse the drink, remembered where he was and with whom he was dealing. He took the shot glass in two swift swallows, Boehme studying him with a crafty expression over his own glass. Regan returned the glass to his host.

"Like you say, Captain Boehme, to business."

Boehme waved the bottle. "Ho! Another, eh?"

"No, thanks."

Boehme wouldn't back off. "Ah! One more won't hurt, now, will it?"

Ken Regan didn't answer. His silence spoke plainly enough for him. Captain Hans Boehme was a master in dealing with people. He'd done it all his life. He couldn't have cared less what or how much Regan drank now or ever again. It was his way of measuring his visitor and Regan knew it. Regan seemed part of a frozen tableau as Boehme held aloft the bottle in one hand and the glass in the other, staring bright-eyed and unblinking at the man before him.

The bottle lowered slowly. Boehme grunted as he pushed in the cork and placed the glasses to one side. His leather jacket creaked as the captain shifted position to face his visitor squarely.

"What about the money?" he demanded.

174

"You'll be paid."

"*Where* is it?"

"You'll get it when it's done," Regan said quietly, firmly. "Not before."

The broad face stared unblinking at him. "How do I know I can trust you, eh?"

"Captain Boehme."

The tone had hardened. Boehme didn't appreciate being spoken to in this manner. He liked even less what he heard next.

"Don't be stupid and don't play games with me."

"Do you know who you're talking to?" Boehme roared. "I'm the master of this vessel, and I won't—" His voice fell away. The man Regan hadn't moved a muscle. Boehme knew, then. Regan didn't *act* as though he had power behind him. Boehme had himself exercized power too long to be fooled. "Well," he grunted. He sniffed and wiped his wrist across his nose. "All right. Let's get to particulars."

Regan nodded slowly. "Are they aboard?"

"Yes, yes. Been here two days."

"Has anyone seen them?"

"Not even I," Boehme said, suddenly sober in his mood. "They came aboard as I told your people, and they haven't stepped from their cabin. They're cooking and all that right where they are. That was my deal. Leave them alone." Boehme shrugged. "We get few passengers on this tub. It seemed an easy way to pick up some money."

"That your company would never see, would they?"

Boehme flushed darkly. "Don't make—"

"Forget it," Regan broke in. "I'm not interested in what you do aboard this ship. My only interest is Cabin Twelve."

Boehme grumbled beneath his breath. Suddenly he turned to sift through papers on his small desk. "Y'know," he said, his back still to Ken Regan, "it's not going to be easy to get them off the *Hacente*."

Regan stiffened. "Why not, Captain?"

Boehme grinned. "They sent this note to me this morning," he said. A loose-lipped smile spread slowly. "The truth is, Regan, I'm damned glad to see you. I

175

was getting nervous about this." He handed the note to his visitor.

Regan swore.

Look at her. She's aged ten years these last few months. More gray hairs than she ever expected to see for another ten yet to come. I hate to see her like this. The whole thing's been rotten to her. But it was the last chance we had. If we hadn't gone along with Mike there was nothing left for us. Couple of jobs here and there, and the pay always getting less and less. With kids willing to fly anything for no matter how much money, what the hell was an old duffer like me gonna do about it? Washed up and kicked out. Every time some son of a bitch found out about it I got the boot again and . . . Mae didn't have a damn thing to look forward to except working in some lousy greasy spoon somewhere until she was like an old dog and they threw her out also. I'd rather see the both of us dead and buried before we got to slop like pigs begging handouts . . . Jesse Buckhorn reached under his bunk for the bottle. He removed the cap, every gesture slow and relaxed. He was going to be here for a long time, and it was no good to grab the bottle like there was no tomorrow. All they had to do was be patient. Sweat it out in this goddamned cabin for a couple of weeks until they made Hong Kong. There he could buy any passport he wanted for himself and Mae, and they would disappear forever. Maybe get some plastic surgery. He rubbed his chin. Not a bad idea. His mind wandered freely through operating rooms and skin grafts and new hair and a new face. *Get rid of this damned scar and fill in all the holes in my skin and—* He took a long, slow drink, the alcohol burning its way down. The glow spread through his limbs. The room wasn't so small and cramped now. He looked at the bottle. To hell with it. He wouldn't be seeing anyone. It didn't matter how much he—

"Please, Jesse."

He jerked the bottle from his lips as if it had stung him. "What the hell, Mae," he complained. "A little drink ain't gonna—"

"You just *had* a little drink," Mae Buckhorn said quietly. "If you have one more now you'll want another, and another, and, oh, Jesse . . ." She wrung her hands and looked around the confining cabin. She took a deep breath. "God forgive me, I don't want to nag," she said quickly. "But we're going to be here for weeks, Jesse. If I don't have you to talk to I'll go out of my mind."

He pushed away the anger as swiftly as it rose within him. "I know that, honey," he said thickly. The alcohol spread through him faster now and he welcomed the warmth. "But I need this. The walls are closing in on me and—"

"Jesse. *Please.*"

The pain showed in her eyes. He didn't want to start off like this. Mae was right. Cooped up in here like two animals in a box, and if they started out on the wrong foot they'd be at each other's throats in no time. *Besides, when she's asleep tonight I can—* He made a flourish of closing the bottle and slipping it back beneath the bed. He glanced at her from the corner of his eye, seeing the relief and the small, quick smile. *I'll make sure she takes one of those sleeping pills tonight. I'll never get to sleep unless I have a couple of healthy swallows . . .*

It won't be so bad tonight. I'll pretend I'm asleep and he'll drink. God knows he needs it. She looked at her husband with deep but troubled love. *He's pushed it from his mind but he lives it again every night. I wonder if I should tell him how he cries out in his sleep . . .* She would never do that. Jesse had been running for years. He couldn't escape even when he slept. Refuge existed only in the bottle.

The bottle. It tore him down, and now it's his only real friend. Before the accident he was the best pilot she'd ever known. He didn't climb into an airplane; he strapped it on his back and went into the high blue and made even the birds envious of his skill. Jesse Buckhorn . . . four-time winner of the national aerobatics competition. Crowd pleaser, daredevil stunt pilot, the barnstorming days come alive again with his dashing

177

figure in leather jacket and helmet, the goggles and white silk scarf. She reached out to him without knowing it. Her husband was dead. Killed, unbelievably, as a passenger in an airliner. He'd been a stunt pilot like Jesse. Tim had been good, but not as great as Jesse. When Tim burned to death she never wanted to see an airplane again. But she couldn't stay away from the gypsy air shows. It had been in her blood too long for her to leave. She didn't know anything else. She went back to standing on a wing while the flashy biplane beneath her whirled and rolled and the crowd thundered applause. She couldn't stay away from the men and women who snapped fingers in the face of death every day.

Jesse swept her off her feet. He knew how Tim had died, flung helplessly to the ground in a ball of flame. Jesse Buckhorn thought about that and this small, brave woman in the sky, and his admiration blossomed into love. Jesse laid to rest forever the ghost of Tim, and she threw herself into his arms. They were married in the hangar with the planes around them and the other pilots wishing them well. The party lasted through the night and they made love in an open field under the stars because Jesse was wild and didn't want four walls around them and—

The next morning he was still as happy as a kid. They had an air show scheduled at one that afternoon and Jesse showed up to fly. They couldn't see he was as drunk as he was happy and so they rolled out his Waco and he roared into the air to give them a show they'd *never* forget.

He did. He forgot his wind drift and he came out of a screaming loop too low and that great flashing knife before the plane tore through the crowd. They couldn't throw themselves out of the way in time, and when Jesse pulled up in horror the whole front and belly of the Waco was smeared with blood and pieces of children.

They'd brought the kids from an orphanage, and Jesse killed twenty-three of them.

She tried not to remember the scene. They took away his pilot's license. Forever. They couldn't prove he'd
178

been drunk but everyone knew. His friends turned from him. He couldn't get a job. With the scar and deep pockmarks on his face he was known everywhere. Mae stuck by him. Only she knew the horror he lived every night in his sleep as that terrible propeller ripped into bodies. He stayed blink drunk for months. Mae worked at any job she could find. She dragged him back to his feet. They moved to Canada and he got a job flying a floatplane in the Canadian back country. A year later a pilot recognized Jesse and spilled the story. The Canadian government threw him out of the country because he was using a forged pilot's license.

Six months later he was desperate. Without Mae he would have killed himself. They heard about a small outfit in Florida that did crop dusting and sometimes flew air shows. Jesse told them he had a couple thousand hours as a duster. Mike Jeffries tried him out and hired him and only shrugged when Jesse said he wanted nothing to do with performing before a crowd. They knew then that Mike Jeffries knew Jesse. They couldn't believe it when Mike didn't fire him.

Then Mike began to feel out Jesse. Jesse Buckhorn was up against a stone wall. Sooner or later an FAA inspector would find out who he was, and this time Jesse would go to jail because he'd been breaking Federal law for a long time now by flying with forged papers. They'd throw him in jail and forget where they put the key. Jesse Buckhorn knew Mike Jeffries was right. But he was trapped. He didn't have any money and he couldn't keep a decent job long enough to . . . He was trapped and he'd stay that way until he killed himself. Only Mae, with her love and faith in him, kept him going.

But Mike Jeffries had a way out. He didn't tell it all to Jesse. Not right off. He felt him out, and they talked for weeks because what Mike Jeffries had in mind took planning, timing, money and the willingness to take *any* risks. Jesse Buckhorn was a brilliant pilot and he had nothing to lose.

For the first time in years he had a chance. He grasped at it desperately.

He flew the plane over Banning that night and Mike

179

Jeffries dropped away into the darkness, and they had the financing they needed for the big one.

Then they had the bombs.

It was too bad about Gene Moore getting killed that way in Kansas City. Gene was a nice kid, but his color would have killed him anyway because he just wasn't made to stand at the back of anything.

Jesse and Mae couldn't believe it when Mike blew the bomb on the top of San Gorgonio. They never believed he'd do it, but he did, and the other bombs were in the cities and it was too late. They talked about turning themselves in, but they knew it was hopeless by then. The bomb had killed thousands of people and God knew how many more thousands died in the panic and riots that swept the cities. If anyone ever found out who they were, they'd have been killed like dogs. So they stuck it out because now there'd be enough money to change what they looked like, get new papers and live anywhere in the world. Jesse never wanted to fly again.

Now they were locked in their cabin and it was just a matter of waiting. Two weeks, that captain said. Two weeks from Seattle to Hong Kong and they'd be free forever. They'd be new people. It took a lot of money, but when Silber was safely out of Lisbon they knew they'd have that too.

They were in terrible danger. They watched television and saw their faces flashed everywhere in the country. They paid the captain five thousand dollars for their passage and his silence.

Jesse didn't trust Captain Boehme. He didn't trust him at all. Jesse and Mae talked it over and they swore they would never be taken alive. Jesse did what he felt was necessary. When he came aboard the ship he brought fifty pounds of plastic explosives with him. As soon as they were in the cabin he locked the door and wired the explosives.

If anyone tried to force his way into the cabin . . .

Captain Hans Boehme blew his nose vigorously and gestured at the note Ken Regan had just read. "Hell of a thing, ain't it?" Boehme shouted. "Do a favor for somebody and now they threaten to blow up my ship if I bother them."

"You knew who they were, didn't you?" Regan asked.

"Hell, no!" Boehme protested. "I figured maybe they weren't lily white and all that but," he shrugged massively, "weren't my affair, and I don't poke my nose into other people's business. I tell you the truth, mister," Boehme said soberly, "when they boarded my vessel I had no idea who—"

"Their pictures have been on television for days."

"Who looks at that stupid thing!" Boehme shouted.

"How'd you find out, then?"

Boehme squinted at Regan. "Find out? Haven't you seen the docks? Posters everywhere. The Customs people even came aboard every ship in this harbor with notices and their pictures. *That's* when I found out. *That's* when I called you people." Boehme assumed a posture of innocence. "It's one thing to pick up a little change on the side, but I don't want to fight the law—"

"How much did they pay you, Captain Boehme?"

"Well, now, that's a private—"

"I'm not from Internal Revenue, man. How much?"

Boehme snuffled in hesitation. "Well, they— goddamnit, Regan."

"How much?"

"Five."

Regan showed his skepticism. "Only five hundred?"

"Five *thousand*."

Regan nodded. "We've got to get them out of that cabin without any fuss."

"Aye to that," Boehme said, nodding vigorously. "Do you really think they set up explosives so that—"

"You'd better act on that assumption, Captain. In fact, it may be worse than you think."

Boehme didn't understand.

"There's still one atomic bomb missing, Captain. I'd hate to think it might be on this ship."

Hans Boehme went white. "What—what d'you have in mind, Regan?"

"Something quiet. Absolutely no fuss. And they can't know what we're doing. We can't risk that."

Boehme showed relief. "Anything I can—"

"I'll leave my friend here. He'll watch their cabin door. Make certain no one bothers him, understand?"

"Aye."

"I'll be back within an hour and we'll get it over with."

"What will you do, Regan?"

"You'll see soon enough." Regan climbed to his feet and started for the door. "One thing puzzles me, Captain Boehme."

"Tell me and I'll—"

"What would you do if Buckhorn found out we were here and he offered you twice as much as we're paying you?"

"I'd never touch their blasted money!"

Regan nodded and a thin smile came to his face. "That's good to hear, Captain. You know why?"

Boehme shook his head.

"Because if you did, your ship would never reach its destination. I'm going to make you a promise, Captain Boehme. If you play any games, I promise you your ship will never be seen again. Just so you understand what I'm saying, so there's no doubt, you would be sunk on the high seas. Without a trace. Relax, Captain. I'll see you in an hour."

Ken Regan made a hurried phone call.

"We found them," he said. "It's possible they have the last bomb with them. No way to tell. Now, here's the situation . . ." He gave a detailed but concise report of where the Buckhorns were located aboard the *Manuel Hacente*. He spelled out the warning Jesse Buckhorn had sent to the captain. "There's only one way to handle this," Regan concluded. "Get the Army CIC team here on the double and make sure they bring what I've asked for. And not a sound, hear? What about the boy? Ten years old? That should be about right. But for Christ's sake, that's your own kid! All right, all right, I understand. Sure. I'll be at the end of the dock waiting."

They had a problem that appeared insoluble. Jesse Buckhorn had booby-trapped the cabin. They didn't know if forcing their way into the cabin would set off an atomic bomb. They didn't dare hazard the risk.

They thought about setting up a high-powered automatic rifle to be used through the porthole. That wouldn't work, either. First, Buckhorn or his wife might see them, and that would be the end of the game. Second, the curtains were drawn and they might not— well, that was out.

There was another way. The ventilator shaft. They couldn't send someone through the shaft because it would make a racket and tip their hand, and if Buckhorn did have the last bomb with him then all Seattle harbor and half the city would disappear.

But they could use the ventilator shaft. Regan's first thought was to use the Army's Green Ring III. The nerve gas was odorless and tasteless and it had no effect on the lungs and the skin. It killed swiftly by attacking the critical nerve centers of the body. It was still too risky. All Buckhorn needed was a few seconds to kill a few hundred thousand people.

Regan knew the answer then. The Army team and a small boy.

Forty minutes later he met the arriving cars at the dock. They boarded the *Manuel Hacente* in silence. Captain Boehme showed the Army team the ventilator shaft system. Minutes later they removed the access panel on the shaft leading to Cabin Twelve. Boehme ordered his crew to work the deck cargo winches to cover any sounds of metal against metal.

With the panel removed the Army specialists set up a silent, rubber-bladed fan in the ventilator shaft. They donned gas masks and the specialists placed a pressurized cylinder within the shaft opening. An invisible, odorless gas swept up through the shaft to fill Cabin Twelve.

"Ten minutes. That does it, all right. This stuff is effective within sixty seconds. They'll be out cold for at least two or three hours."

They moved fast. They still didn't dare force the door. But the porthole . . .

They couldn't open it from the outside and they didn't try. The Army team went to work. Fifteen minutes later their ultrasonic drill had neatly removed the glass from the port and the way into Cabin Twelve lay open.

Jesse Buckhorn never bothered to rig his booby trap at the port. It wasn't necessary. He bolted the thick glass from within the cabin. Besides, no man could ever squeeze through that small opening.

But a ten-year-old boy, his shoulders and arms heavily greased, could get through. The son of an FBI agent rushed to the ship did just that. Inside the cabin he turned on the lights. An Army demolition expert studied the door through the port. "Son, move that chair by the door. Good. Now, see that tape? Right. Just the tape. Take your time. That's it. Just peel the tape back. Now, hold the wires in your other hand. We don't want it touching any metal. That's fine. Wrap the tape around the open wire. Great, great. Just lay it on the deck there. Now, see those bottom wires? All you have to do is repeat what you just did. That's it. Wipe your hands and just take your time. No rush. That's it, son."

Jesse and Mae Buckhorn were unconscious for three hours after the door to Cabin Twelve swung open.

The ordnance specialist examined the explosives. "Plastic charge," he said quickly.

They had two of the people they wanted.

But the last bomb was still missing.

16

"Hey, Alberto!"

The singer looked up.

"Hey, man, here come de judge."

The guitar went silent. "What?"

"The fuzz, man. The *fuzz*. Right behind and it's like they want some talk with us."

"Shit. You been reading too many comic books."

"No, man, it's like I tell you. They got the sparklers on and all that. Got their big eye on us."

"What the hell for?" Alberto protested. "We ain't speeding or nothing."

"Don't matter none. They—" Alberto pushed the guitar aside. They all heard the siren.

"Juanita, I think maybe you better slow down," Alberto said.

The dark girl behind the wheel nodded, coming off the gas pedal and starting the Volkswagen bus to the side of the road. On the small couch in the rear the young couple looked behind at the police cruiser.

Alberto turned to them. "Monk, got any idea why they should stop us?"

Monk nodded "Sure. They're the law and we ain't. Baby, that's reason enough." He nodded again vigorously and nudged his girl. "Like ain't I right, sweetheart?"

"Sweetheart" agreed with a langorous movement of her head. Monk looked unhappy. "Baby, don't talk when the Man asks us questions," he ordered. "You read me?"

"Uh-huh."

"Because you open your mouth and he knows you ain't been sucking Rice Krispies, that's for sure. He talk at you, you just smile and scratch your ass."

"Uh-huh."

185

Monk rolled his eyes at Alberto and Juanita in the front of the Volkswagen. "Man, she's almost out of it."

There was no smile on Alberto's face, and if Monk had looked carefully he would have seen the hard look in the other man's eyes. "She gonna' be trouble?" Alberto asked quickly.

"No, man," Monk smiled. "This ain't the first time the gendarmes they look at her. She ain't been busted yet. I just tell the Man she's, y'know, like stupid."

"Make sure," Alberto said. This time Monk didn't miss the icy tone. He looked with open surprise at Alberto.

"Hey, don't sweat it, man," he protested lightly. He gestured at the police cruiser now stopped behind them. "They *always* stopping people like us, y'know? They see this bus and the flowers and the clothes and the hair and the smiles we got for 'em and like they just never dig the scene. They make like they're looking for grass or shit and every now and then they bust somebody, and—"

"Where's the stuff you had?" Alberto snapped. "Goddamnit, if they—"

"Relax, baby." Monk bared his teeth in a broad smile. "Why you think I got this old hole in the bottom here? Man, like I dumped it all *way* back when." Monk laughed as he shared his secret. "Baby, we is clean."

Juanita didn't miss Alberto's movement. With his foot he nudged a loose pile of clothes beneath the side bench. She breathed a sigh of relief. The movement told her Alberto's decision to play along with Monk and his stupid girl friend. Play it cool. Be nice to the cops. Smile. Accept beforehand they're going to insult you and ignore it. Smile, she warned herself. She glanced through the right mirror. One cop—they were highway patrol, she noticed then—was already out of his car and walking slowly toward them. She saw the instinctive hand movement to assure his gun was free on his hip.

Tony—*don't even think his name*, she hissed at herself—Alberto, she thought in self-correction, had the guitar back in his hands. The clothes were rumpled beneath the bench. He wouldn't be making a play for it unless everything came apart. Within those clothes was a sawed-off repeating shotgun, and he was an expert in its use. She didn't give a damn how many cops went down with a bellyful of shot but she wanted no more of the violence they'd had for so long. She gripped the steering wheel with both hands and looked straight ahead. She could hear the cop's steps on the gravel.

Juanita Aleman. That's your name, she warned herself. Don't forget it. You're Mexican. *Mexican.* When you speak let them hear the accent. Make certain they hear it. Smile, girl. Smile and show your teeth and for God's sake never let them know you're a smart nigger girl with two college degrees and more damned education than the two of those white fools could even count. Because if they find out. . . . She glanced swiftly at Tony. *Alberto! you fool!* At Alberto. In a hundred years you couldn't tell that was a wig on his head. She'd shaped and adjusted it herself until he looked the part, until he *was* what he seemed. A folk singer, not good, not bad, but loose and easy and enthusiastic and he was good with the guitar, which was all that mattered. The wig was perfect for him and he hadn't shaved in a week and those stupid glasses on his face . . .

It was the only way they could get through the police cordons thrown up everywhere. When they heard about Jesse and Mae she felt the fear run cold through her. But Tony had always ridiculed their idea of leaving the States on a freighter. No matter what they paid the captain of whatever ship they selected, he warned, the son of a bitch must know he could get more out of the government and make himself a hero at the same time. Tony warned them and he'd repeated it angrily to her, and all the time he knew just what he was talking about. Trying to get out of the country through the ports or the airlines was insane. They'd go the other way.

But they couldn't just get up and go. Their pictures were everywhere and the whole world was looking for them.

"They'll never be looking for a white man and a Negro girl living together," she told him. "Living and traveling together. Sure, we'll attract some attention,

187

but they'll all be so busy being horrified they won't care *who* we are, and—"

Tony laughed in her face. "Leslie, sometimes, for a smart broad, you haven't enough sense to come in out of the rain. They know what we look like. They're looking for us, remember? And you're not just a colored broad. Sweetheart, you're *beautiful*. You make men clutch themselves between their legs and howl at the moon. We wouldn't get ten miles." He grinned suddenly. "But there's another way . . ."

Tony Maglioni and Leslie Hall disappeared. They had the bread to buy what they needed. Leslie went out alone at night and no one would ever have recognized her. She wore extra clothing to pad her body until she was frumpy and distasteful to the eye. No makeup. Her hair a mess. Flat shoes in which she clumped about. She disappeared into the Watts section of Los Angeles. If you had the bread, you could get anything you wanted in Watts.

Drivers' licenses for Alberto Jiminez and Juanita Aleman. Tony spoke fluent Spanish. They became Americans of Mexican background. Tony played guitar, and together they were endurable in sound. The drivers' licenses said Tony had brown instead of thick black hair. Hair dye took care of that and she made certain not to forget his heavy brows. Her own hair became a dark red, and she got rid of all their clothing, dressing as their new identities demanded.

Tony bought a cheap car and they drove to Watts where they put up in a cheap apartment. Cash on the line, no questions asked. They'd need it only for a day, maybe two. There was a big thing being set up in Roswell, New Mexico. Folk singers, hippies, folk-rock music, the works. A printer ran off some letterheads. She spent several minutes at a typewriter, and when she was finished they had a bona fide offer for a singing job during the music festival in New Mexico.

Transportation was the next problem. "So long as we're playing the part," she told Tony, "why not live it?"

Again they passed the word, and that afternoon they had a visitor. It was the first time they'd met Monk, who was driving with his girl from Los Angeles to Florida in a Volkswagen bus. It fit perfectly. Monk and what's-her-name would provide the wheels and they'd pay the gas and oil and they'd share on the food.

And now there was that triple-damned nosy cop banging on the door for them to come out.

Tony drove. Leslie was still drained from the twenty minutes of questioning by the highway patrolman. Monk played it like he said he would and his girl looked at the cop with a vacuous smile on her face and never said a word. She showed a loose-lipped grin, and the cop muttered something about "stupid kids" and finally they were told to "just keep going and don't stop until you're over the state line." Real friendly people. It didn't matter, Tony Maglioni told himself. They didn't get busted and they were rolling, and he'd drive this son of a bitch straight through until they made Roswell. There they could mix in with the mob and be lost to sight until he could make his move.

Leslie dozed on the seat to his right. Maglioni glanced behind him at the young couple. The thin blanket they'd thrown over themselves when they started making love was in tumbled disarray and he had a fleeting look at white buttocks rising and falling to the rocking motion of the Volkswagen. He grinned and turned his attention back to the road.

At least now he had time to think. How the hell had he ended up dressed like a Mex anyway? The more he thought of it the funnier it became until he chuckled aloud. He heard a sleepy "What's so funny?" from Leslie and he rested his hand on her knee. "Just thinking, Sweet, just thinking." She murmured back into sleep.

It *was* funny when you thought of it. The way he thought of life, anyway. It was all one huge ghastly joke and he tried never to forget that. It helped when his world fell apart around him years ago. Lieutenant Commander Salvatore A. Maglioni, USN. Crack fighter pilot. Once of the best F-4 jocks in the whole damned fleet. Two hundred missions over North Vietnam and a chestful of fruit salad to keep the review boards aware

189

that Maglioni was great stuff for promotion. Even if he was a maverick, he could fly the ass off any pilot he'd ever met.

And then he took a flameout one night coming in for a deck landing. At the worst possible moment. The second engine didn't catch right away and the sea was rough that night and the deck came up and smashed against the F-4 like a huge fly swatter. There wasn't time to punch out of the disintegrating machine. There wasn't time to do anything except hang on and pray, and the moment the blazing machine ground to a halt, to get the hell out. But it wasn't that easy and Maglioni felt something grab his left leg and twist it, and the world blew up in his face. When he came out of it a long time later he knew something was terribly wrong. Even through the morphine he knew. He looked across the white sheets and there was his leg twisted at a crazy angle. He fell back into blackness and when he awoke again he was in another bed and they'd done something to the leg.

What they did, he remembered with a burst of heated anger, was to butcher him. He knew the worst before that fucking surgeon with his sickening sweet smile and friendly pat on his shoulder told him they'd removed a piece of bone from his leg, that the nerves were ruined and they could never again straighten the leg. The saccharin voice tolled on and on with its living death sentence for him. Because it meant he'd never again fly with the Navy. Who the hell wanted a guy with a twisted foot in the cockpit of a screaming fighter? He didn't need the fucking chaplain with his unctuous babbling that was supposed to soothe the now-crippled Maglioni.

And he sure as hell didn't need the review board that pinned the blame on him and attributed the accident to "pilot error." Goddam them all. The radarman who flew the seat behind him was dead; the Navy had lost not only his fighter but another half-dozen planes when his F-4 exploded among them in a terrifying blast. And there he was. The maverick. The review board was a second death-sentence to him, and they cashiered his ass out of uniform.

He'd thought it was bad then. How wrong he was! Two years he was still trying to get a flying job. Anywhere. Doing *anything* so long as it had wings with it. But that goddamned foot was still twisted and they laughed him out of half the airport offices into which he walked so awkwardly. The other half drowned him in sympathy and made him even angrier.

He drifted southward and saw some posters advertising an old-fashioned gypsy air show near Gainesville, Florida. He drove all night to get there in the early morning when they were still working on the planes. He walked amidst the Wacos and Fleets and Stearmans and he thought his heart would burst. Finally he couldn't stand it any longer and it seemed as if his arms and legs moved of their own violition. He found himself in the cockpit of a Stearman and he was turning switches, and as soon as the engine coughed into life he was rolling across the grass, ignoring the people who ran madly after him. He forgot everything except the controls under his hands and feet, and he forgot his leg was twisted, and for thirty minutes he shouted for joy and did everything he could to turn that mother inside out. When he finished he was drenched in his own sweat and gasping for breath, but he'd never felt so alive in his life. He looked down at the field two thousand feet below and the tiny figures looking up. He felt the grin on his face as he chopped power, sucked up the nose and slammed rudder. The Stearman whipped around into a tight spin and whirled crazily for earth. He brought her out of it at the last possible moment, sliding into a landing from the spin recovery.

When the ship bumped to a stop he didn't know he was sitting there and crying.

That's how Mike Jeffries found him.

Leslie Hall looked at Tony behind the wheel. In the darkness she studied his profile as cars passed them. She still found it hard to believe she loved this man. The man who'd laugh at himself and tell the whole world to shove it. The rough-talking maverick who comforted her in his arms when they heard about Gene. A picture of roaring flames and Gene trapped inside the

191

car reached into her mind, and she fought it away. But not before she had a final glimpse of that deeply bronzed and muscled body. Then the flame engulfed everything and she bit her lip to keep from crying out.

They were on the move then. Moving fast to keep everything coordinated. They had the five bombs, and Gene went out alone to set up the first one in Kansas City. They still didn't know exactly what had gone wrong. Some quirk of fate that killed the man she was going to marry.

He had refused them marriage until he was on his feet. Gene came home from Vietnam a hero, a fistful of medals on his chest, a brilliant combat record as a rescue helicopter gunner. In uniform he'd been feted, his back slapped by his comrades. Then he took off the uniform and discovered there weren't any decent jobs for a nigger ex-hero. Gene Moore was a soldier in the finest sense of the word, but no one wanted him. He was a better engine mechanic than nine out of ten of the men who worked on airplanes around the country. No one trusted a black skin working on the engine he was going to fly. He had jobs gassing up planes and wiping windshields and cleaning the hangars. But they wouldn't let him touch the working machinery.

Except Mike Jeffries, who was color blind. Not with his eyes but his heart. And he saw deep inside Gene Moore. Mike didn't need another mechanic, but he knew what Gene was going through. "I don't have a job for you," he told Gene. "If you're as good as you say you are, you'll show me you're so indispensable I won't be able to fire you."

That's all Gene wanted. His chance. Mike gave it to him and a deep friendship blossomed from that first encounter. Mike taught Gene to fly and made a sky-diver out of him. They were a great sight together. Mike didn't lead another man. He inspired him.

Then Gene was dead. Tony Maglioni had been a friend almost as close as Mike. Tony left no doubts where he stood on the color line. "Man tells you he don't mind about another man's color," Tony would say, "never trust the son of a bitch. You got to *not*

192

care. That's the ticket. Me? I just don't give a shit what anybody is . . ."

But he cared about people, and Tony also shaped Gene Moore into a pilot and he took it hard when they read the newspapers and saw the blackened wreck of a car. Because Gene had been in there.

That's when Leslie found herself in Tony's arms. Soon afterward it happened. Miraculously. They were in love. They didn't know how it happened and they didn't care. They didn't even speak to one another about it. They accepted that from here on they were a team.

In a Volkswagen bus with a kid named Monk and his nameless girl friend making love on the floor while they drove steadily to join a music festival. While the nation held its breath looking for them.

No wonder Tony laughed at the world. He was right. Life was just one huge ghastly joke . . .

Bob Vincent propped up his feet on the desk of General Arthur Sheridan. The general showed surprise.

"You celebrating?" Sheridan queried the FBI man.

Vincent smiled. "No. Trying to anticipate would be more like it." He waved a teletype sheet. "We picked up a lead that Maglioni was seen in the Los Angeles area. Out-of-the-way motel. Manager recalled it because he thought he saw a Negro girl going into his room. If he was right it could account for the Hall girl."

"She's the Negro girl?"

"Uh-huh. Mixed company isn't that unusual any more, but it's still not so common it doesn't attract attention."

Sheridan nodded slowly and reached for a cigar. He clipped the end off neatly, spit out a shred of tobacco and peered over the cigar at Vincent. "You didn't come in here just to tell me this."

Vincent pursued his lips. "No-o-o," he said slowly. "I didn't. As a matter of fact I came in here to—"

"—pick my brains," Sheridan finished for him.

Vincent swung his feet to the floor. "Almost, but not quite correct. You recall I once said you didn't have a criminal mind?"

"I remember. I didn't know whether to be flattered or—"

"Consider it a compliment. Now I'd like to withdraw the good words. I need whatever base criminal instincts you have lurking within that spit-and-polish mind of yours."

Sheridan made a face at his visitor. "I still don't know whether I should be flattered."

"We'll hold that in abeyance," Vincent said. "Seriously, Arthur, we need some extrapolating here. The kind we can't get from a computer."

Sheridan waited. Vincent had made the subtle shift from banter to business.

"The best we figure it," Vincent went on, "is that Maglioni managed in some way to disguise himself while he was in Los Angeles. That's not at all difficult. We don't know if the Hall girl stayed with him. Or, if the two are—"

"Wouldn't that make them stick out like a sore thumb?" Sheridan interjected.

"Normally, yes," Vincent agreed. "But we're dealing with people who know very well what they're doing. It's our belief that Maglioni, with or without the girl, managed to get out of Los Angeles. It's impossible to check every car, and it's even more impossible to personally inspect every person. However," Vincent gestured for emphasis, "let's assume Maglioni got out of Los Angeles and headed east. Now, Maglioni has a problem."

"To get out of the country in one piece," Sheridan said.

"Right. Personally I believe the girl will be with him and—"

"Why?"

"We've pegged him pretty well. He's a loner except for a few close friends. That means more to him than anything else."

Sheridan showed his skepticism. "Including money?"

"Strangely enough, yes," Vincent said quickly. "Money has apparently never been—"

"Then what the hell's he doing in this whole mess!" Sheridan said, louder than he intended.

194

"Of all the people I know," Vincent said quietly, "you might understand better than anyone else. Maglioni's an ex-Navy flier who was crippled in a crash. Carrier accident. Most of the pilots who flew with him feel he got a raw deal. He was just about cashiered out of the service. Until he ran into Mike Jeffries, who, by the way, becomes more and more remarkable the more we learn about him, Maglioni couldn't get a job. Flying was everything to him, and—"

"Go no further," Sheridan interrupted.

Vincent nodded slowly. "All right, you have the picture."

"I have it," Sheridan said grimly. "It still spells traitor to me."

Vincent sighed. "That's neither here nor there. I don't want that clouding your judgment."

Again Sheridan waited.

"If you were Tony Maglioni, Arthur, what would you do right now?"

Sheridan didn't answer immediately. He thought of the roadblocks at every border road, of the intensified border patrols to prevent anyone slipping through at night or during bad weather. Even the Mexicans were on the hunt for anyone trying to slip through—the United States was offering a fifty-thousand-dollar reward for any one member of the group they sought. Not one airliner left the country without being searched thoroughly. Every ship, every plane, anything that moved out of the United States went through a fine-mesh screen of painstaking inspection.

Sheridan ran all these facts through his mind. "You say Maglioni was heading east from Los Angeles?"

"To the best of our knowledge," Vincent cautioned. "Which is something less than confirmation."

"There'd be no use in his working his way north," Sheridan mused aloud. He puffed on the cigar. "No, I think you're right, Bob. He'd move east, all right." Sheridan looked up at Vincent. "He'd *have* to," the general emphasized.

"*Why?*" Vincent demanded.

"Because," Sheridan smiled, "I think I know what our boy's going to do. Care to make a little bet?"

"Tony, don't kill him."

He looked at her with surprise.

"Don't kill him," she repeated. "It's got to stop sometime. It might as well be now."

"I don't get you, Leslie." He rolled over on his side to see her face better. "You know what we've got to—"

"I don't *care*," she said fiercely. "Please. Do it for me. Do it for *us*. I, I . . . *please*, Tony."

In the dim light of the moon she saw him shrug. "All right," he promised.

"What—how will you handle it?" she pushed.

"You want a goddamned road map?"

She regretted her last words almost as quickly as she said them. She rested her hand on his arm. "No. I'm sorry. I—"

"We're wasting time lying here like this," he said, his manner curt. He turned back to survey the airfield. "I've got the picture now," he went on. "There's only one night guard. At this hour he isn't going to be too alert. Wait. See him? Down that line of planes. You can see his flashlight."

"I see him."

"All right. You know what to do."

They climbed from the ditch. Maglioni crouched low and took off around the edge of the field, heading toward the east hangar. She waited until he disappeared behind a row of bushes and she started out along the blue-lighted taxiway, walking upright. In the open. Tony figured it close. By the time she reached the hangar the guard would be near the end of his inspection. They'd be close together. Face to face. Man to woman. A white man alone on a deserted airport at three in the morning welcomed any woman. Any color.

She waved her hand. "Hello, there!"

The flashlight turned in her direction. She saw the glint of metal from a rifle barrel. "Oh, God," she thought.

She needn't have worried. Tony could be almost pure animal in a situation like this. The guard played

196

the light in her face and she knew he was smiling. At this hour who'd know? Nigger or not she was built like a brick—

Tony's hand crashed with the force of a two-by-four against the side of his neck. The guard was unconscious where he stood. "Watch him," Tony ordered. A knife appeared in his hand. He ran, limping, to a nearby plane and slashed the tiedown ropes. Minutes later he dragged the trussed-up and gagged man, still unconscious, behind a fence. "Take his rifle," he told Leslie. "We still may have to use it." She didn't argue as he started off for a line of planes. She kept up with him as he looked briefly at the different airplanes. He stopped before a twin-engined machine. "This is the one," he said, smiling. She didn't understand. It was almost as if he'd been expecting this one particular plane to be ready for them.

"We'll try the door just in case he left it open," he said. He stepped onto the right wing to reach the cabin door. "Locked, damnit. Les, start untieing those ropes. One under each wing and one by the tail. Make it fast."

Nice of them, he thought, to leave an Aztec around for us. He ran back to the hangar. There's almost always one towbar left outside and—ah, there. He picked up the metal bar for towing planes in and out of the hangar and returned to the Aztec. He saw Leslie beneath a wing, undoing the tiedown rope.

Maglioni moved between the left engine and the fuselage. In the pilot's left window was a small vent window. Four inches high and not quite six inches long. Hinged on the bottom, held in place by a sliding metal lock. He wrapped his handkerchief about his right fist, aimed carefully and slammed his fist against the window. The catch snapped, as he knew it would. The window fell open. Maglioni pushed the towbar through the window. In the moonlight he could just make out the door handle on the other side of the cabin. He wouldn't need the flashlight for this. He placed the far end of the towbar against the handle and applied leverage. The handle moved. A little more leverage and . . . The door sprung open. Leslie was

197

waiting for him as he came around to the nose. He was grinning. "Let's go, Sweetheart. We're in business. Just check the tanks and—"

He was in the cabin. He flicked the master switch on. The tanks were full. Maglioni strapped into the left seat. "Come on!" he urged her. Leslie climbed into the right seat and he slammed the door shut. She fumbled for the seat belt. "But what about the key?" she asked.

"Don't need one," he grinned. "Just a door lock on the Aztec." His hands moved swiftly, surely. The left engine thundered into life. He pumped the right throttle, nudged the starter. Two engines rumbling, he released the brakes, swinging around the other planes as he taxied to the runway. He didn't bother going through the customary checklist. No time. He moved the controls, scanned the gauges and pushed the throttles through from idle to full power and back. Piss on it. The engines would be warm enough. They were on the runway, rolling fast, no lights. The needle came around quickly and he held it down a moment longer, then came back on the yoke and hit the gear handle. The wheels came up fast and Maglioni took the Aztec out in a high, turning climb.

"We'll fly down the valley. Along the Pecos River," he told her, "down into Texas. Stay on our side of the border until we get to Laredo. There's a big lake along the border just south of there. That's where we'll cross the border. I'll take her down, right on the deck. We'll be too low for anyone to know what we are. Then we stay just east of a mountain range and we'll come out into the Gulf of Mexico near Pesca. Just south of it. There's nothing there for nearly a hundred miles. We'll get out over the water and stay just a few feet up. After that we cross the Yucatán Peninsula into British Honduras. There's a small strip at Punta Gorda where we can dump this thing. Friend of mine will pay cash for it. We can hole up there for a while or get a boat . . . We'll see. Once we're in Punta Gorda we've got it made."

Maglioni took the Aztec to the deck with a vengeance. He hit the lake shoreline at a hundred feet and went down so low the props rippled the water wildly behind them. Leslie held her breath. They beat their way across the lake at nearly two hundred miles an hour, and then the hills rose sharply before them. For sixty miles Maglioni would have to leave the safety of flying just above the surface. The sharp hills and mountains ahead of them, before they reached the flat plains leading to Pesca and the Gulf of Mexico beyond, forced him to reach for altitude. He didn't sweat it. Not this far below the border at night and doing two hundred per. He judged the lake shoreline carefully and came back on the yoke at the last moment, the Aztec scrambling for height. At four thousand feet he leveled out to get quickly beyond the mountains.

A dazzling light exploded silently. They threw their arms before their eyes, blinded. Maglioni squinted, trying desperately to see. The light held course with them, its garish illumination a thin blue-gold of unreality.

"Tony!" He saw the ghostly forms even as she screamed his name. Jet fighters. The Mexican markings swam slowly into focus as his eyes adapted. The searchlight held with him. He squinted again, saw the two fighters with their landing gear and flaps down to stay with him.

He swore. They must have closed off the border to everything except scheduled commercial flights. There was still a chance. If he could stall them—

He knew they'd be on guard channel. He tuned in to 121.5 and jerked the microphone from its socket. "Aztec Six-Six-Four-Yankee," he called. "You read?" He hesitated a moment. "What the hell is this all about?" he called angrily. "I'm on a flight plan to—"

"Never mind, señor," a voice broke in. "It won't work. We must ask you to land. You will reverse course for Laredo at once."

"Now wait a moment! You can't order me out of the air just like that! I have—"

"Start your turn immediately," the voice ordered.

"Tony, I can see the Gulf ahead of us."

He glanced at her. "I know," he said quickly.

"Do we have a chance?" Her voice caught. He felt

199

the same way. Anything was better than going back there.

"We've always got a chance," he said grimly.

He didn't tell her his greatest fear. Two other fighters high above and behind them. That's what *he* would have done if he were running this intercept. Because—

"Unless you turn at once we will open fire."

He almost laughed aloud. Not too long ago he was in a P-51 and he'd said almost those same words . . .

"Okay, okay," he called. "I'm turning." He saw the edge of the mountains dropping away, the level plain beyond. If he could get on the deck—

He yanked back on the throttles to kill power, shoving the yoke forward and rolling sharply to the left. He watched the airspeed and as soon as he dared he banged down on the gear handle. Kill the speed. That was everything. Kill his speed and go for the deck where he could twist and dodge and they'd never be able to find him, and they could—

He knew he was wrong. There *were* two other fighters up there. Whoever ran this show was good.

They had just enough time to hear the sad voice come through the cabin speaker. Almost as if the pilot regretted what he had to do.

"Too bad, señor."

They took the cannon shells directly in the cabin.

17

"Mr. Vincent? This is Mrs. Simpson. General Sheridan would like to see you right away if—yes, sir. Thank you. I'll tell him you're on your way."

Sheridan had the report on his desk when Bob Vincent walked into his office. "Short and sweet," Sheridan said, pointing to the papers. "No bomb. The radiation crews went through the wreckage and then worked their way outward. The counters didn't pick up a thing."

"There's no question?"

"None. Not even the faintest trace of radioactive materials. We had over a hundred people on it, Bob. I wish we could have found—" Sheridan shrugged.

"What about the people in the plane?"

"We put our best crash experts on it. Brought in the CAB doctors and a couple of your own people besides, as you know," Sheridan said. "There wasn't much left. Enough, however, to know two people were in that ship. The fighters gave them a long burst. Twenty-millimeter stuff. Killed them outright. The Aztec exploded when it hit. What about your end?"

Vincent reached for a cigarette. "We're convinced it was Maglioni and the Negro girl. For some reason Maglioni didn't kill the guard at the airport. Strange. A man will involve himself in something that kills thousands of innocent people, yet taking another life with his own hands is anathema to him. The guard never saw the man who hit him. But he had a clear look at the girl and he's identified her from photographs."

Sheridan pushed the report closer to Vincent. "We should be able to confirm identity from what's left of the bodies. But you're right. I don't think there's any question as to who it is. We're cutting them down," he said grimly.

"It's not good enough," Vincent added. "There's still that last bomb. The pressure's really on."

"What the hell do they want? Do they expect us to go out and find them ourselves?"

"Yes," Vincent replied, "if that's necessary. I'll tell you the truth. I'm worried. Jeffries is liable to do anything."

"Any leads?"

"Not a thing." Vincent flicked ashes from his cigarette. "I haven't seen your aide for a while."

"He's at Fort Meade. I sent—"

"Hoving?"

"Yeah. I figured we couldn't afford to overlook anything," Sheridan said. "He has everything on Jeffries we could gather and he's working with the NSA programmers on the computer run."

Vincent kept a blank expression on his face. "Think it will help?"

"Christ, no. Neither does Paul. But we've got to go after anything." Sheridan grimaced. "But why am I telling you that? You're the expert in this business."

"I'm afraid we'll take all the help we can get," Vincent said wearily. "If we don't come up with that last bomb pretty soon I may come to you for a job."

"Done," Sheridan said.

"But I'd rather keep the one I've got right now, thank you," Vincent said dryly. He fell silent for a moment. "I knew I meant to ask you something. That colonel you mentioned yesterday. The one who was—"

"Jeffries' commanding officer in Vietnam," Sheridan finished for him. "Ten o'clock this morning. About an hour from now. He might just give us something to help. In the meantime, I'm hungry. How about a second breakfast?"

Vincent rose to his feet. "Second? What time did you get in?"

"Get in? Hell, until this thing's over I don't go anywhere. I sleep in my office. Let's eat."

With Dave Silber out of the picture General Arthur Sheridan had returned to his offices at Norton Air Force Base. From here he was in direct contact with any military installation anywhere in the world. He was convinced this would be vital in the increasingly tense search for the fifth and last atomic bomb. To his surprise Vincent joined Sheridan at Norton. With the FBI and other agencies scouring the nation for Mike Jeffries and Pat Hughes *and* the last bomb, Vincent could do no more than to sweat out the painstaking search. As much as himself, Sheridan deplored sitting on his hands. They both suffered the irritating urge to act on their own volition rather than react to what the nation-wide hunt might produce.

To the best of their knowledge the group led by Mike Jeffries consisted of four men and three women. All but Jeffries and Hughes were accounted for. Dave Silber made an eighth figure, but he had never been involved directly and he was now out of the way. There were also the unknown contacts in Europe. To hell with them, Sheridan mused. CIA and the other security groups would nail their quarry soon enough. Arthur Sheridan wanted only that last bomb. Vincent wanted Mike Jeffries and his girl friend.

For a while virtually everything moved through the FBI. Yet, at Vincent's request, he and Sheridan lived and worked as closely as Siamese twins. Vincent wanted Sheridan available immediately to judge every new scrap of information, for there was never any way to predict how or when one small bit of news could open the door to a new lead.

Arthur Sheridan was convinced the missing bomb had never been emplaced in a city. Jeffries must know, he argued, that before too long every possible apartment, motel and hotel room, every possible place of seclusion, would be examined. That limited the time in which his control of the bomb would be most effective. It was just the way he told Vincent. Only a fool would give up his ace in the hole and Jeffries, from everything they'd learned about him, was anything but a fool. The thought of Jeffries made him think of John Hoving and the National Security Agency. Goddamn them! They could have had a handle on Jeffries long before now.

The man had been right under their noses all the

time. The thought galled him. Mike Jeffries had been a pilot with Tactical Air Command and for a year had been assigned to TAC Headquarters in Virginia. They'd missed that lead because it was several years back and they were searching frantically for someone either still in TAC or a pilot who'd just completed a tour of active duty.

The signs pointing to Jeffries were buried in statistical data. And, Sheridan grumbled unhappily, those "signs" hardly included Jeffries' combat record in Vietnam. The son of a bitch had the country's second highest combat decoration. Along with his Air Force Cross he had three Silver Star and seven Bronze Star medals and enough Air Medals and clusters to fill a whole chest with fruit salad. Add to that the Purple Heart with a cluster, more than two hundred missions over both South and North Vietnam, and a guy with the balls to keep hammering at enemy targets no matter how rough the flak defenses through which he had to punch his way.

What in the name of God, Sheridan wondered, wipes all that out? It wasn't that old saw of combat fatigue. Every man who knew Mike Jeffries remembered him as a fighter pilot who gave full credit to their profession. He was every inch, every pound, a tiger. Sheridan *had* to know more. His staff located Jeffries' former CO. Maybe he could point out something. It was worth the long shot. Colonel Mark Dupre would be in his office at ten.

"No one could handle the one-o-five like Mike," the colonel said with open respect for the pilot who'd flown under his command. "He made that damn machine do everything the book said and more. He was outstanding when we hit north of the DMZ. He used to come home with the airplane looking as if it had been through a meat grinder." Mark Dupre looked at General Sheridan. "Did you know he had to punch out three times?"

"I didn't know that," Sheridan said. In his mind he created the scenes as they must have been, pulling the handles that set off the rocket charge beneath your seat, ejecting with a howling roar over a vicious airstream.

204

Bad enough over home ground. Worse when God knew what waited for you within the thick jungle into which you drifted.

"Punch out?" Vincent leaned forward, anxious not to miss a thing. "I don't—"

"Sorry," Dupre said. "Jeffries had to eject on three separate occasions. Bail out."

Vincent nodded.

"Something else you might have seen from his records," Dupre continued. "Mike was a paratrooper before he went into flight training. I think he had something like sixty jumps."

Vincent looked from Dupre to Sheridan. "That fits, doesn't it?"

"Uh-huh. Sixty jumps as a trooper is good background for skydiving, I'd say."

"Sorry to break in so many times, Colonel," Vincent said. "Please go on. What happened when he, ah, punched out?"

"Well, he went out twice over the water," Dupre said. "He had time to hang on until he crossed the coastline. If you have to get out of that thing you're flying, then Mike did it the way the book would like it to happen. The rescue choppers picked him up just about the time his feet got wet. But one time," Dupre paused, shaking his head with the memories flooding to him, "he went down in heavy jungle. We knew he landed okay, but we couldn't get to him before darkness. He led the North Vietnamese a wild chase for three days. And nights, I suppose. Anyway, we finally got wind of where he was and we got a chopper to him just in time."

Dupre glanced at both men. "Mike had already killed three men out of a four-man patrol after him. He was out of ammunition by then. When we lowered the sling to him he was beating the fourth gook to death with his bare hands. He made sure that last son of a bitch was dead, and *then* he grabbed the sling and we hauled ass out of there. I know all this because I was in that chopper. The idea of losing Mike Jeffries on the ground just got to us. Every man in the outfit was all for going over there in force to do anything to get Mike out."

Vincent toyed with a cigarette. "All this is very puzzling, Colonel Dupre."

"I don't understand."

"You're describing a man who's about as patriotic as Jack Armstrong and George Washington rolled up in one," Vincent said. "It just doesn't fit the man we're looking for. Did something go wrong somewhere? I mean, what could have happened to—"

Dupre gestured impatiently as he nodded. "I see. Yes, it did, Mr. Vincent." The colonel's face clouded. They didn't interrupt as Dupre sorted out his thoughts.

"The trouble began when the VC opened a big offensive about ninety miles from Saigon," he went on finally. "We were getting frantic calls to do close support for Arvin and—"

"Arvin?"

"Army of Vietnam. They were getting mauled and were screaming for help. We were told to scrub everything going north and get in there fast." Dupre looked directly at Vincent. "Did you know that some of our pilots, more than you might realize, would rather fly missions north of the DMZ than in the south?"

"I've never heard that," Vincent said.

"Some pilots hate close support in the south. You see, if they miss their target, even by a hair, they're going to kill innocent people. We've dropped pretty short sometimes. And you can't always tell where your target is. You get a smoke rocket or grenade for your marker and you try to work all around that. It leaves something to be desired."

Sheridan rolled his cigar in his teeth. "That's the way it goes sometimes."

"Sure," Dupre acknowledged. "I know that too. But some of the jocks aren't that philosophical about it. Mike Jeffries sure as hell wasn't." Dupre paused again, almost as if inviting or daring criticism of either himself or Mike Jeffries. When he received only patient silence he went on. "Mike went out with six one-o-fives on a napalm drop against a village. The Arvin contact told us the village had been evacuated and we were to work

206

it over good to flush out the VC. Mike was already into his run, the other pilots trailing, when he saw people around the buildings. They weren't Cong. He knew that right away. No VC would stand out in the open with a flight of one-o-fives on its way down. Apparently Charlie had forced the villagers back into the place and were forcing them to stand out in the open to be seen by our pilots." Colonel Dupre sighed unhappily. "Mike saw them. The other pilots said he yelled for them to break right, and he booted out of his own dive. He salvoed his ordnance into the jungle beyond the village. But he had a midair with his wingman and—"

"I didn't know that," Sheridan said.

"Hard to say whose fault it was, General. Or even if it was anyone's fault. If you go strictly by the book, then the wingman was wrong. But you've got to consider the conditions at the time, and if you do it's hard to pin blame on anyone. Anyway, the wingman dumped everything he had. The napalm went straight in."

"Damn—"

Dupre nodded and took a deep breath. Going back to this scene, Vincent realized suddenly, was taking a toll on the colonel.

"They killed one hundred and thirty people."

"Jesus Christ. Were they—"

"Yeah, they sure were. Not a VC among them. *All* women and children. Another hundred or more took bad burns. Mike was pulling up and turning and he saw the whole thing. He came back for a low run over the village." Dupre hesitated again. "He threw up in his cockpit, General."

Sheridan refused to anticipate. "How did it end up, Colonel?"

Dupre shrugged. "We had a maniac on our hands."

"Spell that out," Sheridan told him.

"Sorry. Mike wanted to kill his wingman. I mean that literally. But you couldn't blame the kid. He was a young lieutenant and this was only his eighth mission. He was even more broken up than Mike over what happened. After all, it had been his ordnance that . . . Anyway, I took him off flight status for a while. That didn't do a bit of good as far as Mike was concerned.

207

He'd had it." Dupre snapped his fingers. "Just like that. As if someone turned a switch inside him. He'd had the whole war and everything else. He was scheduled for a mission early the next morning. I spent half the night arguing with myself about letting him go. Then I decided it was, it would be better for Mike. I made sure it was north of the DMZ. But it didn't matter. What I decided, I mean." Dupre looked directly at General Sheridan. "He refused to go."

"In what way? How——"

"He just flat refused to go. Told the sergeant who woke him up to get lost. The other pilots discovered he wasn't kidding with them, either. When the sergeant came to me with Mike's refusal to fly the mission I tried to play it cool. I kept reminding myself what happened the day before. In fact, I was hoping I'd provoke him into losing his temper. Get it out of his system. If I could do that with just the two of us then, well, officially it would never have happened."

Sheridan nodded slowly. He liked the way Dupre thought. He felt he would have done much the same himself.

"But I couldn't get him mad," Dupre went on. "I couldn't get a rise out of him. All Mike's anger seemed to have gone into his tirade the day before against his wingman."

Vincent wanted to prompt Dupre. He forced himself to remain silent. The colonel wasn't enjoying what he was telling them. He knew Dupre regretted ever coming here. Even if he had received orders to do so.

"From what I heard, Colonel," Sheridan said, "Mike Jeffries refused to fly any more combat."

Colonel Dupre nodded.

"I heard he told you to take the war and shove it."

"In effect."

Vincent disliked prodding this man. But anything they might learn could help to——"Colonel Dupre, might I ask just what Mike Jeffries said to you?"

A whimsical smile appeared on Dupre's face. "Of course, Mr. Vincent. He told me to go fuck myself."

"In those words?" Sheridan demanded.

"He had a few other choice ones," Dupre answered.

He shifted uncomfortably in his seat. "What really bothered me," he said, "was that I didn't blame Mike. I just couldn't hold it against him. I knew how he felt. You've heard it often enough. What were we doing over there, anyway? Why should he be sent out to kill helpless women and children? All of a sudden his values seemed to evaporate. I mean the values by which he'd lived for so long. I suppose you could say Mike's world fell apart all around him."

Sheridan refused to let go. "He didn't fly combat again, did he?"

Dupre shook his head. "Mike Jeffries was never a man for wasting words, General."

Sheridan turned to Vincent. "I know the rest of it," he said. "They court-martialed him."

Vincent showed his disbelief. "With that combat record?" he protested. "The medals he—"

"They *had* to court-martial him."

"But *why,* in heaven's name!"

"Because he wore a uniform. Because he took an oath. Because he was an officer. Because we were fighting a war. Because—"

"Couldn't they have taken into consideration what happened? His record? What he'd been through?" *My God,* Vincent thought, *I'm defending the man!*

"Don't you think the Air Force did that?"

"Then how could—"

"Mike Jeffries refused to defend himself," Colonel Dupre broke in.

"Refused to—"

"That's right. I assure you, Mr. Vincent, we did everything we could to avoid—" Dupre shrugged. "Mike didn't give us any choice. In fact, he demanded to be tried." Dupre seemed to look off into the distance. "As if by forcing punishment on himself he could make up for what happened in that village."

"And you found him guilty, I suppose," Vincent said angrily.

"Yes. But not the way you think."

For the first time Vincent detected resentment. Dupre had stiffened, as if he regretted admitting this civilian into what should be privy only to those who wore

209

the uniform. *Well, screw you, Colonel. I know what it's like to wear that uniform. I left a leg on Iwo Jima and you can bloody well—*

"But not the way you think, Vincent," Dupre was saying. "We didn't forget those two hundred missions. We couldn't force Mike to defend himself but we could, and we did, defend him as best we could. If we went strictly according to regulation Mike would have received a dishonorable discharge. We avoided that. We, well, Mike was judged unfit because of—"

"Unfit?"

"Yes, damn it!" Dupre snapped at him. "And he *was* unfit. You don't put a man in his condition into a cockpit. You don't give him a machine that may have an atomic bomb in its belly and . . ."

His voice trailed off. They stared at one another.

He was so right.

Vincent stopped before the general's desk and took a deep breath.

"They spotted him."

"Where?"

"Denver. A flight out of Denver bound for Los Angeles. United one twenty-eight. Nonstop. They can't get off until— The girl's with him."

Sheridan was on his feet. "What else?"

"Something crazy," Vincent said immediately. "No attempt at a disguise. They used different names on the tickets, but that's all. I mean, right out in the open. For Christ's sake, *why?*"

"Are they—"

Vincent anticipated the question. "That's what's so crazy. They're booked, *in their own names,* on an Air France flight out of Los Angeles for Paris! In their own names," he repeated.

Arthur Sheridan thought of all he knew about Mike Jeffries. A thought came to him and he felt his blood chill. "Did your people make any move to stop him?" he asked.

Vincent shook his head. "No. It was too late. They were already on the plane. Arthur, do you think they might hijack that airliner?"

210

Sheridan's response was immediate. "No. The only place they could get to with that flight, out of Denver, I mean, would be either Canada or somewhere in Mexico. They wouldn't do that. What the hell for? It wouldn't get them anything."

"We'll get them when they land in Los Angeles," Vincent said grimly.

Sheridan had a strange expression on his face. "Maybe not," he said.

"What?"

"I've got a hunch. I—" He broke off and jerked the telephone from his desk. "Mrs. Simpson. Drop everything. Get me Kirtland Air Force Base. Major Watkins in ordnance. If he's on the phone, break in. I want him immediately, no matter where he is or what he's doing. Good. Yes, I'll hold on."

Sheridan cupped his hand over the phone. "Have you notified your people in LA?"

"Yes. By the time that thing lands we'll be ready."

"You may have more on your hands than you bargained for."

Vincent showed his exasperation. "Damnit, stop beating around the bush! What the hell are you trying to say?"

"I hate to—" Sheridan motioned with his hand as someone spoke to him on the phone. "Major Watkins? General Sheridan, AIG, here. Now listen carefully, Major, because I need your answer right away. This is about the Mark Twelve nuclear weapon. Right. Three hundred kiloton. Now, here's what I need to know . . ."

Vincent heard Sheridan swear. The general hung up slowly and looked at the FBI man. "Bob, contact your people in Los Angeles. At the airport. Tell them under no conditions are they to approach or to bother Mike Jeffries. Tell them to leave that man *alone*."

"What?"

Sheridan glanced at his watch. "I've got a fast chopper standing by on twenty-four-hour alert." He turned from Vincent to stab his intercom button. "Mrs. Simpson, tell base ops I want that alert helicopter in front of my office *now*. Then call FAA for priority ATC clearance into Los Angeles International. Tell them—give

211

them the emergency code. I'll talk to them from the chopper on the way over."

"Arthur, will you—"

Sheridan grabbed Vincent's arm and started for the door. "No time to explain now," he said quickly. "I'll tell you when we're in the air. Let's go."

People looked at them as they walked toward the long corridor leading to Air France. Their appearance compelled attention. A tall, square-shouldered man with tanned, almost leathery skin, deep blue eyes beneath a crop of tousled hair. A strong man, confidence in his walk. The woman at his side tall and willowy, as beautiful as he was ruggedly handsome. Long blonde hair, shapely legs matching his stride. People looked at them. A beautiful couple.

Pat Hughes carried a small overnight bag. At her side Mike Jeffries walked with a trench coat carried loosely over a leather case in his right hand. There was no hesitation in their walk. They knew where they were going, what they were doing.

Vincent made his moves carefully. His men made no attempt to stop Mike Jeffries and Pat Hughes. They were allowed to depart on the United jetliner. They walked into the main terminal, left the building and then walked along the oval concourse to the international terminal. From here they moved toward the final long corridor that would take them to the check-in counter of Air France.

"Mike, do you—"

"No sweat, baby. Just keep right on like we're doing."

"They've spotted us, Mike."

"I saw them a long time ago."

"I'm frightened."

"Don't be." He smiled at her, a flash of white teeth against the tanned face.

They kept walking. They were well into the long, bright corridor.

"Well, well," Mike Jeffries grinned. "They're going to make their play just about now." He glanced behind him, then looked ahead. The tourists and the business
212

travelers were gone. No women. No children. They'd vanished into thin air. Near the far end of the corridor a small group of men waited. Another group had moved behind them into the corridor.

Jeffries knew who they were. Who else could they be? He'd expected them. They continued along the corridor until they were a dozen feet from the group waiting for them. Jeffries saw an Air Force uniform. One star. He thought he recognized the man, that he'd seen him somewhere a long time ago. It didn't matter. He didn't know any of the other faces. That didn't matter, either. He knew they were FBI. Several men standing back from the others had guns in their hands.

He didn't know them, but they knew him. They'd studied his face, and hers, a thousand times in photographs.

The man in front faced Jeffries. He didn't bother with any preliminaries.

"It's the end of the road, Jeffries. The party's over."

Mike Jeffries smiled at him.

He's too sure, Vincent thought. *I hope to God Sheridan's wrong . . .*

"You can come with us quietly," Vincent said. "Or we can take you any way you want. Walking, or carried out."

Jeffries laughed. Quietly. Sure of himself. He noticed the general staring at him.

"It won't be anything of the sort," Jeffries said. His voice was surprisingly rich. "We're leaving on that plane."

Vincent motioned with his hand. The agents started closing in.

The smile was still there.

"You only have four bombs," Jeffries said. His eyes were steel as he faced Vincent. "Don't be stupid."

"We know we have four," Vincent said. He felt stupid, as if this man were manipulating him like a child. "What about—"

The bag. The bag in his hand. My God. Sheridan was right. He's got the last bomb in that bag!

Vincent stared wide-eyed at the leather bag. Mike Jeffries read his thoughts.

213

"That's right," he said. "We're getting on that plane. You're not going to stop us. You're not even going to try. Because if you do . . ." He smiled again and shrugged. "If anyone comes within six feet of me," he went on, "or if they so much as touch her, you lose this city."

They stood in silence. Then Vincent heard Mike Jeffries saying almost the same words Sheridan used in the helicopter.

"There's a manual override in the detonator," Jeffries said, his voice echoing hollowly down the long corridor. "The first five interlocks are released. I'm holding down the last switch. If I release the pressure you can kiss Los Angeles good-bye."

Goddamnit to hell . . . ! He's right. Oh, sweet Jesus . . . we can't touch him. If we shoot him, anything . . . if he just relaxes the pressure, just a bit, Sheridan said, the bomb detonates . . .

Jeffries moved closer to Vincent. His eyes never left those of the man he faced. "We haven't a thing to lose," Jeffries said.

Still Vincent didn't move. He felt frozen to the spot.

"Try me," Jeffries said, his voice so soft it was almost a whisper. "Just try me."

Vincent felt as if he were going to be sick. He motioned with his hand to his men. "Let them through." His voice was hoarse.

Mike Jeffries and Pat Hughes started down the corridor. Jeffries stopped suddenly, turned again to Vincent. "Don't underestimate me," he said coldly. "If that airplane stops anywhere but Paris, if anyone bothers me on the plane or gets in our way when we get off, that's the name of the game, mister. I let this thing go."

They walked away in silence.

Vincent spoke to his men. "Leave them alone. Don't interfere with them. We can't do anything about . . ." His voice trailed away.

Twenty minutes later they watched the Air France DC-8 thunder into the sky.

18

General Sheridan turned to the Customs officer. "Can you put through an emergency call for me? Good. The White House. Get the DC operator and tell her it's General Arthur Sheridan. Use Code Alpha Quebec Six-Six. Tell her that. It will get you right through."

"Uh, yes sir. Excuse me, General. Who's the call to?"

"The President. President Dowling. I'll wait right here."

The Customs official started to say something to Sheridan, thought better of it and grabbed for his telephone.

Sheridan moved with Vincent to a corner of the office. "There's only one way," he told Vincent. "We *can't* let that thing land in Paris."

Vincent's face was agony. "Damn you, don't you think I know that? But what can we do!"

"Add it up, that's what," Sheridan said, ignoring the feelings of the other man. "Just add it up."

"What are you—"

"There are a hundred and forty people aboard that airliner," Sheridan said. "There are a couple of million people in Paris. Just add it up."

"Are you suggesting . . . We can't do that!"

"And why the hell not?" Sheridan exploded. "If you've got any better ideas let me have them *now*."

"You're saying we ought to shoot down that airplane!" Vincent protested. "Shoot down a French airliner! My God, man, do you know what would happen if an American fighter shot down a French—"

"We don't have to shoot it down," Sheridan said. "But in the end it's the same thing."

"Arthur, you can't kill one hundred and forty people in cold blood!"

"If it's necessary, the hell I can't. When you've got to make a choice between one hundred and forty people in an airplane and maybe a million people on the ground, you really haven't got any choice at all."

"And you don't have the authority to do any such thing," Vincent retorted.

"I'll argue that with you some other time," Sheridan threw back at him. "But we don't have to do anything right this moment. We've got time until that ship gets out over the North Atlantic, until it's well away from everything. In the meantime——"

He turned as the Customs official extended the telephone.

"Sir, this is General Sheridan. Yes, sir. Here's the situation . . ."

He hung up the telephone and turned to Vincent.

"The President told me to judge every factor."

Vincent waited.

"He said he'll support fully, as though it were his own orders, whatever I decide is necessary."

Vincent didn't trust his own voice.

"We can be back at Norton in less than an hour," Sheridan said. "I'll decide by then."

He's lying, Vincent said to himself. *He's already made up his mind.*

"Robin Hood Six, Robin Hood Six, this is Queen Mary. How do you read? Over."

The pilot in the lead F-106 interceptor squeezed the transmit button on his control column. *"Queen Mary from Robin Hood Six, got you five by five. Go ahead."*

The radar controller studied his scope with the practised ease of a man who's expert in his work. A hundred miles off the Greenland coast, cruising at fifty thousand feet, the F-106 pilot and his wingman came in perfectly on radar.

"Priority intercept, I repeat, priority intercept," the controller said. *"Confirmation Bravo Tango Alpha."*

"Confirm Bravo Tango Alpha." The voice ghosted out of the Arctic stratosphere. *"I read you as priority intercept, Queen Mary."*

216

"Confirm wingman."

"I've got it," came the voice of the second pilot.

"Roger, Robin Hood. Vestor three zero zero, angels three-five. Confirm."

The two fighters eased into a new heading of three hundred degrees and started into a shallow glide that would take them down to thirty-five thousand feet. The lead pilot confirmed their new heading.

"Robin Hood Six, Queen Mary."

"Right, Mary."

"Robin Hood, your orders are: Do not arm missiles. I repeat, do not arm missles. Did you copy? Over."

The pilot's exclamation carried through his microphone. *"Queen Mary, I read you as negative on arming missiles."* He repeated the words slowly and carefully. *"That is negative on arming missiles. Over."*

"Roger, Robin Hood. I copy your confirmation negative on arming missiles."

Then eyebrows raised in the two fighters high above the world.

". . . will close to within two zero miles, as confirmed by airborne radar and this controller. At that point you will switch radio frequency to Squawk Channel Niner Six, I repeat, Squawk Channel Niner Six. At target distance of two zero miles and Squawk Channel Niner Six you will activate Radio Code One-Two-One-Six-Two. I repeat, Radio Code One-Two-One-Six-Two. Confirm."

The pilots read back their orders for final confirmation. They were mystified at procedures they'd never before followed. Nor could they understand why the radar controller ordered them to lower their sun visors before activating the radio code on Squawk Niner Six.

Ten minutes went by.

"Robin Hood, you are now four zero miles from bogey. Four zero miles from bogey. Maintain three zero zero and angels three-five. Confirm when you have visual on contrail or target. I repeat . . ."

"Daddy, look!" The little girl pressed her face against the window. "Oh, look! Mommy, can you see it? Can you?"

Far off to the right of the jetliner, two spider-strands of silver curved majestically in their direction, gossamer reflections of Artic moonlight.

"Isn't it *beautiful?*"

"Roger. Coming up on two zero miles. At my mark we will be two zero miles from bogey. Over."

The F-106 pilot looked straight ahead. Twenty miles away he saw the ghostly needle leading the long contrail across the top of the world.

"Confirm sun visors down, Robin Hood."

"Confirm."

"Roger. You will now activate Radio Code One-Two-One-Six-Two."

"Roger."

The pilot moved his thumb to press his transmit button. He still didn't know why those idiots wanted them to lower sun visors in the middle of the night. He could hardly . . .

The last bomb exploded.

ABOUT THE AUTHOR

MARTIN CAIDIN, who is the author of seventy books, is recognized internationally as an authority on astronautics, aviation, science and crime. His first novel, *Marooned,* is a thrilling account of a space rescue. It has had great popularity all over the world, not only as a novel, but as a superb motion picture. *Almost Midnight,* Caidin's ninth novel, will be produced by Irwin Allen as a major motion picture for Avco-Embassy.

From 1950 to 1954 Martin Caidin served as nuclear warfare specialist for the State of New York. He analyzed the effects of nuclear and other weapons on potential targets in the United States.

As a commercial multi-engine pilot, Caidin flies his own plane all over the country. He has flown two-engine and four-engine bombers to Europe. For a time he flew his own World War II Messerschmitt in Europe and the United States. Although he lives within sight of the launching towers at Cape Canaveral, he is giving much of his attention these days to the problems we have fashioned for ourselves with our nuclear weapons.

RELAX!

SIT DOWN

and Catch Up On Your Reading!

☐	THE HARRAD EXPERIMENT by Robert Rimmer	(4690—$1.25)
☐	THE FRENCH CONNECTION by Robin Moore	(5369— 95¢)
☐	HER by Anonymous	(6669—$1.50)
☐	THE BELL JAR by Sylvia Plat	(7178—$1.50)
☐	THE EXORCIST by William Peter Blatty	(7200—$1.75)
☐	WHEELS by Arthur Hailey	(7244—$1.75)
☐	RAGA SIX by Frank Lauria	(7249—$1.25)
☐	HIM by Anonymous	(7369—$1.50)
☐	THE DAY OF THE JACKAL by Frederick Forsyth	(7377—$1.75)
☐	THE FRIENDS OF EDDIE COYLE by George Higgins	(7504—$1.50)
☐	THE TERMINAL MAN by Michael Crichton	(7545—$1.75)
☐	MEMOIRS OF AN EX-PROM QUEEN by Alix Shulman	(7565—$1.75)
☐	THE LEVANTER by Eric Ambler	(7603—$1.50)
☐	SHEILA LEVINE IS DEAD AND LIVING IN NEW YORK by Gail Parent	(7633—$1.50)
☐	THE ODESSA FILE by Frederick Forsyth	(7744—$1.75)

Buy them at your local bookstore or use this handy coupon for ordering: